# THE SIDEWALK

Barbara Brunk Sharkey

Novels by Barbara Brunk Sharkey

*Counselor Stories*

ISBN  978-1-312-92342-3

Cover Photo:  Barbara Sharkey
Back Cover Photo: "Lano Beach - Savai'i" by NeilsPhotography on
Flickr is licensed under CC BY 2.0

To my husband and best friend Richard.
To all my family, near and far,
here now, and gone before.
To the Obies of the world, who encourage others and
share their abundant joy in everyday life.

Chapter One

*Saturday, February 10, 2001*

**M**ADIGAN looked out her living room window for what must have been the ninetieth time that Saturday morning. No one was in view. She twirled a strand of her short dark hair around a finger in a fretful mannerism more suited to an eight-year-old than someone who had just turned thirty-two. She checked her watch again—noon. *They said they'd be here **early** Saturday.* Her hand was reaching for the phone when she heard the distinct sound of a slow-moving vehicle with a thunderous muffler. She went back to the window and looked out again.

An old gray pick-up with many repaired rust spots had slowed to a stop in front of her house, and two elderly men appeared to be conferring in the cab, first looking at her house number, then at the driveway.

*Is this them?*

Slowly, the passenger door opened and a large man with short, curly gray hair in old denim overalls disembarked as if movement was painful. The driver's side opened and another man, similarly dressed and only slightly less rotund, got out more agilely. As they stood beside each other, Madigan decided the driver was the younger brother. He was definitely less gray. The two inspected her driveway, then glanced up at the house.

Pulling back from the window quickly before she could be seen, Madigan struggled to remember the exact words her good friend Marilyn had used when she recommended these "practically perfect" workers to fix the driveway. *Two brothers from an island you've never heard of in the South Pacific who do wonderful work for reasonable rates.* Had she mistakenly assumed the brothers would be young men in their twenties or thirties? Men who would arrive in a truck with their business name neatly stenciled on the side, rather than this banged up clunker with the camouflaged rust spots?

With a swift in-breath, Madigan pulled herself together and opened the door just as the older man was about to knock. She nearly got his large fist on her forehead.

"Oh!" she gulped.

"My fault entirely," the man replied graciously with a generous smile and kind eyes. "Are you Madigan Gardner?"

"Yes, and you must be James and Martin." Madigan tried not to stare. His richly-lined face was such a roadmap of a long life, possibly not always easy, that she couldn't avert her eyes.

"I am Martin." The man's deep voice, politeness of speech, and lovely rolled vowels were mesmerizing. "That is my brother, James. We have come about the driveway. You have many cracks, as your message said. And the water pools at the bottom of the garage door?"

"Yes."

"Some of the soil beneath the concrete has probably been washed away, and now the driveway is settling. And your beautiful tree," Martin paused and pointed to the large maple in Madigan's front yard, "its roots may also be part of the problem." He was soft-spoken and direct, making Madigan feel a little better. Her friend had sworn that Martin and James had done a perfect job on her sister Susan's driveway and sidewalk. With a gentlemanly nod, Martin invited her

2

to walk out with him. Although Madigan was nearly five-seven, she felt dwarfed beside the man. *It's not just his height,* she thought. *It's his girth.*

"We could do a nice job for you," James said, his tone gentle, no pressure, and he had the same nice eyes as his brother.

"How much would it cost?"

"Do you want this same look to the concrete, the same brushed surface you have now, or something a little less plain?"

"This is fine, I guess." Madigan hadn't thought about the surface.

"Then it wouldn't be too much. But for a little more money, we could make it nicer. Perhaps a little edge on the side to make it special?"

"Okay, but how much would it cost?"

"We don't charge as much as the others, and we do exceptional work," James continued to carry the conversation while Martin stood encouragingly beside Madigan.

The familiar feeling of contractor frustration began to well up in the young woman, seeping into her voice. She looked pointedly at Martin. "What would the cost be?"

Martin looked at James. "The usual, yes?"

"About that." James then looked at Madigan. "Five hundred dollars. You will have a nice new driveway, and the water won't be under your garage door. We can fix that."

Madigan was a little stunned. She had been expecting a much higher price. "Well." *What else could she say?* "That would be great. When could you do it?" She was prepared for a downside to the reasonable price—perhaps a several-month wait.

"We could start next week," James replied.

"Really? Like, Monday? Or when? Do I need to be here?"

"You don't need to be here. Is there an electrical outlet outside?" James was doing all the talking.

"Up by the front door. Do I need to sign something? A contract?"

"There's no need for a contract. You pay us cash; we'll do the job; everyone will be happy."

"What about permits? Don't you have to get a permit or something?"

"We'll take care of that. We have a good relationship with your Building and Planning Department. You are lucky to be two miles north of the city line. It's much easier dealing with your town than the city's department."

"Well," Madigan was desperately trying to think of other things to ask. "Do you want a down payment or something?" She looked at the older brother Martin for an answer, but it was James who spoke.

"No. We'll work a little, then we'll get some money, then when we finish, you'll pay the rest."

"That's how you always do it?" Madigan turned once more to Martin.

"Yes, that's how we do it." James smiled.

*What was that accent? She'd heard it in a movie somewhere. A mix of British and island rhythms.*

Martin, still silent, this time at least nodded his head in agreement.

"All right." Madigan pulled her hair apprehensively. "I'll see you Monday, then." Not quite sure what else to do, she turned and withdrew up the three steps to the small porch and then into the house.

"Good day to you!" Martin called cheerfully to her retreating back.

Once inside again, Madigan warily peeked out the window. Martin walked around the driveway a few more times, examining the cracks, then he and James went back to the truck. Martin was having an even harder time getting into the truck than he'd had getting out.

4

She watched James as the engine refused to catch. Finally, it did and the noisy relic pulled slowly away from the curb.

An uneasy feeling settled in the vicinity of Madigan's stomach. Could it really be this easy, that they would just come and fix her problems? *Why didn't I ask them how long it would take? Or for some other references? Why did I say yes without thinking it over?* Thankfully no money had changed hands. She picked up the phone to call Marilyn for Susan's number to double-check that these seemingly pleasant men were really on the level.

Monday morning arrived with no sign of James or Martin. Madigan left happily for her job in the city's administrative offices anyway, expecting to come home and find the old concrete gone. Instead she arrived home to find the driveway looking exactly the same as she had left it. She immediately phoned Marilyn.

"They didn't show up!"

"Hello to you, too. Calm down. They'll be there tomorrow. Probably something came up at another job. I told you they work a little differently than others. But they're quite dependable once they get going." Marilyn seemed bemused by her friend's annoyance.

"Once they get going? What does that mean?"

Marilyn was patient, knowing that Madigan, the accountant, couldn't stand being in limbo. Things left up in the air agitated her.

"You've got to remember we're talking island culture here. The pace might be a little different from what you're used to, but the end product is well worth the wait. You'd still be making phone calls trying to get someone else to come out to look at your driveway if you weren't using James and his brother."

"That's true," Madigan hated to concede the point. "But I like to know what's going on. Don't they ever call if they're not coming?" She ticked her pencil against the counter edge, not caring to cede control in this or any other situation.

"Not really. But don't worry. It'll be okay. My sister told you she adored them, right? Good things sometimes take awhile."

"I know, but—"

"And the weather wasn't great today. I seem to remember that they don't really work in the rain."

Madigan considered the number of days some degree of precipitation fell during the spring months in Seattle and noticed her stomach tensing again.

"Madigan? Are you still there? I know you're used to your perfect world where everything runs on schedule, but I promise: Everything will be fine. Honest!"

Each day that week Madigan arrived home from her office, hoping to see the old truck in front of her house. On Wednesday, Thursday, and Friday, she called the phone number she had first used to contact them, but got no answer, and the answering machine no longer picked up. She went through her evening routine: dinner, one designated chore, a shower, an hour of TV, and then upstairs to bed, still in a cranky mood. Lying in the darkness with the streetlamp gently lighting the room, she finally decided it wasn't worth the stress. She would hire someone else, though a part of her badly hoped she had somehow misunderstood, and they had meant they would begin the *following* Monday. The more she thought about it, the more she convinced herself that this must be the case. She decided to wait until Monday night, then she would find someone else if James and Martin still hadn't come.

Saturday morning at nine o'clock Madigan was stepping out of the shower after her three-mile run when she heard the roaring muffler. Wrapping up in a bathrobe, she hurried to the bedroom window to peer out. There they were! And not just one truck but two, and two younger men with the older brothers. Both trucks parked in front of her house and Martin again slowly descended. Madigan hurriedly dressed and went outside.

"Good day to you!" Martin greeted her, his happy grin completely infectious.

She tried to appear annoyed, or assertive, or simply insistent that this wasn't the way their relationship was going to be, but the words tangled up, and she only managed to spit out, "Good morning." But she hoped he could read her thoughts: *I was expecting you last Monday!*

"It is a *good* day today! No rain, and we were able to get the other truck. You'll see a lot of work done today." A second later, James joined him.

"Good day, Miss Gardner."

"Madigan. Please call me Madigan."

"Good day, then, Madigan. This is my son, Young James, and my other son, John. And, of course, you know Obie. My sons will help us—"

"Obie?" Madigan scanned the group for a third new person.

"Martin. He has always been called Obie by the family," James explained. "It stands for Older Brother, O-B. He is the oldest boy. The others started calling him that when they were little and the name stuck. As I was saying, my sons will help us today with the heavy work and lifting."

Young James and John seemed close in age and not much older than twenty. They flashed quick smiles and nodded in Madigan's direction, then pulled a jack hammer and extension cords from the back of their truck.

"This will be noisy, but not for too long," James apologized in advance. "You'll need to move your car out of the garage and park on the street. You won't be able to get in and out for a little while."

"Okay, I'll get my keys." Her heart beat faster in exhilaration—how quickly things were moving! She took the front steps two at a time. Going into the garage from the kitchen, she carefully squeezed between her ten-year-old blue Ford Escort and the brown moving boxes piled up high on every side, then rolled up the heavy garage door. James looked at her in surprise as they stood face-to-face.

"Why are you doing that by hand?" he asked, his brow furrowed with concern. "Don't you have an electric door opener?"

"It's broken. I need to get it fixed."

"Let me look at it, and we'll fix it for you. This door is too heavy to roll up and down every day."

"I don't mind that as much as standing in the puddle that's usually underneath it."

"That for sure we will fix. Today we'll find out what the problem is."

With barely enough space to open the car door, Madigan slid into the driver's seat. James stood aside for the Escort as she backed out onto the street, and then pulled ahead of the trucks to park in front of her neighbor's. She rarely saw them, but figured they wouldn't mind for a few days.

Madigan studied James and his sons as she walked back to the garage. The sons were young, yet James looked nearly sixty and Obie even older. The younger men were tall like their father, but did not have his wide girth.

Young James and John went quickly to work with the jackhammer. Their impatient client began to feel relieved at the sight of an actual work crew breaking up the old concrete. *Maybe this is how it will get done, the younger ones helping.* The noise became deafening. She carefully walked around them and into the garage, pulling down the door.

After half-an-hour, she looked out again. No matter how far she tried to get from it, the noise was so loud it was beginning to make her head hurt. Maybe she would go pick up some things from the store.

She yelled to Obie, who seemed to be supervising from the side of the driveway. "I'm going to do some errands. I'll be back in about an hour."

Obie walked her to the car. "Your garage is very full." He raised one arm to the height of the stacks for emphasis.

"Yes," she was surprised by both his observation and his comment about it. She had become used to the tight fit and had forgotten how it might appear to someone else.

"So many boxes. You have some trouble fitting the car in, yes?"

"Well, yes. It's…." Her chest tightened and that hard black spot in her heart began to hurt. "Well, most of it is from my parents' house in California. After they died unexpectedly, there was so much to deal with. I only have one brother, and he lives in Colorado, so I ended up moving most of their things here until we go through them together."

"Hmmm," Obie ran his fingers through his tight gray curls. "Your brother wants these things?"

*How did we get on this conversation?* Automatically defensive on this subject, Madigan answered to herself. *Does Lee want the stuff? Probably not. But he was supposed to come out and sort through it. That was the point. He was supposed to go through it with me.*

"I don't know what he might want."

The answer was truthful but forceful enough to end the conversation, although Madigan knew she sounded rude, making her blush.

"Maybe his wife, perhaps she doesn't want so many things?"

This small truth registered its mark as if a perfectly thrown sharp stone had knocked a chip off the hard rock in her chest.

"You're probably right," she softened. "I'm sure a lot of it is junk. My brother's house is on the small side, and they have kids. But

9

maybe there are a few things he would like to have. At least, I've always thought he would."

"I only mention it because one day we might have to move a little bit of it to work around the doorway. But we'll be careful with your boxes."

The way Obie said "your boxes" made Madigan feel like an old woman in a dark, drab parlor surrounded by things marked "Don't Touch." She looked at him quizzically, to see if he was making fun of her, but his expression was guileless. Madigan realized he was simply stating a fact: They would be careful with her boxes.

Embarrassed now, she thanked him.

"I do need to get the garage cleaned out. Maybe getting the driveway done will be an incentive." She opened the car door. "I'm running to the store. Can I get you anything?"

"No, thank you." He gave a courteous nod and closed the door for her.

"Bye, then. See you later." She pondered this unusual man, so eloquent and gentlemanly in an old-fashioned way.

Madigan left at ten o'clock. When she returned at eleven-thirty, her work crew had evaporated like the night's rain on the pavement. Most of the concrete had been broken up and taken. Both trucks were gone, but there was a small pile of irregular chunks near the curb. Looking at the dirt trough that had once been her driveway, she noticed a huge hole in front of the garage, and some tree roots poking up here and there.

*I guess they went to the dump, or maybe to lunch.* Madigan considered what to do with the rest of her day as she carried in her groceries, plunking them down on the counter. She put away the frozen things, then felt compelled to go look in the garage. Without the car parked in the middle, there was room to walk around. What was in all these boxes, anyway? It had been five years since her parents had been killed by a drunk driver in a terrible car accident. The boxes hadn't been touched since the movers had set them down. *Maybe it's time to start. But first I'll call Lee.*

Madigan had an unexpectedly pleasant conversation with her older brother's wife, and then with Lee himself. She told him she was going to start going through the boxes, and he mentioned a few things he'd like to have if she came across them. He said maybe he could drive out in early summer. His kids had never seen the Pacific Northwest. Madigan agreed to put aside anything she thought he might want to see. The rest she would keep or sell, and split the proceeds with him.

As Madigan hung up the phone, tears unexpectedly welled in her eyes. *I didn't realize a part of me has been packed away for five years.* She had ceased even to see the boxes, despite wedging herself through them each day.

In a determined mood she finished putting away the groceries and ate lunch, always keeping an ear out for the trucks. Back in the garage, she surveyed the mountainous piles, trying to figure out the most logical way to undertake the overwhelming task. Seeing that any approach at all could do nothing but help, she grabbed the closest box, choking on the grimy dust on its top, and carried it to the kitchen table. Old pots and pans filled it. A two-quart saucepan was on top with her mother's cast iron skillet below. No wonder the box had been so heavy. She hadn't thought of that skillet in years. The image of her mother rose from the box: standing at the stove in her favorite yellow apron, sizzling onions in this skillet, the aroma filling the kitchen. Madigan closed the flaps to shut out the memory. That was the problem. Everything was a memory. What do you do with boxes and boxes and boxes of memories?

Madigan sat on the edge of a kitchen chair and studied the box as if the dirty cardboard might offer an answer. She pulled her hair pensively. *Maybe the first step is just to see what's there.* A simple inventory. She would make a general list of what was in each box, then she and her brother could go over the list together. It was encouraging to have a plan of action. What could have been a tiny smile pulled at the corner of her lips as she found a sheet of lined paper and rummaged around in the drawer by the phone for a wide-tipped black marker and a pen. When the box went back out to the garage, it bore a big "#1" and "Pots and Pans" on its side and top. She placed the box with a thump in the middle of the floor where the car had been; there was no other place to start a new stack.

For the next three hours, Madigan dug through boxes, marking them and creating her master list. Surprised at how late it had become, and that her work crew had not returned, she lingered over a big box with some of her mother's picture albums. Another beside it was filled with loose pictures in large manila envelopes. Those two boxes she carried wearily to the kitchen. It seemed a good time to stop.

Glancing at the clock, she looked out the window. There was no sign of them at all.

Nothing had changed on Monday, but when Madigan arrived home from work on Tuesday, encouraging evidence that the work had progressed was evident: A few wood forms lay along the edge of the driveway and the dirt had been smoothed and graded a bit. *That's one thing that's gone right today, anyway,* she fumed. Parking in front of the house, Madigan slammed the car door with more force than necessary, her boss's words still heavy in the back of her mind. The speaker at one of their annual motivational seminars had compared certain types of criticism to handing out slugs—exactly like Donald's negative managerial style. She felt constantly covered in a slug trail of slime that wouldn't wash off. *How can he expect me to do anything when he has cut the department to nothing? What am I supposed to do when no one will stay?*

The week had been spent trying—unsuccessfully—to keep her friend Marilyn from transferring out of accounting. Then, today, Donald had blamed *her* for the decline in his staff. As if Madigan were the reason they were looking for openings anywhere, to do anything, they were so anxious to get out of the department any which way.

Once inside the house, she changed out of her suit, microwaved a meal, and looked at the paper. After dinner she threw her sheets and towels into the wash. Still angry when she went to bed, she spent a restless night tossing and turning, worrying about work. Exhausted by morning, she called in sick, though she hadn't missed a day of work in almost a year. Her assistant hardly knew what to say. Pulling the covers up over her head, Madigan was still in bed at ten a.m. when she heard the distinctive sound of James' truck arriving out front.

"Good day to you, Madigan!" The brothers hailed her as she came out to see them. "We noticed your car was still here. Do you have a holiday today?"

"You could call it that," she responded grumpily. Obie's cheerful question had sounded like an accusation to her tired ears: *Why aren't you at work?* "It looks like you're making some progress." She tried to keep the sharpness that fit her mood out of her expression.

"Good progress," Obie agreed, pulling out a shovel and ignoring the tone in his client's voice.

Since Madigan didn't feel like small talk, she cut the conversation short. Stepping back in the house, she decided to take advantage of the unseasonably warm February day by going for a jog. Maybe answers would come while she pounded the pavement.

When she returned, both Obie and James had stopped working and were sitting on overturned five-gallon buckets under her maple tree eating lunch. The delicious smell of chicken bar-b-que wafted her way.

"It's a lovely day," Obie said as she passed. "You should sit under your magnificent tree and enjoy it. The fresh air will do you good."

"Thanks, no. I've got things to do."

Her mood still dark, she half-heartedly scanned through the want ads at the kitchen table. A bit later she checked and they were still sitting under the tree. Madigan went back out.

"Is there anything I can get you?" Her curt offer clearly showed her goal was to spur them to movement rather than to extend hospitality.

"No, thank you. We're just resting for a few minutes." Obie's answer was as smooth and unhurried as Madigan's question had been harried and short.

"Oh." She stood for an awkward minute, then went back into the house and had a dry peanut butter sandwich. After studying the want ads a little longer, she read the rest of the paper. After another thirty minutes with the men still reclining beneath the maple's big branches, she changed her tactic, carrying a pitcher of ice water and two glasses out to them.

"Thank you," James replied politely as she offered him some. "That will wash down the chicken." He and his brother each took a glass and smiled appreciatively as they took a sip, but they made no move to get up.

"So how much longer do you think it will take to finish the driveway?"

"Only a few more days. Things are going well," James answered.

"Okay." Madigan went back to the kitchen and put the newspaper aside. She pulled out the box of her parents' loose photos and began sorting them, making one pile for her brother and another for herself. At one-thirty, there were still no work sounds coming from out front. She came out onto the porch.

"Would you like some more water?"

"No, thank you. We have some of our own. But yours was delicious," Obie answered this time.

Madigan couldn't stand it another minute. "What are you doing now?" she asked with some exasperation, but trying not to sound rude.

"We are resting." Obie's half-closed eyes proved the point, not about to be pressured off his comfortable spot. "We always rest after lunch. Because of the heat of midday. We've learned on the island, it's not a good time to do heavy work. Everyone rests after lunch."

Madigan thought about this. It was 51 degrees outside, uncharacteristically warm by Seattle standards for February 21, but it could hardly be described as midday heat. She looked at her watch and went back in the house. At two, she came back out and sat on the steps. Maybe sitting and watching would start the work flowing again. However, they continued talking quietly under the tree.

"How long have you been here in the States?" she asked during a lull in the conversation.

James answered. "I've been here three years, since I started my business. But Obie has been here only one year."

"And have you always worked with concrete?" Her curiosity was aroused.

"We've had many different jobs over the years," Obie replied. "We did all kinds of construction on the island. When there is no one to do it for you, you learn to do everything. What about you? What do you do?"

"I manage an office. For the city. Accounting." Her forehead furrowed to its worry look.

"And are you happy there?" Now Obie was the curious one.

"It's not a matter of being happy. It pays well and is what I know how to do. I've been there ten years…since right out of college. I have pretty good seniority for my age." A sense of pride filled her voice.

"But you are not happy?" Obie asked again.

"My boss is a problem sometimes."

"Ah, yes," Obie nodded with understanding. "My boss is a problem, too, sometimes." He looked at James and they both roared with laughter.

Madigan stiffened, thinking they were poking fun at her, but finally couldn't keep from smiling along with their enjoyment of their own joke. She tried to compare her boss Donald with these gentle men seated across from her. The non-stop, pressure-cooker, tearing-out-your-hair-in-frustration days she spent at work measured against the day these two were spending, sitting calmly under her tree. She shook her head.

"So you think you can finish by next week?" she asked again hopefully.

"Yes. No problem," James answered, the astute businessman in control of the calendar.

Madigan was about to leave, but the sun felt so good on her face that she leaned back against the railing of the steps and closed her eyes. *I'll only rest for a minute,* she thought, but relaxed so completely that she drifted off. Awaking with a jerk to the sound of the truck's engine, she slowly realized James was heading down the street. Obie's hand came out the passenger window and gave a slow wave.

Madigan looked at her driveway. It didn't look that much different than when they had first arrived in the morning.

## Chapter Two

### *Thursday, February 22*

E ARLY Thursday morning, James and Obie were pounding two-by-fours to frame the driveway when Obie noticed a curly-haired little girl peeking at them from behind the tree next door.

"Hello!" he called without looking over directly.

"Hi," a small voice answered, then a petite girl in a bright purple outfit stepped from behind the tree. She looked about seven, the same age as Obie's young cousin's daughter. "What are you doing?" she asked.

"We are making a new driveway for Madigan." Obie straightened, resting his back for a minute.

"Why?"

"Because her old driveway had many cracks in it."

"Our driveway has lots of cracks in it, too."

"It does?" Obie could easily see the cracks from where he was standing.

"What's that for?" The girl pointed to a round machine in the back of the truck.

"That's how we mix the concrete."

"And then what?"

"Preparing the area is the hard part. That's what we're doing now. Pouring the concrete is easy; it just looks hard. Then smoothing is the most fun of all, like icing a giant cake."

"Can I watch when you do it?"

"Of course." Obie was going to say more, but the head disappeared as abruptly as it had appeared. In a moment she was back, this time with a slightly older boy, both with jackets on and dressed for school. Sitting on their own steps with the stuffed backpacks beside them, the curious pair watched as Obie and James worked.

"When are you going to pour the cement?" the boy called.

"Concrete. Cement is what holds it together. Not today, but soon."

"I want to see it."

"Maybe you will," Obie straightened up again. "Maybe it will be Saturday." Obie looked at James and raised his eyebrow in an unspoken question. James nodded.

Obie spoke to the children. "If we have extra concrete when we pour, maybe we will make you some little stepping stones where you can write your names. Then you can put them in your garden. Do you have a garden in the back? Would you like that?"

"We don't have a garden, but we have a fort under the trees in the backyard," the boy replied enthusiastically.

"Lauren! Kevin!" A woman's voice called sharply from inside the house.

"We have to go to school now," Lauren sounded disappointed. "Mom's giving us a ride. See you later."

"Good day to you!" Obie called after them, a smile crossing his face as the memory of his own children at that age, also a boy and a girl, flashed before him.

The garage door opened and a silver sedan backed out. The children waved at Obie and James from the back seat. Their mother

18

barely paused to check for traffic before backing into the street and taking off down the road.

"In a hurry today," James said to his brother.

"I think every day," Obie replied, hammering in another nail.

The neighbor's garage door surprised Obie and James by going up at three-thirty before they even saw her car. All in one continuous motion, the mother made a quick turn into the driveway, pulled into the garage, and the door went down. Several minutes later, Obie heard young voices: Lauren and Kevin raced each other down the street from their bus stop, their backpacks banging on their shoulders as they flew up the steps and into their house. Within minutes, Lauren had returned to her spot on the top step with a glass of juice and a granola bar.

"How come you're still doing those boards?" she asked.

"The preparation for pouring takes a long time. It needs to be just right so that the concrete will lie smooth," Obie answered. "How was your school today?"

"Boring. My teacher is mean. We didn't get to go to recess because everyone was talking so much."

"That's too bad."

"And then, we had to write the spelling words five times each. I hate that."

"But how will you learn them if you don't practice?" Obie paused with the next board in hand.

"I don't know. But I hate writing the same word over and over again."

"Which grade are you in?" Obie peered into her eyes with genuine interest.

"Second. And the words are so hard."

The girl's mother called to her from inside the house.

"I have to get ready for baseball," Lauren said with a sigh, needing a few more minutes to stuff in the last bite and wash it down.

"Is it not early for baseball season to start?" Obie asked.

"Oh, it's called Early Bird Baseball. It's at the Y. Well, the park beside the Y. It's not the real thing yet. You get to pick your sport, and Kevin and I both like baseball the best." The sticky bar garbled her words.

"You are a great baseball player, then. And how about that? Is that boring?"

"Only if I'm in the outfield." A last sip cleared her mouth. "Usually I get to catch. Coach says I have a good arm. I think it's because of Kevin." She stood up and brushed off the crumbs. "He taught me to throw when I was little. Him and my dad. See you later —I gotta go." With that she was gone.

The garage door went up again and out went the silver car. Lauren and Kevin, baseball caps on their heads, waved again from the back seat.

"Busy day," James said.

"Yes. Busy people."

The last piece of framing on the children's side of Madigan's drive was in place. The brothers sat down under the maple. The leaves were still tiny bumps on the branches, but the magnificent size of the tree was a peaceful canopy. They rested and talked quietly, then packed up their things and left.

Madigan waited expectantly on Saturday morning, hoping her crew of four would arrive together to pour the concrete. Pleased to see the additional work done on Thursday, she had assumed that job completion was in view with the extra help of Young James and John on the weekend. But Saturday passed and Sunday, too, with no sign of any of them.

At six-thirty Monday morning, Madigan was awakened in the pre-dawn darkness by the noise of a rumbling truck slowing in front of the house, but it wasn't the sound of James' truck. She scrambled up and peered out her bedroom window. An enormous dump truck was maneuvering in the street, beeping as it backed over the sidewalk and a little ways into her drive. Madigan dashed down the stairs and through the front door, pulling on her bathrobe as she ran.

"Wait!" she yelled over the noise of the truck. "WAIT! What are you doing?"

Too late, the back of the truck rose, opened, and emptied a load of gravel and sand into her driveway. The driver finally noticed her and hopped out of his cab.

"What is this? This is a mistake." Madigan gasped.

"Madigan Gardner? 3505 Trail Run Road? I have an order for five cubic yards of gravel and sand mix."

"What?"

"Your contractor probably ordered it. It's paid for. Sign here, please." He held out a clipboard with a slightly dirtied order form attached.

"But—"

"All you have to do is sign there by the *X.*" He pushed the clipboard into her hands.

"It's just that I wasn't expecting this. I didn't know—"

"Don't worry, it's standard for this kind of work. Good foundation under the driveway, otherwise it's going to crack again."

Madigan scrawled her signature, barely able to keep it on the line, her hand was shaking so. The driver got back in the cab, lowered the bed of the truck, and pulled slowly onto the street. Madigan stared at the mountain of gravel and sand in her driveway. *What will they do with all this?*

Her shock first gave way to the familiar feeling of total helplessness but then irritation took over. She stormed into the house, first trying the phone number she had for James and Obie, with no success. Then she called Marilyn.

"Do you know what time it is?" Her friend's groggy voice left little room for doubt: too early.

"Do you know that a huge dump truck delivered a load of sand and gravel into my driveway? The mound's as big as a car! I thought we were almost finished. It's been two weeks since I could use my garage. How long will it take them to move all this? I'll still be parking on the street for the Fourth of July."

"Madigan, get hold of yourself. You're trying to get the drainage right, remember? Not having wet feet at work every day because of the puddle in front of the garage door, remember? That was the whole point of a new driveway." Marilyn pulled the covers up over her stirring husband and tapped around the cold floor with her toes, searching for her slippers.

Madigan's heartbeat began to slow. "But they said nothing about this. They say nothing about anything."

"I know. And it all gets done. Relax. It's going to work out. I promise."

Feeling sheepish at her overreaction, Madigan's voice softened. "I'm sorry I called. The noise woke me from a sound sleep and I panicked. It's not like I have a contract with them or anything. I mean, I haven't even given them any money yet. It's just so . . . ."

"Not quite the city's style of doing business, is that it?" Feet now secure in her bunny slippers, Marilyn took the phone into the bathroom so she wouldn't rouse her spouse any further.

"Exactly. It's so loose. I never know what's going to happen when. It drives me nuts." Madigan pulled at a section of hair and twirled it around her finger.

"A little uncertainty in your life is probably good for you." Marilyn turned on the bathroom light and examined her face in the mirror.

"How I miss your daily dose of sarcasm. How's risk management treating you?"

Happily observing that the dark circles under her eyes were receding since she'd transferred, Marilyn shared that good news and more: "My boss isn't nearly as good as you were, but *his* boss isn't nearly as bad as Donald. So overall I'm way ahead."

"Thank you *so* much."

"You've got to get out of there, Madigan. He's going to suck every ounce of joy out of you. If you even have any left at this point."

"Tell me about it. I don't know how he thinks brand new replacements are going to be able to do the work when we were already way behind with experienced staff. It's impossible." Another hair strand was wound even tighter around her finger this time.

"Get out of there. Why don't you move to purchasing or come to risk management with me?"

"There aren't any lateral transfers left. I'd lose my seniority and have to take a pay cut."

"Better than losing your mind."

"Easy for you to say. You've got two paychecks to depend on at your house."

"You're right, but I'd still do it." Marilyn clicked off the bathroom light and prepared to return to bed.

"Gee, you've done a lot to pep me up. Thanks for the uplifting start to my morning."

"Hey, you called me, remember?"

"Yeah, you're right. I'll talk to you later."

Madigan observed her sand pile. The thought of another long day at work made her head ache. Her head actually did ache, she realized with some surprise. Maybe she was coming down with the flu. She glanced at the clock: seven exactly. *Get dressed,* a little voice in her head prodded her. *I can't face it today,* her inner voice responded. Then she could hear Donald from the day before, criticizing her

23

efforts at every turn. *The man spends the whole day handing out slugs to people. And what do I do? I take them and get slimed.*

Madigan lay back down on her bed. How much less *could* she live on? That was the question. She called in and left a message for her assistant. Then she took a warm shower, put on a pot of coffee, and hauled out all her financial records. She found her calculator and grabbed a blank tablet from the drawer. By the end of the day, she'd know what her options were.

It was ten o'clock when she heard James' truck. The sight of Obie easing himself from the high cab seat was comforting to her, and she went to greet them, noticing for the first time the hint of a tattoo on Obie's midsection peeking out where his shirt was sliding up from his overalls.

"Another sick holiday?" James came around the back of the truck from the driver's side.

"Yes."

"We're thinking your job is making you sick." Obie joined his brother at the tailgate, tucking his shirt back in place.

"I'm beginning to think that, too. Listen, I need to know how much money you want and when you want it. I'm trying to figure out some things."

"Pay us half now—two-fifty. That will cover the gravel, sand, and wood. Then pay us the rest when we finish," James answered.

"And you'll be finishing when?"

"Pretty soon. Today we're making a new bed for the driveway, and we'll get the drainage just right."

"Will you take a check?"

"Cash is better for us."

"I'll have to run to the bank, then."

Obie cleared his throat. He had moved to the sidewalk.

"One more thing," James continued. "Your sidewalk. It's cracked and broken in many places. The tree roots have pushed up the slabs.

24

Someone's going to trip and get hurt. Do you want us to pour you a new sidewalk, too?"

"A new sidewalk?"

"Look here," Obie pointed out the worst spot. "Now imagine your driveway is going to be all beautiful and new right out to the street, and then you'll have this ugly sidewalk the rest of the way along your yard. It's not so much to do, ten squares. That's nothing."

"How much more would it cost?"

"Two hundred dollars more, that's all," James replied. "And it will look so much better."

"I don't know. I'd have to think about it. How much longer will it take?"

"No time. No time at all. One extra day. We'll get the boys to pull up the old concrete one evening, then we'll build the frame quickly, and we can pour all of it at the same time. Very easy."

Madigan didn't know what to do. They were right, of course. The sidewalk was awful. And the original price for the driveway was less than she'd been expecting.

"Oh, fine. Go ahead and do it. But you better hurry. I'm probably going to be unemployed soon. You should get your money while you can." She encouraged them with a smile.

"She's a nice lady," James mused, pulling his shovel from its assigned slot in the truck bed as Madigan disappeared into the house. "Very smart, I think. Too bad she doesn't like her work. She needs something else."

"She needs a lot of things she doesn't have right now." Obie grabbed his shovel and slowly attacked the mountainous pile of sand and gravel while his mind wandered to various possibilities for action on Madigan's behalf.

After running to the bank at noon, Madigan brought out a pitcher of lemonade. The brothers sat under the tree eating a chicken and rice dish that smelled deliciously of coconut.

"Here's three hundred," she handed James an envelope. "I like round numbers."

"Thank you," James smiled and stuffed the envelope into the top pocket of his overalls.

"Do I need a receipt? Will you remember that I've paid you?"

James pretended to be stricken. "You don't trust us? You are still worried about the money?"

Madigan sat down on her steps, unapologetic. "You must know how different you two are from anyone who has ever done any work for me. I'm sure I'm not the first person to mention this."

"We know." Obie smiled. "James is teasing you. Americans worry so much about everything. Everything! Where we come from, we say we'll do the job, we do the job. It's simple. You say you will pay us, we believe you will pay us. We have no reason to cheat you; we believe you have no reason to cheat us. You are the friend of Susan's sister. Susan is a good person. Her sister must be a good person. You are the sister's friend, so you must be a good person. It's easy for us."

Madigan shook her head. "I wish it was that easy for me. You haven't been in the States long enough. When you've lived here a long time, you might not be so trusting."

"When we've lived here a long time," Obie observed dryly, "we will be dead." James burst into laughter.

Madigan tried not to, but a smile tugged at her lips. It was impossible not to be touched by the underlying affection these two had in working together and their easygoing philosophy.

"How did you get started in concrete, anyway?" Madigan asked. "It doesn't seem like a usual career on a small island."

"When we were young," Obie answered, rubbing his tight curls with his hand, "there was a lot of money on our island for constructing roads and structures for the government. They wanted everything to be modern, so we built, built, built. Many of us learned how to make and pour concrete. But when there was no more money, the building stopped."

"And what brought you to the U.S.?"

"Our brother's wife had a cousin whose daughter married a young American who was living on the island for a while," James answered between bites of his creamy rice. "When he returned to the States she came with him. That was ten years ago. They had a good life, she sent money back to the family. She liked it here and got a good job. So when there wasn't much work on the island, I came. First I came by myself and worked for a year, then I brought over my wife and children. My girls are still young, eleven and fifteen. And you've met the boys. They go to school and work. Everyone is happy at the opportunities we have here."

"What about you?" Madigan asked Obie.

"I came over one year ago. Back home, our children were grown and had moved to Hawaii to work in the hotels there. Then my wife got sick…and she died. I was lonely. First I went to Hawaii, but it didn't work out." His usual joyful lilt was missing. "My children are anxious to be modern now. It's too much of everything for me. So I came to help my brother." His cheerful smile returned.

"You live with them?"

"It costs too much money to live alone. But sharing one house is manageable."

"How many of you?"

"James and his wife Lilly, and his sons and daughters. And our relative's daughter and her husband and their little children. That's all."

"Hmm." Madigan considered this. Three generations. Three families living together under one roof. And she couldn't even get her own life straightened out.

27

"How's the garage going?" James' question interrupted her thoughts.

Madigan smiled. "Some progress. I'll be done before you will, I think!" They all laughed. Though the joke was on them, the brothers joined in heartily.

"See, you laugh when you stay at home with us. We don't think you laugh enough when you're at work," Obie playfully counseled her.

Madigan was caught off guard. Obie strolled into her personal life so easily, this unusual man with a calm appearance who saw something in every little nuance, even in the way she walked out the door each day. She hated to admit it, but he could be right.

"I'm going to go finish what I was working on," she said, rising. "When will you be pouring?"

"Saturday, if we have Young James and John."

"Okay. See you then."


Once again at three-thirty, Obie heard the voices of Kevin and Lauren as they scampered down the street from their bus stop and disappeared into their house. Back out with pretzels and apple juice, they began playing basketball in the driveway. The free-standing hoop, held down by sandbags and positioned with its back toward Madigan's driveway, allowed missed shots to career over Obie's head as he moved gravel and sand from the barely shrinking pile up to the garage door in the wheelbarrow.

"When are you going to pour?" Kevin came to retrieve a ball for the fifth time.

"Maybe at the end of the week," Obie replied patiently like one used to living with young children.

"Look out!" Lauren yelled as her ball nearly hit James. "It's hard to play basketball at our house," she said apologetically as she came to recover the ball. "The driveway is so cracked, the ball always takes a bad bounce and rolls into the street. Plus, if you miss the basket, the ball ends up over here."

"I can see the problem," James sympathized.

"Could you fix our driveway?" Lauren looked hopefully at him.

"Mom and Dad would never go for that," Kevin shouted to her from his spot on the steps where he was trying to launch a long shot.

"Do you think your mother and father would like to have it fixed?" James paused while leveling a new section with a rake.

"Maybe. I could ask them." She gazed longingly at the new straight lines of the frame for Madigan's driveway.

"You ask them, and then we can talk about it. Tell them we can do a nice job. We could even put up a real basketball hoop for you."

"But would it cost a lot? They complain all the time about money."

"We don't charge as much as other people. They'd be happy. Ask them, then we can talk to them if they are interested."

"Wow, a real court! We could paint lines on it and everything!" Kevin's voice was ecstatic.

"If you get a real court, you can practice all the time. You'll become big basketball stars, and you can buy your parents a new house. They won't worry about money anymore!" James joked with a smile.

"Like your boys, James? So where is your big new house? The one with the master suite for me?" Obie teased back.

An old BMW roared down the street, stopping four houses down. A long-haired girl with a backpack hopped out and ran into the house.

"High school's out for today, I guess," Obie noted.

"Are you ready to stop?"

"Yes, I'm tired." He stretched his shoulders upward in an effort to relieve the throbbing in his lower back. "How about you?"

29

"Let's go. We're almost finished moving the fill. There's always tomorrow."

Madigan glanced out her window in time to see the truck pull away from the curb. The mountain of gravel and sand was less by only a quarter or so. Obie was in the passenger seat as usual. His hand came out the window as he gave his slow wave.

*How does he even know I'm looking?* she wondered, but found herself returning a little wave to the retreating truck's tailgate.

At the kitchen table, the numbers stretched out before her. She could definitely live on less. She could go to work tomorrow and request a transfer and be done with Donald. *Why shouldn't I? He's ruining the department and taking me down with him. If I had any backbone at all, I would have been the first to leave instead of the last.*

Madigan felt a small burst of energy and took the stairs two at a time to change into her running clothes.

# Chapter Three
## *Tuesday, February 27*

T HE sudden buzz of her intercom startled Madigan as she sat at her desk fidgeting nervously with a pencil the next morning.

"Roger would like to see you in his office," her assistant Denise announced.

"Thank you." She had been waiting for this. She had filed the paperwork as soon as she had arrived at seven-thirty. She knew Roger appeared promptly at eight-thirty each day, and she had been waiting for him to work his way down through the pile on his desk to find her transfer notice. *Well, this is it. Last chance to back out.* She stood and smoothed her skirt.

She avoided Denise's inquisitive stare and made her way to the other side of the building. She said good morning to Roger's assistant who motioned her ahead. At Roger's door, she could hear her name being announced on the intercom.

"Good morning, Madigan," Roger looked up from his desk. "Sit down, please. I received your transfer request this morning." He fixed her with a discerning gaze. "Would you tell me more about why you want to leave accounting? You've been there ten years. You're the most experienced person I have."

*Oh, here's the hard part,* Madigan's heart began to pound. *Getting out without trashing Donald.* She took a deep breath and tried to remember the lines she had rehearsed in front of the bathroom mirror only hours ago. She spoke slowly and distinctly.

"I'm sure that you are aware, from the number of recent transfers out of my department, that things have been difficult for the last six months. I am left with all new employees and an impossible workload. Any solutions I propose are not acted upon, and I've become frustrated. I need to do something different for a while." *There! I did it!*

"Six months, you say. That would put it about the time Sylvia retired and Donald took over as department head."

"Yes."

"Your relationship with Donald has not been good, then?"

Madigan waited a moment before answering.

"Look, Roger, we've known each other a long time. You know I'm not the type to complain about my boss. But it isn't working for me. It's no secret I was hoping to be promoted to department head myself when Sylvia retired. She had groomed me for the job, and I thought it was all set. Despite that, I've done everything I could to help Donald succeed. He came from a different department with no idea how to run things in accounting. He's made me lose all my staff. It's ridiculous."

Roger's serious expression did not change. "What would you say if I told you Donald will be leaving us? And that the department head position will be open again? And that this time I am able to offer it to you?"

Madigan sat, stunned, certain she had heard correctly but unable to imagine this outcome to the conversation.

"I don't understand," she was finally able to muster. "Is he leaving because—"

"He's leaving because he wasn't qualified for the job in the first place, but he had to be moved from his previous department. We had to keep him employed through another six-month review period before we could fire him. Even now, we may have to move him again, but I was trying to keep him in one spot until the six months was up or you threatened to quit, whichever came first. I'm sincerely sorry, Madigan, to have put you through this. Obviously, I couldn't say anything to you, and I knew you would try your hardest to make things work. Our labor attorney insisted we follow protocol precisely to avoid a wrongful termination suit. But the good news is that tomorrow you may move your things into your new office. The announcement of your promotion will be made at four today." Roger smiled conspiratorially. "Any time after that, you may begin enticing your old staff back."

"What about the new hires?" Madigan grasped for reality. She was alternately processing the news and leaping ahead to new possibilities.

"Keep them for now. You've been understaffed for three months. They'll help you catch up with the backlog, and then we can fit most of them into other departments as needed."

"Denise?"

"She'll move with you, of course. Donald has gone through four secretaries in six months. The one he has now can stay and take Denise's place with your replacement. Looking at seniority, that would be Marilyn, if you can get her to come back."

Completely speechless, Madigan made a conscious effort to snap her mouth closed so she would not appear like a fish out of water.

"Unless you want to follow through with your transfer request." Roger held up her form, a slight twinkle flashing in his eyes.

"No," Madigan finally stood, politely receiving the page. "No, I will be quite happy to stay in accounting. Thank you. Thank you very much."

"I know you'll do a good job, Madigan." Roger stood and held out his hand. "I wanted to give you the position six months ago, but my hands were tied. I'm glad it has all worked out. I was worried you would get fed up and quit, especially after Marilyn transferred."

"I'm glad I stuck it out, although I had no idea this is how it would end…could end."

"Try to stay away from Donald today, if you can." Another smile slipped beneath Roger's professional demeanor. "You don't have much of a poker face."

"I will lock myself in my office, I promise." Madigan reined in her million dollar smile and floated back across the floor, pausing at Denise's desk.

"Be in my office at four o'clock today. Until then, I don't want to be disturbed."

"All day, you don't want to be disturbed?" Denise repeated in surprise.

"I'm going to go through the pile on my desk, and I don't want any interruptions. And order me a ham and turkey for lunch, would you please? I'll eat at my desk."

"Sure." With one hand reaching for the ringing phone and her brow wrinkled in confused concern, Denise swiveled her chair a full 180 to watch her boss nearly skip the few more feet to her office.

Madigan closed the door gently and gave a quiet whoop of celebration and joy.


When she returned home that evening, the first thing she did was to call her brother to tell him her good news. But before she could even finish the story, Marilyn and her husband had appeared at the front door, offering a bottle of champagne complete with red bow.

"The driveway's going well, I see," Marilyn observed upon stepping over the threshold.

Madigan glanced out. It hardly seemed to matter that the pile of sand and gravel looked untouched.

"Why such a long face today?" Obie asked the next day after school when Lauren slumped onto her front steps.

"We found a puppy. And Mom won't let us keep it. 'Cause Kevin is 'lergic to dogs. But I want to keep it." She burst into tears.

"A puppy? What kind of puppy?"

"A mix of things, Mom said. Mostly lab, maybe shepherd. He's black and brown and he's so cute and soft."

"Where is your puppy now?"

"In the garage. Mom's going to take it to the shelter while we're at baseball." Lauren burst into tears again.

"Hmmm," Obie looked at Lauren sympathetically. "Ask your mother if we can see the puppy."

Lauren jumped up, and in a moment, the garage door opened. Kevin led out a small puppy dancing and pulling on a twine rope. Obie found a scrap of bread in his lunch and held it out. The pup pulled his way over to him and ate the bread hungrily.

"Where did you find him?" Obie bent over to pet its head.

"He was in the woods on the side of the playfield at school. He came right up to me. I was the first one to see him," Kevin answered. "I asked all around, but nobody knew where he came from."

"Isn't he cute?" Lauren sat down and the puppy came back to her. "But Mom says we can't have a dog because we're too busy and Kevin is 'lergic."

"Allergic, you idiot. It's not my fault. I told Mom we could keep him outside."

"Oh, I don't know about that," Obie stroked the soft fur. "A pup like this needs to be inside at somebody's feet at night. What do you think, James?" Obie glanced back at his brother who had stopped spreading sand to watch. The younger brother shrugged.

35

"Tell your mother we will take the puppy for her, if she wants. We'll be sure it gets a good home. We know lots of nice people." Obie looked at James again, but James refused to meet his eyes.

"Really?" Lauren's face immediately brightened. "Maybe you could keep him yourselves! You could bring him when you come to work here. Then we could see him every day!"

"Maybe." Obie patted the soft fur again and chuckled as the pup's entire hind end wiggled hard under his hand. "You never know what might happen."

The next day Obie and James arrived about three o'clock. They tied the pup on a long line to the tree in front of Madigan's house. They were still there when Madigan arrived home at 6:30.

"You're working late tonight," she said cheerfully as she got out of her car at the curb. "Is there something special about Thursdays?"

"You are smiling tonight," Obie replied. "Is there something special about Thursdays for you?" He grinned back at her.

"Very funny. I happen to have a new job. I got promoted Tuesday evening!"

"What about your boss who gave you headaches?"

"No longer employed by the city." Madigan's satisfaction was obvious.

"No wonder you are happy, then. No more sick days."

"Right—" Suddenly Madigan noticed movement under the tree. "What is that? What do you have over there? Oh, it's a puppy?" She came forward and set her briefcase on the steps and the pup ran up to greet her. "How sweet you are," she murmured to the dog. "Where did you get him? *Is* it a him?" Holding the pup away from her suit she took a quick peek beneath. "Oh, yes, you *are* a sweet little boy. Where did he come from, Obie?"

"The children next door found him at school, and their mother wouldn't let them keep him. We said we thought we could find him a home." Obie approached and now the puppy ran to him.

"I bet James' girls must love him. Look how soft he is." The pup returned and was begging to be picked up. Madigan scooped him up in her arms, too captivated to worry about her suit.

"You don't have any pets, do you?" Obie asked, a bit too innocently.

"No, I can't really have any animals. I'm so busy. Working all day."

"This is a nice puppy. Well-behaved already. The children were so disappointed they couldn't keep him. The little boy is allergic, his sister says."

"Well, that's too bad. He sure is a sweetie. That's so nice of you two to take him." Madigan put the puppy back down. "Are you still on track to pour on Saturday?"

"We think so. There is still some sand to move and compact with the roller. Then we must pull up your old sidewalk. But we'll try," James replied optimistically.

Saturday morning Obie and James arrived with the puppy. They tied him up by the tree again. Kevin and Lauren heard the truck arrive and bounced out of the house excitedly to play with the dog.

It was ten o'clock when Madigan leaned out of the upstairs window and yelled, "Where are your sons, James? I thought you were pouring today."

"We're waiting for them." James leaned back and looked up at Madigan. "Today we're only going to be able to get up this old sidewalk. We'll have to wait to pour until next week."

Madigan rolled her eyes and closed the window. Nothing surprised her anymore, but these never-ending delays didn't seem to matter as much, either.

"I wanted to watch you pour today," Kevin said, disappointment in his voice.

"Me, too," Lauren added, though totally engrossed in playing with the pup.

Soon Madigan came out and sat on her steps. The day was warming up. The puppy crawled into her lap.

"My name is Madigan," she introduced herself to the children. "I've seen your family coming and going, but we've never really had a chance to talk."

"I'm Lauren, and this is Kevin."

Obie turned from his work. "You live beside each other and you have never met?" he asked in amazement.

"We haven't really been outside at the same time, I guess," Madigan explained. "And our backyards are fenced."

Just then the children's mother came out her front door. Seeing the group on Madigan's front steps, she joined them. "Time to go," she announced to Lauren and Kevin. Then she stuck her hand out to Madigan. "Hi, I'm Liz Haffner. I know we've said hello over the years, but we've never had a chance to introduce ourselves."

"I'm Madigan Gardner. And this is Obie and James," she introduced her crew, one of whom was hard at work with sledgehammer, and one of whom was supervising. "And I guess you've met this little guy already." She patted the puppy's head.

"The kids were distraught that we couldn't keep him. They smuggled him home on the school bus. I didn't even know he was in the house until I heard Kevin sneezing. Thank you so much for taking him," she called to James, who stopped his work for a moment. "Are you still looking for a home, or have you decided to keep him yourself?"

"We are keeping him for now," James answered. Obie was suddenly busy looking for something in the truck.

Liz walked over to James, drawing Obie's attention. "The children mentioned that they had asked you about our driveway. I would love to have it re-done, if it wouldn't be too expensive. Could you give me an estimate sometime when you have a chance?"

"We have looked at it already," James replied. "We could do a nice job for you."

"How much would it cost?"

"Do you want that same look to the concrete? Or something smoother to play basketball on?"

"The kids would love a real play court. Would that be expensive?"

"Not at all. It's simply a different surface to the top. And if the basketball hoop is attached above the garage, and the driveway is widened a little, you'd have a real half-court. Then the balls wouldn't roll into the street or Madigan's yard so much, because the children would be shooting toward the house."

"I'll ask my husband. But how much would it cost?"

"Not much. We are very reasonable. For a two-car driveway, twelve hundred dollars. A good hoop would be another three hundred, and we would put it up for you."

"How soon would you need an answer?"

"Any time is fine. We'll be here for at least a few more days."

"Okay, I'll let you know." She turned back toward her own house. "Come on kids, we need to go. Nice to officially meet you, Madigan."

"Nice meeting you, too. Bye, Kevin. Bye, Lauren." The pup was still curled up in her lap. "No one has come looking for him?" she called out to James. "What have you named him?"

"We don't have a name for him yet. Why don't you name him? It's been a good week for you," Obie encouraged her.

Madigan felt happy. It *had* been a good week. She pulled the pup closer and stroked his back as she tried to think of a name.

"I name you Roger," she announced ceremoniously. "After a very good boss."

She let the puppy chase the rope end for a while before she realized there was no work going on. She looked up at Obie expectantly, but he continued leaning against the truck.

"Waiting for the boys to come with the truck and the jackhammer. So we can break up the other concrete," he gestured with his hand as if reading her mind.

"Are they coming for sure? It's almost noon."

"They're coming, but they have some things to do first. Don't worry, they'll be here. We'll wait for them."

Madigan planted a kiss on the puppy's head, then put him in the grass, stood, and stretched. "I've got things to do inside. I'll see you later."

Obie smiled at James.

Madigan was in the garage going through more boxes when she heard the engine of the newer truck. Soon there was knock on the front door. Obie held the wriggling pup in his arms.

"Young James and John are here," he began apologetically. "We are going to use the jackhammer, and the noise will be painfully loud for the dog. Could Roger come in with you for a while?"

"Sure, I guess so. Come on, baby," Madigan held out her arms. "Does he need water or anything?"

"I put his bowls in your backyard. You could feed him lunch in a little bit. It's in his bowl already."

"Okay. Glad to help."

Madigan sorted boxes and Roger sniffed around the garage, startling each time the jackhammer sounded on the front sidewalk. After some food and a game of chase in the backyard, he collapsed into a small brown and black ball in the grass. Madigan carried him back to the garage and laid him on an old towel. She worked as the dog slept, enjoying his quiet companionship. Suddenly, she realized it was *too* quiet. She ran into the house and looked out the window.

Everyone was gone. The sidewalk by the street had disappeared, and only a few chunks of concrete remained stacked along the curb. James' truck was still there, but his sons' had disappeared.

Madigan returned to the garage.

"Now where have they gone off to and left you here?" she asked the sleeping pup. "I suppose they went for lunch. They better not forget you." She leaned over and stroked him. Roger reminded her of the dog she'd had as a child. He had died when she was only seven, and they'd never replaced him. The pup slept despite her touch, his feet trembling as if he were chasing something in a field.

Madigan worked for another hour with no sign of the guys. Finally, at four o'clock, she heard the truck.

"Where have you been?" she asked a little indignantly, bringing Roger out front.

"Sorry. The dump was all backed up today and traffic was bad both directions. It took longer than we thought. I'm glad we didn't have the dog in the truck all this time." Obie looked appropriately remorseful, gazing at her from beneath his thick grey eyebrows.

"Well, here," she modified her tone as she handed him the cuddly lab mix.

"He will make a lovely pet, don't you think? So calm and sweet."

"I think you're right. He reminds me of a dog I had when I was little."

"Hmm." Kindly crinkles edged Obie's eyes and mouth.

"Looks like you might be doing a job right next door. That would be lucky, huh?" Madigan continued, suddenly sorry she had been complaining again.

"You'd be surprised how often it works that way," James said as he loaded tools carefully into his truck. "People see how new and clean the concrete looks, then they look at their own old driveway, and decide they want it new, too. Side-by-side, it happens often."

"So what's next?"

41

"All we have to do is prepare the ground under the sidewalk with the leftover sand and gravel, compact it, and make the framework. Next week we can pour."

"What about tomorrow?"

"Not on Sunday," Obie answered firmly. "We never work on Sunday. There's church morning and evening, and rest in between. Even most of the cooking is done on the other days."

"Two church services?"

"On the island, everyone worships in the morning and evening. And during the day, people visit one another—a day of rest."

"Okay, then. I'll see you one day next week, I guess."

"Good day, Madigan," Obie said fondly.

She watched him put Roger on the truck seat and then heave himself up into the cab and take the pup back on his lap. Roger *was* a cute puppy. But there was no way she could have a dog. No way.

Chapter Four

*Thursday, March 8*

MADIGAN did not see Obie and James again until after work five days later, when she found them smoothing gravel and sand in the sidewalk bed.

"I wondered if you were ever coming back," she said, exiting the car at the curb. "We're practically halfway through March already."

"We decided we really could not pour without my sons' help," James said placatingly, undisturbed that the "quick job" was stretching into its fourth week. "There seemed to be no reason to come and sit here when we have other small jobs we can do. Now we'll get everything ready."

Madigan surveyed the scene. The driveway had seemed ready for days. The front sidewalk was framed, and the mountain of gravel and sand reduced to less than a quarter of its original size. As she walked toward the house, a bundle of fur raced from behind the tree.

"Wow, you've really grown!" Madigan put down her briefcase and scooped the puppy up, again unmindful of her business clothes. His small tongue gave a lick right up her cheek. Instantly a feeling came over her, one she had not had for a long, long time. That lick...it was just like the one her childhood dog had given her many times. And that puppy-breath smell. Roger settled down into her arms as if he belonged there.

"You are so cute," she said, gently putting him down and retrieving her briefcase.

"We are having a little problem with him," James confided quietly.

"Oh?" Madigan paused.

"Our cousin's daughter, the young mother in our house, does not want a dog right now. Her children are little. It's a fuss for her, the clean-up. The pup is a little rough on the baby."

"How old is the baby?"

"Nine months. He's crawling and beginning to pull himself up. The pup...Roger...tries to play with him like he is another puppy. It's a little too much."

"What are you going to do?"

"We're going to find him a good home." Obie had materialized silently behind her.

Madigan whirled around and looked Obie straight in the eye.

"Oh, no, don't even think about it. I told you, I work too much." Roger had caught the tip of her shoe and was trying to play. She shook her foot out of his mouth, which made him grab it again. "There's no way I can have a dog. He'd be lonely during the day." She reached down and pushed the pup back, trying to preserve her good shoe while feeling slightly cornered.

"You have two good puppy sitters living right next door," Obie reminded her. "I think they'd be happy to play with the dog and care for him after school. They have nearly half-an-hour every day, even with baseball."

"You two have had this figured out from the start, haven't you?" Madigan looked accusingly back and forth between James and Obie. "You had no intention of keeping him at all, did you?" The deviousness of their plan was quite brilliant, not that she would ever admit it to them.

Now Roger was attacking James' boot. The husky workman looked at the ground and wiggled his foot in gentle play, shrugging. "It was Obie's idea to take the dog."

"Did we find him?" Obie asked with mock defensiveness. "We didn't bring him here from the woods. But we're keeping him from the pound where he would be frightened by all the big dogs. We even took him to the vet. He's had his first shots. Now we're simply trying to find him a good home. You can't be mad at us for that."

Roger came back to Madigan's shoe and finally she scooped him up. He sent another lick up her face. She sighed, knowing it was all over.

"It's so...so...conniving of you!" She felt Roger's quick heartbeat against her hand and held him closer. "I'll try it for a few days. I'm not making any promises."

"We put his bowls and bag of food in the backyard for you," Obie said helpfully. "That's all we have for him so far."

Madigan tried to be mad, but it was impossible with the warm bundle in her arms.

"I guess this is where I take my new puppy to the pet store like in all the commercials. Puppy bed, leashes, toys. It's *expensive*, you know."

"You're the one with the big promotion, remember?" Obie's wise eyes met hers. "Now you are a happy worker, like us. You have plenty of money to help a little dog who needs a home."

*Why does Obie have to be right about everything? Of course I have enough money to take care of a puppy. What have I been doing with it for ten years? Nothing. One vacation a year. Gifts for family. A few new outfits. That was it.*

"Fine. I'll keep him. But it's up to you two to make sure there are no paw prints in the new concrete."

45

"No paw prints, I promise," Obie agreed solemnly.

All heads turned at the sound of Liz's garage door going up. Before their mother could pull into the garage, the kids popped out of the back seat, and Madigan met them halfway.

"Hey, guys," she held Roger out for Lauren's embrace, "I have a proposition for you."

Obie and James exchanged looks behind Madigan's back. "Well, that is *one* thing she needed," James said under his breath.

"And it was so easy," Obie added with a smile.

They were putting their rakes in the truck when Liz came out of her house to speak to James. Obie listened as the usual conversation over money and a contract followed. He always let James handle that part. On the island, their word had always been enough to close the deal. He did not understand how to negotiate the finer points in the easy way that James did.

"When can you start?" Liz was asking James.

"We need to finish Madigan's, but on days when we can't work here, maybe we could start to pull up your driveway. You'll need to park out on the street for a while. Will that be a problem?"

"No, I don't think so, if it's not for too long. Let us know when you want to start."

"Next week, I think. Your husband goes to work every day?"

"Yes, he leaves quite early and isn't home till late. That's why you never see him. *We* barely see him. And all I do is work and drive the kids around."

"It's a busy life," Obie observed.

"I'll tell my husband you might start next week. And congratulations on finding a home for the dog. I never would have thought she'd want a pet." Liz nodded her head in her neighbor's direction.

"Why is that?" James inquired.

46

"Seems like she works all the time. In the three years we've lived here, I've never seen her as often as I have in the past month. We didn't even know each other's first names."

"Hmmm." Obie's favorite expression escaped him.

"I guess that seems kind of sad. But time flies; it's as if we just moved in. Well, thanks for finding a home for the dog. And even better that it's right next door so Lauren and Kevin can play with him. It's perfect."

"We thought so, too."

"See you next week, then."

"Tell the children we'll probably pour on Saturday. All we need to do yet is tamp down the sand and gravel. They want to watch."

"They've been anxiously waiting!"

However, Saturday came and went with no sign of Obie or James. Madigan, by now used to this scenario, did not panic but, instead, savored the day with Roger. In the morning, Lauren and Kevin came over to play with him in the backyard. The sound of young voices and a barking dog so near was new to her, but not disagreeable. Roger, being an especially smart little black lab-shepherd mix, was already getting the idea of going outside to the bathroom. She kept her back door open when she was home and blocked him in the kitchen with plenty of newspaper covering the linoleum when she was gone. At night, he slept in the crate in her bedroom. Liz had a house key so the kids could come in after school. The arrangement seemed to be working for everyone.

Trying to think of something special to do Saturday afternoon, Madigan took Roger to a large off-leash park she had read about where the dogs could run freely. She was overwhelmed with the attention Roger attracted from the moment they arrived as they made their way to the puppy area. The range of people and dogs in the park amazed her. Several people sat on folding chairs and chatted as they watched their dogs cavort together. Others walked or jogged the perimeter while their pets played.

Roger alternated between bravely wandering away from her, then skirting back behind her legs if any bigger dog got too close. After twenty minutes of running, he was totally exhausted and came back to her. She picked him up, and he nearly fell asleep in her arms. *How have I gone all these years without the joy of a warm puppy? And how have things changed so much in only one month?*

Pouring day finally came on Tuesday. Young James and John arrived with Obie and James at noon and worked till nearly three, carting the concrete by wheelbarrow from the portable mixer to the driveway where Obie and James carefully spread it with their hoes and square trowels. By the time the children got home from school, Young James and John had left. Lauren and Kevin quickly dropped off their things inside, raced to Madigan's back door to get the dog, then brought him around to the front yard as he tugged and pulled on his small leash. They settled down on their steps to watch.

"Why don't you have a big cement truck, like everyone else does?" Kevin asked almost immediately.

"It costs too much," Obie answered, pausing to straighten his tired back. "It takes several people to handle the concrete when it comes out so fast, to spread it just right before it sets. This way, we mix a little, we do a little, we get it exactly right, then we do a little more."

"The driveway's nearly finished," Kevin's voice showed he was impressed.

"It's been a long day. And we need to finish it tonight."

Lauren disappeared and brought back a flowery summer pitcher filled with strawberry lemonade and four small plastic glasses. Obie and James joined the children on the steps for a moment between batches, relaxing and sipping the sweet drink while Roger jumped and tumbled beside them. Unsettling this calm scene, the BMW with the long-haired girl came flying down the street again, this time followed by the boy in a souped-up Honda. They both parked and then disappeared into the girl's house. Obie's eye was caught by the boy's casual arm around the girl's shoulder as the front door closed behind them.

"Are you enjoying having the puppy next door?" Obie returned his attention to the children and leaned over to pet Roger.

"Oh, yes," Kevin answered happily. "It's probably the closest I'll ever get to having my own dog, unless I outgrow my allergies."

"Your papa, what does he do that he is gone such long hours every day?" Obie extracted his finger from Roger's sharp-toothed grip.

"He's a scientist at the university. He runs a lab and teaches graduate courses."

"No wonder he is busy, then. I don't think we have seen him yet."

"It's the lab part. He's always checking his experiments."

"But he'll be coming to your baseball games soon, no? Maybe we'll meet him then."

"He wants to come. He can't always leave the lab."

"That's too bad." Obie stood up slowly. "Well, we're doing one more mix today. We'll make those little stepping stones I promised you. But don't move them today. Let them harden for a few days."

"Thanks!" Lauren caught Roger's leash and led him to Madigan's back door. "We've got to go to practice now, Kevin."

"When can you start at our house, do you think?" Kevin's impatience was directed at James.

"Pretty soon. We need my sons' help to pull up the old driveway."

"I can't *wait* to have a real court to play on. And Mom said you're going to put up a new hoop for us, too?"

"Would you like that?" James smiled, remembering his own boys' enthusiasm as children.

"Oh, yeah! This hoop isn't high enough. And it always falls over. It didn't cost much."

"The new backboard will go above the garage door, solid and sturdy. Then the court will come this way," James motioned with his hands. "We'll widen the driveway a little, so you will end up with nearly a half-court."

"Could we paint lines on it?"

"Whatever your parents agree to."

Lauren came back, swinging the key on its string. "See you later." Kevin waved and raced his younger-but-faster sister up to their front door.

"The puppy was a stroke of luck, no?" Obie smiled as he waited for the concrete to churn in the small mixer.

"She has not even complained about taking it," James replied with amazement.

As they finished the narrow, decorative side sections of the driveway, a newer-model, dark red van pulled hurriedly into the driveway on the other side of the children's house. A pretty woman in her early twenties hopped out of the driver's side. The passenger door opened, revealing a young man who looked slightly older, balancing himself on one leg as he exited and then pulling out some crutches. His right leg had a large brace on it. He slowly made his way around the front of the van and awkwardly navigated the six steep steps up to the front door. A long scar from temple to chin marked the right side of his face. Ahead of him, the woman unlocked the door, then hurried back into the van and left. Obie and James heard the front door shut as they went back to their work.

"He looks like he was seriously hurt," James wondered aloud.

"Hmmm," Obie replied.

"A car accident, I suppose."

"Hmmm."

Half-an-hour later, Madigan pulled up. Cheerfully hopping out of her car, she was at first slightly distracted. Obie and James waited expectantly for her reaction as her glance fell from their faces down to the finished driveway at their feet, and then a little gasp escaped her. Both men broke into broad smiles. Madigan stood beside the car taking in the smooth surface, the perfect slope, and the whimsical pattern of small stones up each edge of the drive.

"It's gorgeous. I had no idea it would turn out like this." She admired the straight lines and bent to better inspect the fine work on the edges. "Where did you get these little stones?"

"They were left over from another job," Obie beamed. "We wanted to surprise you, do you like it?"

"I love it. It's perfect. I mean, I had no idea it could look so…so special. It's unbelievable." At that moment they could hear Roger's loud crying from inside the house. "Let me get him, and I'll be right back," Madigan excused herself and soon reappeared with Roger.

"Keep him off the—" Obie started to yell as Roger made a beeline for the slick concrete, but Madigan scooped him up.

"Just seeing if you can take a joke," she laughed. "The driveway is stunning. I can't believe how nice it looks from inside the house." Roger sent an excited lick up her face. "Did the kids get him out today? He seems so lively."

"Right after school they had him out for about thirty minutes. How is the kitchen floor?"

"Not too bad." Madigan couldn't take her eyes from her driveway. "I love this pattern with the pebbles on the side. I can't believe it's done. It goes so slowly, and then all of a sudden it goes fast."

"Construction always seems that way. So much preparation. But, listen, now," James instructed her solemnly, "you must spray this down every morning and evening for two weeks before you can drive on it. You must keep it damp so that it doesn't crack as it dries."

"Twice a day for two weeks? I've never heard of that."

"It takes five minutes, and it's very easy to do," Obie encouraged her.

James began to carefully rinse and clean his tools. "This week, when my sons can come with us, we'll pull up your neighbor's driveway. Then we'll finish your sidewalk."

Warning bells went off in Madigan's brain. "You don't think you should completely finish over here before you start on theirs?"

"We need to do the pulling up when my sons are available," James explained. "We can finish your sidewalk any time, now that the driveway section is done."

"As long as you don't leave me unfinished forever." Madigan was not entirely convinced that waiting to finish her job was a good plan. The idea for replacing the sidewalk in the first place had been presented to her as a way to prevent an unsuspecting pedestrian from tripping. But someone falling into an entire stretch of torn-up sidewalk seemed much more likely than someone catching a toe on the original slightly uneven slabs.

"Don't worry. We can easily work on both projects at once. It's a much better use of time," Obie assured her seriously.

Madigan studied Obie's face and considered the absurdity of these two lecturing her on time management. But what did it really matter about the sidewalk, since she would soon be able to park in her garage again?

"And we'll fix that garage door opener," James said, as if reading her mind. "Let's look at it right now."

Surprised they had remembered, Madigan led the way through the house and Obie rolled up the garage door from inside. James stood under the ceiling motor and looked at it.

"It doesn't work with either the wall button or the car remote?"

"No. It just stopped working one day. I replaced the battery in the remote, but that didn't help."

"Do you have a little ladder or something I could stand on?"

"I have a two-step stool in the kitchen. That's all I have, but it might be enough."

James moved a few boxes aside to position the stool, then examined the unit carefully. Obie traced the wires along the wall to the "open" button.

"No problem here," he reported to James.

"I don't see anything wrong here, either," his brother answered. "Go get the remote," he told Madigan. Retrieving it from the car, she handed it to James, then stood in the open garage door and admired the new, very gradual slope to the driveway.

"Looks like you fixed my puddle problem."

"I hope so," James mumbled as he fiddled with the manual override. "Try it now from the wall button."

Obie hit the wall button and the door lurched to life and began to close.

"How did you do that?" Madigan jumped out of the way.

"Let's see if the problem is still with the remote," James said as the door came to rest on the floor. "Try it now." He flipped her the remote.

Madigan pushed the button, and up came the door. "I don't believe it. I'm going to go try it from outside."

James stepped off the stool.

"Loose wire?" Obie asked.

"I don't know. I gave everything a little jiggle. I'm not sure if anything was really wrong."

Madigan appeared on the front lawn. She aimed the remote. Down went the door. And then back up.

"I can't believe it. Do you know how long I haven't been using this? Before you started the driveway, I mean."

"It might have been a loose wire, or dust," James was sympathetic.

"Maybe your aim was off," Obie suggested. Madigan shot him a disparaging look.

"If it stops working again, tell us," James continued. He and Obie walked through the house and met Madigan in the living room.

"I'm going to take Roger to the off-leash park for a run."

"Good day to you, then. Don't forget to spray your driveway tonight," Obie reminded her.

"Oh, right." With Roger wiggling in delight in her arms, the task had already slipped her mind.

Chapter Five

*Wednesday, March 14*

BACKING out of his garage at 7:30 the next morning, the children's father stopped and lowered his side window when he caught sight of Madigan impatiently spraying her new concrete.

"It looks really nice," he called to her.

Madigan released her hold on the spray nozzle to hear more clearly.

"It looks terrific," her neighbor called again, leaning across the seat to make eye contact.

"Oh, thank you." Madigan moved closer to his car and leaned down. "They finally have this part done, anyway. I hear your house is next."

"So I've been told. I'm afraid I was outvoted. I didn't think anything was wrong with our driveway, but I'll admit, compared to yours, it does look pretty bad."

"It's amazing what fresh concrete can do for the looks of the place. Now I feel like I need to paint the garage door and plant some flowers or something. And say, I wanted to tell you how much I appreciate the kids helping out with Roger."

"Roger?" His look was quizzical.

"The puppy?" Madigan pulled back a strand of hair that had fallen forward and waited for some recognition in his face. "The dog they found at school but couldn't keep? The one that Obie and James took home, but I ended up with."

"I guess I haven't heard about that yet. What exactly are they doing?"

"Each day after school, they let the puppy out and play with him for half-an-hour or so. It's a great help, since I sometimes don't get home until seven. It would be a really long day for him to be alone, otherwise."

"I'm glad it's working out," he said, still sounding puzzled. "Well, got to go." He leaned back toward the steering wheel and the window went up.

"Bye," Madigan said to herself as she finished spraying the concrete. This was the first time she'd even had a conversation with him since the day they had moved in. It seemed odd that he didn't know anything about Roger.

Late Saturday morning, Madigan was about to drive off when Obie, James, Young James, and John pulled up in the two trucks. They parked ahead of her, in front of the children's house. Madigan rolled down her window and waited as Obie got out of the truck and came back to speak to her.

"Good day, Madigan! Good day, Roger! And how are you this fine day?" His cheerfulness was infectious, as usual.

"I'm good, thanks. And you?"

"I'm well, also. Your driveway is looking fine. You're keeping it damp."

"The rain has helped. What are you doing today?"

"We're taking up this driveway. Have you seen the children's parents outside yet this morning?"

"The kids were up earlier, out here playing with the dog. I think Liz is still home. I don't know about the dad."

"We need to get their cars moved out of the garage. Would you go ask them for us?"

"I'm leaving for the dog park...." Obie stared at her patiently as James began getting out tools. "Oh, fine." She put her head back in the window and turned off the ignition. "Stay, Roger. I'll be right back." She cranked the window up a little more so he couldn't escape and ran up the lawn to her neighbor's front door. Ringing the bell she could hear the shouts of the children inside.

Lauren peeked out the window and then opened the door. Madigan looked past her into an immaculately decorated house.

"Hi, Lauren."

"Hi, Madigan. Where's Roger?"

"He's in the car. We're going to the park. Is your mom home?"

"She's upstairs."

"Would you please tell her that Obie and James are here to start your driveway, and they want to be sure the cars are out of the garage."

"Okay, I'll tell her—"

"Who is it?" Liz's legs came into view as she descended from the second floor. "Oh, Madigan, hello. Come on in," she welcomed her neighbor inside.

"Thanks, but I'm actually on my way to the park. Obie and James asked me to run up and tell you that they're ready to start on the driveway and you'll need to get your cars out of the garage." *And why am I being the messenger when they could have come up and asked themselves?*

"Oh, thanks. Frank has already left for the lab, but my car's still in there. I'll find my keys and be right out."

Madigan held the screen door open and couldn't help admiring the decor. "Your house is gorgeous," she said as Liz hunted for her

57

keys. "I had no idea these old homes could be made to look so lovely."

"Thank you. Interior design is my work. Part-time, sort of around the kids' schedules." Disappearing momentarily into the kitchen, Liz returned, still hunting. "And what do you do, Madigan? I know you keep hours that are nearly as bad as my husband's."

"I work for the city. In the accounting department. All those checks you make out for city service wind up in a spread sheet on my desk."

"You're an accountant, then. Wow, that's a lot of responsibility. They won't let me near the books at my work."

"My job is more management, now. Trying to predict the needs and trends, analyze data, that kind of thing. But the bottom line is kind of balancing the books on a large scale."

Lauren leaned against her mother. Liz's hand automatically went to her daughter's head, stroking her hair gently.

"Her boss's name is Roger," Lauren confided. "She named the puppy after him."

"Really?" Liz looked back at Madigan in surprise. "And was that a compliment to your boss or something else?"

"Oh, it's a compliment," Madigan finally stepped inside. "I was recently promoted after six pretty bad months. That's why my hours had been so long. But things are getting much better." She glanced outside as a bang came from one of the trucks. "I'd better not keep you or you'll be trapped in your garage till who knows when."

"How long do you think this might take?" Liz gave up on the coat pockets and searched her purse once more.

"You'll have to ask James." Madigan laughed. "He and Obie do have a slightly different sense of time, but their work is excellent, and reasonable. And they're so congenial to have working at your house. The time element might be their *one small* downfall. I think it was five weeks ago today that they first came to look at my driveway."

58

"Five weeks?" Liz's head jerked up, and she nearly dropped her purse. "We might be out of the garage for five weeks?"

"I'm sure yours will go much faster," Madigan consoled her. "The weather is better, and they seem to be on a roll here, starting yours and finishing up mine."

"How did you say you heard about them?"

"The sister of a friend of mine at work used them and was happy with the outcome. My new concrete is so flawless it makes everything else look shabby. Now I feel like I need to spruce up the front yard. "

Liz rolled her eyes. "I'd *love* to have an excuse to get a landscaper in here. But Frank thinks it's a waste of money. Not that *he's* ever home to do any yard work." Liz began looking for her keys again, finally finding them under some papers on the credenza in the hall. "All right, tell them I'm moving the car."

Madigan returned to where Obie was petting Roger through the open window.

"Sorry it took so long. She's coming."

"She seems like an agreeable lady. Maybe you'll make a new friend." He flashed his disarming smile so quickly that Madigan couldn't take offense.

"Yes. She seems like a charming person. But you shouldn't worry so about my social life, Obie." She patted his arm as she slid into the car. "I'm headed to the park. Will you be here when I get back?"

"Definitely. We have a long work day ahead of us to get the driveway up. And don't despair, your sidewalk is going to be finished soon."

*Yeah, right.* Madigan had heard that line before. She pulled around their trucks, waving to Young James and John. It was odd, she thought, again noting the seriousness of the sons contrasted against the easy sociability of their father and uncle, how the variable and inconsistent rhythm of their work no longer bothered her at all.

The Haffner's garage door rose and Liz backed her car out of the driveway. Since there was no place else to park, she pulled in front of the next neighbor's down the block.

"Good day," Obie said engagingly to her as she got out of the car. "It's a fine day."

"It is. And I see you were able to get your assistants."

"Yes, this one is my nephew Young James," he said, pointing to the shorter of the two young men pulling tools from the truck, "and that is his brother John. They are James' sons."

"Nice to meet you both," Liz called. They nodded and James came over.

"Good day, Mrs.—"

"Haffner. But please, call me Liz."

"Good day, then, Liz. Today we'll get up all the old concrete and take it away. Then we'll level the driveway, build the outside framework, put in some sand and gravel if we need it, and finally pour. Like at Madigan's. We'll do a good job for you. Have you decided about making the driveway a little bigger for the basketball court?"

"Yes. I want you to do that."

"We'll take about a foot from the lawn along each side. And then perhaps a smoother surface than we used on Madigan's, so that you can paint lines on it?"

"Whatever you think. I know nothing about it."

"We'll check with you again before we pour," Obie suggested. "Perhaps your husband will have an idea that he wants it just so?"

Liz smiled. "No, I can guarantee you that he will have no opinion about concrete."

"All right, then." James rubbed his hands together as if in anticipation, "we'll get started. It's going to be noisy today!"

"The kids have practice, then we'll do errands. We'll be gone most of the day."

60

"And your husband will realize about parking on the street?"

"He probably won't remember until he sees there's no longer a driveway, but I told him you might be starting sometime soon." Liz headed to the house, calling for her children to come.

Happy to find an empty parking space not too far from the gate at the dog park, Madigan grabbed Roger's leash and hopped out of the car. She kept returning to this park because of its huge exterior fence. She was still a little afraid of losing Roger, since he had already been lost once in his short lifetime. He galloped beside her, caught a whiff of something in the grass and stopped to smell it, waited till he was about to be tugged, and then galloped ahead of her again. As they got to the double entrance gate, Madigan scooped him up and carried him through.

The park was full. She put Roger down and unclipped his leash. He was instantly off, running after another dog that looked like a lab mix. The bigger dog stopped, allowed Roger a small sniff before it bumped him with its nose and tumbled him to the ground. Instantly he was up and after the dog again, as if a great game had been discovered. Within minutes, he was distracted by another dog and ran in that direction. Madigan followed along, welcoming the outdoors and sunshine. Dogs were running, barking, playing, lying down beside their owners. Everywhere you looked there were dogs. And a bit of unscooped poop, Madigan realized, as she narrowly missed a pile.

At the Haffner's, father, sons, and uncle labored to break up the concrete of the double-width driveway for the next two hours. The speed of the young men was twice that of their elders, but Obie and James worked steadily until their lunch break. Young James and John were back at work almost immediately, while James and Obie rested.

"Will you need us to help dig up the grass to widen the drive?" Young James asked his father.

"I don't think so. We can use the cutter."

The younger men hauled three more wheelbarrow loads to their truck before John announced that it was full. "I don't think we can take all of this today," he called over, looking at the remaining pieces.

"Pile the rest of it by the curb. We can get it later."

As James spoke, the dark red van pulled sharply into the driveway beyond them. The driver's door opened and the young woman got out. She didn't wait for her husband this time, but went hurriedly into the house without a word to him or them. The passenger door opened and the man slowly turned and maneuvered his legs out before gently lowering himself to the ground from the high seat. He balanced with his crutches in one hand while closing the door with the other, with no weight at all on his right leg. He glanced over, and seemed surprised to see them right next door.

"Well, hello. Now you're doing another driveway."

"We're making a new basketball court for the children," James answered.

"That's good. I've noticed they lose their ball into the street a lot."

"The new hoop will be up against the house, so they can shoot that direction. And without so many cracks, perhaps the ball will not bounce so wildly."

"Good idea. That other driveway came out superbly. You do fine-looking work."

"Thank you."

"I'm Michael, Michael Stevens." The man held out his hand toward James, who came across the Haffner's lawn and extended his own after giving it a quick wipe down his overalls to remove the concrete dust.

"I am James. That is my brother, Obie, and my two sons, Young James and John."

"Good day to you," Obie waved from his perch on an overturned bucket at the top of the driveway in the shade.

Michael grimaced a little as he leaned back against the van and shifted position.

"You are in some pain there," James said.

"I took a fall about four months ago at work. Doing construction. You know the new building downtown at the corner of 5th and Sitka?"

"Yes. We go past that every day on the freeway on our way here."

"I was on the third floor. Fell off the scaffolding."

James' and Obie's eyes widened in recognition.

"You are that man?" Obie asked incredulously, coming over. "At Thanksgiving? I remember that. That was a bad, bad fall. Something happened to your safety line, but you landed on a convertible, correct? You are lucky to be alive. That car saved your life."

Michael blushed a bit at the unexpected recognition. "I know, I know. I should feel very lucky. But it's a little hard right now. I healed up pretty well at first, but I'm having a lot of trouble with this leg."

"You are still off work, then?"

"I was in the hospital and rehab for weeks. I've had two surgeries on my left leg, and four on my right. They were both broken, but this knee was mangled much worse than the other." Michael's hand came up protectively to the scar running down the right side of his face as he talked, but he didn't say anything about it.

James nodded towards the house. "Your wife, she's working?"

"Thank goodness, yes. She's got a good job as a buyer for Larsson's. Her hours are flexible, but she's getting tired of chauffeuring me around. And I'm tired of it, too." He gave his crutches a hard tap on the ground to emphasize his point.

Obie looked at his right leg in its brace. "You can't drive with your left foot?"

63

"No, my car's in the garage. It's an old Toyota, a stick, so I can't drive it. I could drive the van, but Veronica doesn't know how to use a clutch, or we'd trade cars. And I can't teach her like this."

"I've taught many of my nieces and nephews to drive a manual transmission. It's not so hard," Obie mused. "What kind of car did you say it was?"

"Toyota. It's a small four cylinder. It's a great car to take to construction sites. It's already beat up."

Obie thought out loud. "Your wife. If she knew how to drive it, would she?"

"I think so. She'd be so happy to be free of me, she wouldn't care how it looks."

"You think about this. If you want me to give her some lessons, I would be happy to. I guarantee it, I can have her driving in one hour." Obie smiled encouragingly.

Michael burst out in laughter, then realized he might appear rude. "I'm sorry. You haven't gotten to know Veronica yet." He hesitated, then spoke more soberly. "But I'll mention it to her. If she gets fed up enough with hauling me around, maybe she'll take you up on it."

"There's no hurry. We'll be here for some time. We still need to finish Madigan's sidewalk."

"Is that her name, Madigan?" Michael looked toward the broken sidewalk. "What's her last name, do you know?"

"Gardner. Madigan Gardner," James answered.

Michael pushed himself off the car with difficulty. "It's been nice speaking with you," he said sincerely. "I'd better get on in there. Veronica's not too happy with me today."

"That's too bad. Tell her about the driving, maybe it will help," Obie offered optimistically.

"I doubt it...but thanks."

Obie and James watched as Michael made his way laboriously up the six-step stairway.

"Is there not a back way that is easier?" James called to Michael as he cleared the top step. "Or through the garage?"

The injured man turned back. "No, they're both worse. There are ten steps in the back. And the ones up from the garage inside are especially narrow. Stairs are the hardest thing. I don't have much flex even in my good leg."

"Hmmm." Obie studied the old steps carefully. James observed him with a keen eye as the screen door closed behind Michael.

"I know that expression on your face and exactly what you are thinking," James muttered quietly to Obie as they returned to the Haffner's driveway. "You think you can teach the girl to drive, and then we can make a ramp for the husband instead of those bad steps. A ramp that would be easier for him."

Obie smiled his all-knowing, older brother smile. "No, that is what *you* are thinking. *I'm* thinking what a terrible fall. He's lucky to be alive. I do not see how he survived tumbling from three stories up. But your ideas are good. Excellent, in fact."

"Obie, we cannot—" James protested.

"Hey, we're done!" Young James interrupted from the back of his truck. "We can't take any more. We'll head to the dump and then home. What about you?"

"I think we'll stay a little longer," James replied. "Maybe start to pull up the lawn a bit."

"All right. We'll see you at home."


"Who *are* these people?" Although inside their house, the shrill voice of Michael's wife could be heard through the open front door even over the noise of the newer truck leaving.

"They're the guys that are doing the driveways and sidewalks on the street. They started two houses down, and now they're doing the Haffner's. They're going to put in a basketball court for the kids."

"And exactly how did they offer to teach me to drive?" Veronica Stevens stood in their kitchen with her hand on her hip, her eyes blazing.

"I don't know," Michael shrugged. "It came up, somehow. I said something like I thought you were getting tired of chauffeuring me around, which might have been obvious to them anyway, after the way you stormed into the house, and one of them asked if I couldn't drive with my left foot."

"I really don't appreciate being talked about with complete strangers."

"Fine. I'm sorry. But it might help things if you could drive my car. You'd have some freedom again. And quite honestly, I would, too. That's all. Maybe someone else could teach you. A driving school or something."

"A *driving* school?" Veronica whirled around to grab her purse, her shoulder-length blond hair spinning out in a perfect arc of indignation. "A *driving school*? Never!" Her blue eyes pierced him as if he had suggested something revolting. She stomped out of the kitchen, down the hall and out the front door, slamming it behind her. Obie and James simultaneously turned toward the noise and received a dirty look before Veronica climbed into the van, slammed *its* door, backed out of the driveway at a precarious speed, and then raced down the road.

"I don't think that idea went over too well," James said quietly to Obie as he pushed the grass cutter through the old sod along the driveway.

"No. Maybe not."

Madigan hadn't been home long before Obie knocked on her front door. Roger raced ahead down the hall, and she had to corral him to prevent him from sprinting out the door.

"Hey," she invited Obie inside. He stepped in and put his large hand on Roger's head.

"Good afternoon, Madigan. I have come to ask an important question."

"Yes?" Madigan felt her heart skip a beat at the seriousness of his tone. *Oh, no, there's something wrong with the driveway.*

"Do you know how to drive a manual transmission? A 'stick,' as it is called here?"

"Sure," she replied absently, trying to glance past him to see what disaster might have happened in the yard. "My brother taught me. My first car was a little blue Beetle. Why? Do you need me to drive the truck or something?"

"Oh, no, nothing like that. But your neighbors over there, beside Liz, the young couple, do you know them at all?"

"The guy on crutches? No, I've never met them. They've lived there about two years, I guess, maybe not that long. I did notice that he was injured."

"He is the man who took the bad fall off the new office building downtown at Thanksgiving. Remember? The worker who fell three stories and survived? That is him, living right beside you, almost!"

"Oh." Madigan vaguely recalled the news stories. "I had no idea. I've never seen him out much. But what does this have to do with driving a stick?" She finally put the wriggling Roger on the floor.

"Michael cannot drive his own car right now because it is small and a manual transmission. But he would be able to drive his wife's van, even with only his good left foot. But the wife, she cannot drive a stick. If someone could teach her to drive, then they would each have a car again. Wouldn't that be a good idea?"

"Well, sure." The words escaped her before she realized where Obie was headed with the conversation. "But wait," she backtracked, "I don't even know them. She's not going to want me to teach her to drive. I'm not sure I could teach somebody else."

"I'll help you. I taught all my nieces to drive in no time."

"I don't know, Obie." Madigan pulled the shoe Roger had found from his mouth. "I mean, sure, I guess, if she's looking for someone to help her learn, I'm willing. Hopefully, his car will be easy."

"Of course. Or you could use the truck. You can't hurt it."

Madigan tried to envision teaching a woman she didn't know how to drive a manual transmission in the old work truck with its bad muffler announcing their presence on every back street.

"Learning on the car she's going to be driving would be the best," she suggested diplomatically. "But, I don't think it's going to happen."

"So it's all set then. When we see Michael, we'll tell him you are willing to help."

"Well—"

"Next Saturday morning would be good for you?"

"Obie, don't be disappointed if it doesn't work out." Madigan felt suddenly protective of Obie's exuberance. "You are so caring to want to help them."

"We'll see. You never know."

Madigan peered into his kind eyes. What was it about him? He inspired confidence, and calm, and…imaginative hope.

"Saturday would be fine," she said. "You can let me know."

Chapter Six

*Sunday, March 18*

OBIE took his last bite of coconut curried chicken and wiped his mouth on the cloth napkin reserved for Sunday's noon-time meal.

"Thank you, Lilly," he said politely as he pushed himself away from the table. "That was excellent."

"You're welcome, Obie." Lilly looked with affection across the table at her brother-in-law of thirty years. His wife had been her cousin, and they had always been close. "You seem tired today, Obie. Go rest this afternoon."

"Yes, that sounds good." Excusing himself from the table, Obie pulled on an old sweater and headed into the backyard of the multi-bedroom home. The March sun was angling over the trees and falling in a circle on the grass. That morning the sun had shone through the windows of the church, warming the congregation in a glow of spring light, a welcome relief from the usual gray skies.

Lowering himself into his favorite wooden Adirondack chair in the yard, Obie faced the flower bed he labored over in his spare time. A faint breeze flowed from the south, and he leaned back comfortably and closed his eyes. Inside he could hear James, Young James, and John as they watched the basketball tournaments on TV. The voices of his youngest niece and the other children also carried to him as they played in the front yard.

Obie's thoughts began to wander. Sunday was his favorite day of the week with its time for island ways: no work other than simple cooking, and the family went to church together morning and evening. On the island, there would have been much visiting back and forth throughout the afternoon with circles of old men gathered in the shade on porches telling stories, while mothers stood in groups talking as they watched their children play nearby in the sand.

But here, in this northwest part of America, there was almost no one to visit between the morning and evening services. People were too busy. And the services themselves were not even at the same church. In the morning, his family worshiped with the Methodists, and in the evening they attended an Episcopalian service. The different congregations did not matter that much to Obie. It was one God. His family would honor the Sabbath and rest on the seventh day, no matter what.

Obie thought of the island. He felt himself sitting on the beach, the warmth of the sun on his dark skin, the surf rolling up in endless swells as far as he could see. He imagined the warm sand under his hand as he stroked the beach, the immensity of more grains of sand and droplets of water than could ever be envisioned. He had always found peace beside the water, since he had been a little boy. This was the peace he longed for, the peace he could not always find in this busy United States. Sometimes, in the quiet of church, he could find it, but not often enough.

He missed his wife. He thought of her, always, on Sunday afternoons like this as he sat in the backyard.

They had had a good life together, until her illness. And even then, God was merciful. She had not been unbearably sick until the final week.

*Ah, Lord,* he thought. *My back is tired. My hands begin to shake. I am thankful to still be some help to my brother. My children are raised and no longer need me. There is distance between us. Lead me: My life is yours, to do with what you will.*

His breathing became slower and deeper, and when Lilly looked out the kitchen window a few minutes later, she could tell that he was fast asleep.

"Shh!" she shushed the children as they ran into the kitchen for a drink. "Be quiet now. Uncle Obie is resting."

Lilly got the children some juice and sent them back out front. Finished with the dishes, she sat down quietly on the little back porch with the book she had started and a cool glass of water. She heard her husband and sons at the television, the younger children in the front yard, and saw the rise and fall of Obie's chest before her. She whispered her daily prayer: *Thank you, Lord, for these my blessings. My children are healthy and strong. We have steady work, a place to live, and food to eat. Thank you, Lord, for these your gifts.*

She thought for a moment about her cousin Maria and how Obie missed her. Lilly and James had worried so about him the year he was alone on the island without his wife. They had been pleased when he went to live with his children in Hawaii. But it had not worked out. The young couples had adopted too many modern ways for Obie. They did not respect the Sabbath. They did not acknowledge him as the leader of their homes.

So Obie had come to live with them. And she was glad.

Chapter Seven

*Wednesday, March 21*

O N the next dry day, Obie and James were spreading the gravel and sand at the Haffner's when Michael and his wife arrived home. Once again, she left him in the van and hurried into the house. Painfully, Michael got out and paused to watch them work.

"Good day, Michael," Obie said warmly. "How are you doing today?"

"Back from therapy. Veronica's heading back to work."

"Your neighbor has offered to help your wife learn to drive your car," Obie seized his opportunity.

"She has?" Michael was surprised

"Oh, yes. She would like very much to help," Obie stretched the truth a bit. "We thought perhaps your wife would prefer a woman her own age instead of old men like us."

"She's not too busy with the children? It seems like it would be an imposition."

"The children?" Obie was confused.

"Not that neighbor, the other neighbor." James quickly figured it out. "Madigan, over there." He pointed to the newly refinished drive.

"I don't think we've even spoken to each other before."

"When I explained the situation, she was insistent about helping. She was *very* sorry to hear about your accident and would like to be of service," Obie encouraged.

Michael scratched his head. "It would really be great if Veronica could drive my car. I'll ask her. You might be right about another woman teaching her."

The front door opened and Veronica descended the steep stairs with her large purse swinging beside her. Without a word, she started the van and backed out. Michael hopped quickly out of the way to avoid being hit by the side mirror.

"She's not so happy today?" Obie observed, watching the exhaust settle.

"She's not happy a lot of days, I'm sorry to say," Michael sighed.

Obie looked at the young man, leaning on his crutches, his face a picture of defeat in every manner. "The sun is warm today. Why don't you sit out here with us for a while?"

"Thanks, but I've got things to do. There's a stack of forms I'm working on. You can't believe the paperwork."

"And these forms won't still be there in an hour? Sit and soak up some sunlight." He walked over to his lunch pail. "James's wife Lilly packs sandwiches for an army. Have some."

"No, really, I couldn't." But Michael, unexpectedly, was struck with the idea that he had absolutely nothing to do and there was no reason at all why he couldn't sit here with these men for a few minutes. Overcoming all his own arguments, he looked around for something to sit on.

Obie hurriedly took a pair of two-by-fours and set them over two five-gallon buckets to make an impromptu bench. James brought another bucket for himself and one for Obie from the back of the truck. While Obie steadied him, Michael carefully lowered himself onto the makeshift bench. Then Obie took a seat, opened his pail and passed over half a chicken sandwich and a small apple. James reached into the plastic grocery bag at his feet and pulled out a large container of potato salad and one of macaroni salad, along with some plates and forks. And finally a bag of potato chips.

"Thank you," Michael said, casually observing the disparity between the packed lunch and what was coming out of the store's bag.

"My wife Lilly is a nurse. Since living here, she has been trying to improve our eating habits. She is a wonderful cook but doesn't understand the joy of...," he held up the creamy salads, "something cold and moist in the middle of the day."

Michael chuckled and felt the sun's warmth on his head and shoulders. His muscles relaxed in a way pills and therapy hadn't yet done.

"You must be missing your work each day, no?" Obie began.

"I miss it a lot. I've always been a pretty active person." Michael's right hand came up and traced the scar on his face unconsciously.

"The doctors didn't think you were going to live for the first few days after the accident, did you know that?"

"That's what my friends told me. I really have no memory of that first week. They had me pretty doped up."

"You must be a strong man. That's why you lived," James concluded.

"Strong and stupid. I shouldn't have fallen in the first place."

"But the papers said the harness was bad," Obie pointed out supportively.

"Not exactly. It was a couple things. But—well, anyway, there's no going back at this point."

"Right. So, what will you do now?" Obie smiled.

"It's getting through all this paperwork. Veronica wants me to sue my company, but I don't think that's even possible in this state. There's disability, and that's what I'm working on now. I have to show

74

I can't work. We're lucky we've got some savings that will float us for a while."

"No, no," Obie interrupted. "I mean, what will you *do* now?"

"Do?"

"How will you spend your time? You won't fill out papers for the rest of your life. Will you become a stay-at-home father and raise your children the way some men do? Will you find other work?"

"I don't know what other work I can do. I've always done construction." Michael was uncomfortable with the direct questioning.

"You took no other training in your schooling?"

"I didn't finish college." Michael accepted the can of grape juice that Obie was holding out to him. "I went for two years, then spent a summer making good money doing construction. I was really good at it, so I quit school."

"What did your parents say about that?" James wanted to know.

"I actually don't see my parents much. It wasn't a problem."

"That's the bad thing about America," James said to Obie. "All these people don't see their families. Where we come from, everyone is family. You spend a lot of time together—"

"Of course, it is a small island," Obie interrupted.

"—and families take care of each other," James continued, ignoring Obie. "You would already have another job on our island. You would not sit at home having to wait for your wife to drive you places."

"I don't sit at home—" Michael began to protest before realizing, of course, that was exactly what he did: sat at home waiting for his wife to drive him places. Hadn't he been sitting at the kitchen table by the window and watching these two work for the last six weeks? Their arrival on the street had been the most interesting thing to happen since his last surgery. He took another bite of his sandwich instead of finishing his sentence.

75

"What did you want to do when you first started college?" Obie's curiosity seemed boundless.

"I don't know," Michael wiped his hand on his pants. "Engineering. Or teaching. I was always good at math. And I like to build."

"So there are lots of things you could be now. Engineer. Teacher. Architect. Contractor. Which one do you want to do?"

"I'd have to go back to school for a long time to be any of those."

"That's a problem?" Obie asked him earnestly. "You have no time on your hands? You are too busy watching us work out here to go back to school?"

The last bite of sandwich caught in Michael's throat and he nearly choked. *Oh, no, had they seen him watching them out the kitchen window? They couldn't have.*

"It's a little early yet to make decisions." He took a sip of juice, regaining his composure. "My rehab isn't finished. I'm still hoping my leg will improve, and I can go back to work."

"You were not sufficiently damaged the first time, you want to try diving off a building again?" Obie asked in his serious and straight-forward, head-of-the-family manner. His eyes rested on the scar on Michael's face.

Michael's heart tapped some extra beats, and he spilled the last drops of juice on his shirt. *What an odd thing to say.* He dabbed at the juice with the napkin James offered. He was accustomed to Veronica's never-ending prodding, of her words of disappointment that he wasn't trying hard enough, her impatience that his recovery was so slow. But Obie's questions seemed to be after something much different, and they unnerved him.

Michael put the can down on the board beside him, found his crutches and struggled to stand.

"Thank you for sharing your lunch. I'll ask Veronica about the driving."

With Michael out of earshot, James turned to Obie. "You talked too hard to him."

"Maybe," Obie took a sip of his drink. "But he is sitting in that window all day doing nothing but watching us while his wife slams the doors. Something has to change over there."

James just shook his head.

Chapter Eight

*Saturday, March 24*

MADIGAN knocked gingerly on Michael's front door. It opened to reveal a striking blonde a little taller than herself.

"Veronica? I'm Madigan."

"Oh, hi."

After an awkward pause, Madigan managed, "I heard you were looking for some help learning how to drive a stick."

"I am. Since Michael's accident, things have been crazy around here. We both really need to get back to having our own cars. Or each other's cars. Anyway. It's nice of you to offer to help, especially since we don't know each other."

"We'll see how good a teacher I am," Madigan said, wondering exactly how her offer of help had been extended. "I can still remember the day my brother taught me. It should be much easier since you already know how to drive. Not so much to concentrate on at once."

"Okay. I've got Michael's keys. The car's in the garage. You'll have to back it out. I'll move the van out of the driveway."

"I thought we'd head over to that church parking lot on 85th. It ought to be empty. Then we'll work our way up to the hills."

Veronica led the way through the house. Madigan followed down the hallway and past the kitchen.

"Hello," Madigan greeted the man sitting at the table. "You must be Michael. I'm so sorry about your accident. I had no idea that was you...my neighbor."

Michael looked up from the morning paper.

"Yeah, well, I haven't been out much in the wet weather since it happened. I really appreciate your helping Veronica. I can't even fit in my car right now with my leg in this contraption."

"I'm glad to help," Madigan replied, surprising herself that she actually didn't mind as much as she thought she would when Obie announced that her Saturday morning had been scheduled for something other than the dog park.

"Watch yourself on these steps," Veronica said as they went down a level into the garage. "Everything's a mess."

"Wow!" Madigan caught sight of Michael's car. "Is this an old Toyota? It's almost identical to my brother's car that I learned to drive on. I can't believe it. This will be a snap. They're quite easy to drive."

"That's good. I really need my own wheels back." Veronica hit the button raising the garage door, tossed the car keys to Madigan, and walked out to move the van. "I hope it starts. Michael's friends had been coming over to drive it a little to keep it running, but it's been awhile."

"Let me see." Madigan bit her lip as she pushed in the clutch and pulled the gear shift into neutral. She turned the key halfway, and the dashboard lights blinked on. "So far, so good," she murmured. The car came to life as she finished cranking.

Veronica returned and slid into the passenger seat. "Michael thought it would be okay. He'd just replaced the battery before his accident. Although the car looks like a piece of junk, he's always kept up the engine. He says there's no point in taking a nice car to construction sites, all sorts of stuff happens. But he does like having a decent motor. It's going to kill him to drive the van. He thinks it's a slug."

"Here we go." Madigan backed the car out of the garage. As she rolled into the street, Obie and James arrived. "Well, look who's here." She gave a wave and headed down the street. She was sure she saw Obie grinning. *How do they get me into these things?*

Veronica learned quickly. As Madigan's brother had done with her, she spent most of the time letting Veronica experiment with where the catch point was and helping her learn to listen for the changes in the engine as she accelerated. Soon, Veronica didn't need to look at the RPM gauge on the dashboard, but could hear by the revs when she should shift from first to second. After Veronica had gotten the Toyota up to 25 mph several times in the parking lot, Madigan decided it was safe to try the streets. They went around the church on the side streets for fifteen minutes in increasingly larger circles, even getting into third gear, and Veronica only stalled once.

"Hills are the hardest. Do you want to try today, or wait for another time?"

"Let's do it today if you have time. I've got hills on my way to work, so if I don't learn today, it means I still won't be able to take this car to work."

"Okay. What about that hill behind the elementary school? It's not too steep and it doesn't have any traffic on a weekend. Do you want to practice over there?"

"Sure."

Madigan settled more comfortably as Veronica confidently navigated her way to the school.

"I'm really sorry about Michael's accident. I remember hearing about it on the news and seeing it in the paper. I had no idea you guys lived on my street."

"It's been hard." Veronica flipped her hair behind her ear between shifting. "I feel like I'm going crazy sometimes. He won't do anything.

80

He needs to go to physical therapy more often if he's ever going to get back the use of his right leg. It's like he's given up."

"Do his doctors think he's going to be okay?"

"They weren't sure he was going to live. But he surprised everyone. He's a really strong guy. And he was in great shape. He's always done tons of sports. We were on the tennis team over at the athletic club. And we used to bike and ski."

Madigan realized why she had never gotten to know them—they had probably never been home. "What do you do, Veronica?"

"I'm a buyer for Larsson's."

That explained a lot. Larsson's was the top department store in the city. For early on a Saturday, Veronica was almost too immaculately groomed.

"Sometimes I need to carry samples with me. That's why I have the van. I don't know how I'll do it in this car, but it's going to have to work. I can't keep leaving work to come take Michael to his appointments. He's got to become more independent."

"Well, hopefully this will help you both," Madigan responded quietly.

When they reached the school, Madigan had Veronica turn around, then stop at the bottom of the slight incline.

"Now this part gets a little tricky. But it all depends on you having complete faith in where that catch point is, and that you believe the car is going to get in gear and go forward before you roll too far backward. You have to have quick feet. Some people learn by using the hand brake, but my brother was a purist...and you've learned everything else so quickly, I think you'll get the hang of this, too. Let me show you."

After switching seats, Madigan demonstrated by going a little way up the hill, stopping, then going again. "You have to be fast off the brake and onto the gas, and let the clutch pedal come up to the right spot. And don't panic that you're not going forward, or you'll stall for sure. Now you try it."

The hill process took a little longer, but Veronica soon had it.

Madigan took one more turn at the wheel, showing Veronica how to use the parking brake to hold the car on a hill if necessary. Then Veronica drove them back home, pulling up in front of her own house.

"Would you mind running in and telling Michael I'm going to stay out for a bit and practice?"

"Uh, sure. You might work on reverse. We didn't have much time for that."

"Will do. Thanks again." Veronica took off the moment the door closed. Madigan looked over at James and Obie, who had stopped working and were obviously waiting for a report.

"What can I say? She's a quick learner. I think she's got it."

"You're a good teacher." Obie seemed delighted.

"I don't know about that. But she can definitely drive the car now. Have you seen Michael? I'm supposed to tell him she's going to stay out and practice."

"In the kitchen," James said. "As always."

Madigan stuck her head in the front door. "Michael? It's Madigan."

"Come on in. Looks like it was a successful mission."

"Oh, yes. Your wife is a fast learner." Madigan found him at the kitchen table.

"She's so coordinated. You should see her on the tennis court."

The wistfulness in Michael's voice made Madigan change the subject. Feeling uncomfortable standing and talking down to him, she perched on a chair.

"How long have you lived here, Michael? I was trying to remember when you moved in."

82

"It's been almost two years. The down payment was a wedding gift from Veronica's parents. They're pretty well off. They didn't much care for the fact that she was marrying a construction worker, but they helped with the house anyway. Veronica's first act of rebellion was going to school at Berkeley, and the second one was marrying me. But they've come around, since I was making good money and could support her. They've got a big house overlooking the water on the Peninsula."

"Wow, that *is* money." Coming to a pause in the conversation, Madigan took a blank sheet of paper from the table to write her phone number. "Here. If you or Veronica ever need help, let me know. It's sort of weird how we didn't really know each other before this month...." *before Obie and James.*

"They're rather different, aren't they?" Michael shared the same thought as he gazed out the window again.

Madigan's eyes followed his. The two workers were nailing two-by-fours at Haffner's.

"Oh, yes. Quite different." She rose. "Do you want me to go with you when you try to drive the van for the first time?"

"Oh, no, I'm sure Veronica will be back eventually to help. But thanks again for teaching her."

"No problem." Madigan showed herself to the front door. *Something is weird in here,* she thought, but she couldn't quite put her finger on it.


"So when are you going to finish my sidewalk?" Madigan and Roger strolled over to the resting spot of the brothers after lunch. "Not that I'm anxious. It's only been six weeks." Roger immediately ran up to Obie, who put his hands out to protect himself from the slobbery kisses of the growing pup.

"Madigan, Madigan," James feigned hurt and indignation. "Surely you are not counting the weeks? This is art! It cannot be rushed."

"Art? The driveway, yes. The sidewalk, not so much, I think."

"A few more days, and you will be able to drive on your new driveway and put the car in the garage," Obie observed. "You have it all cleaned out now, right? In these long six weeks?"

"Okay, you've got me on that one," Madigan laughed. "But really, are you going to pour the sidewalk soon?"

James spoke softly now. "What would be the best thing to do—and I'm being completely honest with you—would be to wait so that we pour all the sidewalks together at the same time."

"But the Haffners aren't doing their sidewalk, are they?"

A look passed between the brothers, and Madigan suddenly understood.

"Ohhh, I get it. Another hook 'em-with-the-driveway and then throw-in-the-sidewalk routine. At this rate, it will be Christmas before you're done."

"No, no," James consoled her. "I promise. Yours will be finished before Christmas."

"We can't pour if it's freezing, anyway. Rain, sometimes yes—freezing, no," Obie contributed seriously, his double chin tucked back with sincerity almost to his collar bone.

"But you don't work in the rain!" Madigan threw her hands in the air in mock exasperation. "I give up. Well, we're going to the park. See you later?"

"Probably next week. We're almost done for today. And thank you for helping Michael's wife." Obie flashed his most grateful smile.

"No problem." Madigan held the car door open for Roger to hop in. She surveyed the scene in the Haffner's front yard and tried not to think that things did not look particularly different from when Obie and James had arrived. As she pulled away from the curb, she observed them talking. *When do they actually work?* she wondered. *It's amazing anything gets done at all.*

James and Obie watched her car go down the street.

"She's going to the park every Saturday now," James commented.

"Yes. It's good for her."

The brothers sat in silence for a few more minutes.

"We should get the last of this grass up today," Obie proposed.

"Yes," James answered, "at least get it started."

"Do you think we might need a little more gravel and sand?" Obie enjoyed the feel of the afternoon sun on his back and shoulders.

"Perhaps." James closed his eyes for another moment of rest.


Madigan drove to the dog park, happily singing along to the radio. She parked in her regular spot and carried Roger through the double gates, closing each carefully behind her. Then she put him on the ground and took off his leash. Now over his initial shyness, he romped gladly around her. Madigan started to meander along the outside edge of the park, slowing whenever Roger stopped to investigate or play.

Around the corner, a striking yellow lab mix lay in the sun, chewing on a bone. Roger raced up, tried to make a running grab for the bone, then circled back to Madigan.

"That's not your bone, Roger. Leave the dog alone." Madigan gave his head a rub.

Mistakenly encouraged, Roger took another running dive at the bone. This time the lab gave him a good shove with its head and sent him tumbling onto his back.

"Sunny!" came a sharp call from behind Madigan.

"Roger! Get back over here!" Madigan yelled.

A man in sweats jogged up beside her. "Sorry about that," he panted. "Sunny, that's no way to treat a pup."

"Don't worry about it. Roger has no manners whatsoever. Your dog was lying there minding her? his? own business."

"Her. This is Sunny." He bent down and rubbed his dog's head. "And I guess you must be Roger?" He extended his closed hand and Roger came over warily to sniff it. The man reached slowly in his pocket and pulled out a treat. "Okay to give it to him?"

"Oh, sure," Madigan laughed. "He's a real cookie monster."

The man opened his hand slowly, and Roger pounced on the biscuit, gobbling it down in one bite.

Madigan chuckled. "See what I mean? No manners at all."

The man straightened up. "I'm Peter. That's a nice looking pup you've got. Sort of a Heinz 57?"

"Yes, I think so. My neighbor's children found him in the woods by their school. It's a long story, but I ended up with him. How about yours?"

"Sunny's a pound puppy. She's half lab and half everything else. She's almost six. She's been a great dog, calm but protective when she needs to be."

"Hello, Sunny, I'm Madigan." She bent down and allowed Sunny to sniff her hand before stroking her on her head. "What a nice girl you are."

"I haven't seen you here before," Peter observed conversationally.

"I've only had Roger a few weeks. Someone at work was talking about how much fun these off-leash parks are, so I decided to give it a try. It amazes me how most of the dogs get along together so well."

"I like it because Sunny's started to have a little tenderness in her hips. The vet told me not to take her jogging with me anymore. So here, she can lie in the middle, while I jog the perimeter."

"Maybe I can work up to that. Right now, I'm afraid to let Roger get too far away from me. He might steal every bone in the park."

"Don't worry. Dogs have a way of teaching each other manners." Peter looked down at his dog fondly. "Well, old girl, are you ready to

86

go?" Sunny stood up somewhat stiffly. Roger immediately grabbed what was left of her bone.

"Roger!"

"He can have it. She's got more at home." He picked up the old leather leash from the ground where Sunny had been lying. "Come on, girl. See you next time!" he said, giving Roger a last head pat.

"Nice meeting you, and thanks for the bone." Madigan watched the two walk toward the parking lot. "Good choice, Roger. If you're going to steal a bone, at least you picked a nice owner." She reclined against the adjacent tree while Roger chewed on the bone, closing her eyes and enjoying the warm sun on her legs, one hand gently resting on Roger's back. *Lovely day.* She smiled as she felt herself completely relax and she breathed deeper and slower. *Sitting doing nothing in the sun.* Then she could immediately hear Obie's voice in her head: "Oh, not 'nothing', Madigan. You are storing up sunshine for a rainy day! *Very* important work."

## Chapter Nine

### Monday, March 26

L IZ arrived home after work to find Obie and James grunting as they wrestled a huge box out of the back of their truck.

"Hey," she greeted them. "What's that?"

"Your basketball hoop," James answered, clearing the back edge of the truck bed. "We'll put it up today."

"Before you pour the driveway?"

"Yes. We don't want to make ladder marks on the new concrete. So we'll do this first."

Liz smiled. "The kids will be so excited. That's all they've been talking about." She glanced down the street toward the bus stop. "They'll be home any minute. I'm going to fix them a snack before we have to leave for practice."

"You must have practice almost every day, then," Obie said, holding up his end as they moved the box to the lawn.

"Kevin practices Monday and Wednesday, and Lauren is Tuesday and Thursday. But the field has a great playground, and the other players' siblings are there, so they each like to go. And I like to exercise while I wait." Liz disappeared into the house.

"She must be a walker," Obie said to his brother.

"Why do you say that?"

"She is not so drenched in sweat when she gets home like a runner would be."

"The things you notice, Obie," James shrugged. He pulled out a smaller box containing the hoop and hardware from the back of the truck, glancing toward the sound of running footsteps and Lauren's voice.

"Whatcha got?" she asked as she came to a stop beside them, her breath in gasps from the run. "Beat you!" she said to Kevin as he appeared equally breathless beside her.

"No fair. You were sitting up front. I had to wait for all the little kids to get off the bus. You had a head start."

"That's what you get for always wanting to be at the back of the bus. Anyway," she turned again to Obie, "what's this?"

"The basketball hoop, right?" Kevin jumped with joy.

"That's right. This is the backboard."

"Can we see it? Let's open it!"

"It's going to take a little while. Don't you need to take care of Roger? And your mother is waiting for you inside." Obie was not anxious for too much help at that moment.

"We'll get Roger and be right back." Lauren flew into her house and returned immediately, swinging Madigan's key on its string.

Kevin was still inspecting the box. "Cool. It's a HotShot®. Those are supposed to be really good backboards. What color is it?"

"The clear fiberglass," James answered. "Those are the best, right?"

"Yeah. Will it be hard to get up?"

"I don't think so. You have good supports already above the garage." James scanned them with a practiced eye.

Kevin helped Obie open the smaller box with the directions and hardware.

"Thanks so much for doing this," he said quietly. "My folks would never have been able to figure it out."

"It's not so hard. More a matter of time for them, I think," Obie sympathized.

"Naw, my dad's not good at sports. He never watches any games on TV or anything."

"That's how you judge sports ability in America, by how much TV a man watches?" Obie replied pointedly.

"Aw, you know what I mean. He isn't that interested. He's always at the lab, worried about running his assays."

"But his work is important. Do you know what his research is about?"

"He tried to explain it to me once. Something to do with nerves. Someday it could help people with—oh—I forget. It starts with an M...M.S., that's it. Do you know what that is?"

"Of course. That's important work he's doing. He could help many people."

"But he still doesn't know anything about sports. I don't think he played much as a kid."

"Things were probably different when he was growing up. Maybe there weren't so many chances to play."

"That's what he said. I think he was kind of short. Grandma said he never grew until he was in his last year of high school, and then he grew six inches."

"We haven't seen him. Is he tall?"

"I think he's six-four. I hope I get to be that tall."

Liz called from inside the house.

"Well, I gotta go eat and help with Roger."

Obie found some pliers and a screwdriver in the back of the truck and pulled out the large staples holding together the corners of the bigger box. James helped him slide out the backboard.

Lauren arrived with Roger, who scampered around the yard, went to the bathroom, then ran up to Obie.

"Roger! You are looking like a fine young fellow today. Growing and growing!" Obie gave him a pat.

Roger sniffed the boxes and backboard, grabbed the screwdriver in his mouth, and took off across the lawn.

Kevin came back out with an apple in his hand and took up the chase. James unfolded the directions and studied them for a moment.

"Can I help?" Lauren asked, her eyes lighting up with excitement.

"It's not too difficult. Like others we have put up. First we need to measure."

James pulled out two long ladders from where they had been neatly tucked along the sides of the truck. Lauren settled down to watch, and Roger collapsed at her feet. Obie began connecting the metal frame together.

"Do you have kids?" Lauren asked him.

"A boy and a girl, all grown up. James has his older boys, and also two girls who are a little older than you and Kevin."

"Did you put up a hoop for them when they were little?"

"Back on our island, there are many hoops, though not so fancy as this. At James' house here, there is not quite enough room for a hoop."

"So you live with James?"

"He is my youngest brother."

"What about your wife?"

"She passed away three years ago."

"Oh." Lauren was quiet for a moment. "Where are your kids?"

"They live in Hawaii. They are married and have good jobs in the hotels there."

"Do you get to see them?"

"It's been a year since I've seen them."

"That's too bad. I bet you miss them." Her eyes were filled with sympathy.

"Yes, I miss them." Obie thought back to when his daughter was Lauren's age, curious about everything, peppering him with questions as she watched him work. His heart twinged a bit that a gulf wider than the Pacific seemed to separate them now.

"Lauren!" Liz stuck her head out the front door. "We need to leave in ten minutes. Take Roger home."

"Okay, Mom. See you later," she smiled at Obie. As she stood to leave, the old BMW roared down the street, followed by the Honda Civic. Both parked in front of the third house down.

"That's Sierra. She's in high school," Lauren said to Obie. "Mom says she always drives too fast on the street. And that's her boyfriend. He comes over every day."

"Oh."

When the children returned from baseball practice two hours later, the backboard was in place against the house and James was up on a ladder, attaching the net to the hoop.

"It's done!" Kevin burst from the car. "I can't believe you got it up so fast!"

"James' sons came by and gave us a hand," Obie confessed. "Two old men both standing high on ladders is not always a good thing."

"Who are you calling old?" James objected. "We did the work. The boys only held the ladders."

Liz was impressed, whatever the truth was. "So how much longer till the court is done? And don't you need some money?"

"Money would be good today. Seven hundred dollars will cover the first half." James carried the ladder to where she was standing at the end of the driveway. "But first, let me ask you this. See your sidewalk? It's old, has cracks, and is bumpy from the tree roots. Someone might trip and fall one day. Now imagine how nice the new driveway is going to look. A lovely new surface like Madigan's. But on each side of the new, this ugly old concrete. Perhaps you would like us to pour you a new sidewalk, too? Like Madigan's?" James attention

92

was diverted momentarily as Sierra's boyfriend came out of the house and got into his car.

"How much more would it cost?" Liz asked.

"Not much. This is only about fifteen squares. Say another three hundred dollars. It's not that much because we will already be pouring for Madigan and we can do it all together."

Liz examined the old sidewalk. "It's not attractive out here, you're right. Sure, go ahead. We might as well get it all done at once. I've asked around and your prices are quite reasonable. Why is that?"

"Low overhead. We don't have an office, and we don't call for the big cement trucks to come. They charge for every minute they are sitting at your house. We mix and pour what we need as we need it."

"I'll check with my husband, but I'm sure he won't care. Yes, go ahead."

"We'll do the driveway first. I know the children will be anxious to have the court finished. Maybe we can get it done this week."

A small sedan came down the street and pulled into the garage at Sierra's house.

"Sierra's mother," Liz said when she saw Obie and James both watching.

"Good timing," Obie said quietly to James.

"Uh-huh."

Madigan arrived home. "You guys are here late today." She pulled her briefcase from the car. Then she spotted the new hoop. "Hey, that looks good."

"And guess what?" Lauren bounded up to her. "We're going to get a new sidewalk, too, just like yours!"

"Oh, really?" Madigan glanced at Obie and James who suddenly got busy collecting their tools. "That's a great idea," she said to Liz. "You certainly wouldn't want anyone to get hurt tripping over the rough spots in the sidewalk."

"That's what James said," Liz replied, totally missing the irony. "And I never realized how bad the sidewalk was until he pointed it out."

"Yes, that's how it happened at my house," Madigan smiled. "And I can't wait to see how great they'll both look when they're FINISHED TOGETHER." She made sure she aimed the word "finished" in Obie's direction.

"You have been faithful keeping your new concrete wet," James said, hoisting his ladder into the truck. "It's been two weeks already. Tomorrow you can drive on it. Don't park on it if the car is leaking oil, it will stain easily for a while. But now you can get into your garage again."

"Nice change of subject, James. But when *are* you going to do the sidewalks?"

"I'm certain we will do the sports court this week. Then maybe the sidewalks next weekend."

"I'll believe it when I see it." She turned to Lauren, "So how was Roger today?'

"No pee or poop inside."

"Progress then, at least on one front. See you all later."

"Can we use the hoop?" Kevin asked Obie.

"Of course. You'll have to work on your passing game until the driveway is in."

"Are we going to have to stay off the driveway for two weeks like Madigan?"

"No, a few days is enough until you can walk on it. Two weeks is for cars."

"Oh, good, I can't wait."

Obie picked up the cardboard pieces that were lying in the yard, stopping when he found the directions. He handed them to Lauren. "Here, put this in a safe place. It will tell us how to measure to paint on the court lines, if you want them."

94

"Okay."

"Perhaps your mother would like to do that. She likes to paint, doesn't she?"

"Kind of. I don't know if she's ever done a driveway before." Kevin took the diagram from his sister.

"But she could add that to her website," Lauren piped up. "Sports courts by Liz! Doesn't that sound good?"

"Very professional. Show her the papers. You'll need to decide what kind of lines you want—only for basketball, or also for four square. James' youngest daughter plays that all the time with her friends."

James had loaded the last of the tools. "Speaking of home, I'm ready to go, Obie. It's late. Lilly will be wondering what's keeping us."

"I'm coming." Obie picked up the last of the cardboard pieces, threw them in the back, and slammed the tailgate shut.

"See you tomorrow!" Lauren called happily as Obie climbed into the passenger seat with some effort.

"Probably the day after. It's going to rain tomorrow."

"Okay, Wednesday. Thanks for the hoop!"

After several false starts the truck was rolling down the street when Liz ran out the front door.

"Wait! I have your money!"

But they were already beyond the sound of her voice.

Chapter Ten

*Wednesday, March 28*

F RANK Haffner was approaching his car, settled snugly between his wife's and Madigan's on the street, when Obie and James arrived in the early morning.

"Good day to you," Obie said as he eased himself out of the truck and closed the door.

Frank's fingers were on his door handle. "Good morning. The hoop looks great. You have it secured up there solidly."

"We tried to be sure it won't come down for some time," James said.

"Well, thanks." Frank opened the door and was sliding in when Obie called out.

"How goes the science fair?"

There was a moment as Frank folded his long frame all the way into his car before the words seemed to register, then he reversed direction and popped back out. "Science fair?"

"Isn't there a science fair for the children this year?" Obie asked innocently.

"Is there?"

"I think so. The children have said you are a scientist. I assumed they always entered the science fair."

"I haven't heard anything about it."

"Oh. I am wrong, perhaps."

"I'll ask Kevin about it tonight." Frank seemed puzzled as he got back into his car.

"Good day!" Obie called cheerily, helping James pull out the bags of concrete mix.

James waited until the car had pulled away. "What science fair? The children have said nothing about a science fair."

"I saw it in the paper last night."

"But that was not the children's school!"

"I know. But every school has a science fair in the spring."

"You don't know what you are talking about." James dropped the heavy bag up by the mixer.

"I am talking about a father who does not know anything about sports. But he should know something about science. See what happens. At least he will have to ask Kevin about it." Obie followed with a bag of his own.

"Obie, you are messing with them too much," James said sternly.

"I see a father who is missing his children. You and I know more about their days than he does. Who are we? Complete strangers. He did not even know about the dog."

"It's different here. You're not on the island anymore."

"It's not so different that a father shouldn't know what his children are doing."

James left it at that, and they pulled the remaining bags out of the truck in silence. At eight, Kevin came out, still slightly rumpled from sleep.

"Wow! So you're going to do it today? Start to pour?"

"The weather is good. Today is the day. We want you to have your court."

"Can I help?"

"You could grab the tools and put them up by the house."

"Okay."

"Kevin," Obie spoke nonchalantly as he rested by the bags, "do you have a science fair at your school?" James shot him a warning glance.

"I think so."

"Can anyone enter? Do you have to be a certain age?"

Kevin thought for a moment. "Last year some third graders entered."

"Don't you think it would be fun to enter a project? Why don't you ask about it? Here you live with an important scientist. He could help you with an idea."

"I don't know. Dad doesn't have time for that kind of stuff. Mom always helps us with our homework." Kevin carefully placed the hoe he carried by the mixer.

"There are so many amazing things to discover in science. Like right here," Obie tapped a dusty bag with his foot, "how do all these tiny substances mix together to make such a strong material?"

"You think I should do a project on concrete?" Kevin was dubious.

"No, no. I'm saying it's interesting, that's all."

Liz stuck her head out the front door. "Breakfast is ready." She turned her attention to James and Obie. "Good morning," she called. "So today's the day?"

"James' sons will come to help after their classes. But we can get started."

James took a last swing through the driveway with the heavy rake, smoothing it to his satisfaction. The children came out and walked down to the bus stop, and Liz left a few minutes later. About 9:30, Veronica sped off in Michael's old Toyota without even a glance in their direction.

They had been mixing and pouring for two hours when Michael came out on his front stoop and called to them, "I could offer you something cold to drink, but I wouldn't be able to get it out to you."

"Thank you, Michael." Obie paused to stretch his back. "We've got plenty to drink. How is the driving going?"

"Veronica's doing great. Thanks for setting that up with Madigan."

"But you?" Obie wiped his damp forehead with a blue handkerchief from his pocket.

"I haven't been out yet, but I have therapy later today. That'll be my first attempt."

"We'll be here all day. Call us if you need help."

"In all honesty, the biggest problem is these steps."

Obie looked surreptitiously at James before he spoke. "We have been wondering. Would you like us to make you a ramp? What do you have there, six steps? About four feet in height? To be in code, that would mean—"

"I've already figured it—the ramp would end up all the way into the street, for ten feet horizontal to every foot of rise."

"If it went straight out, yes. But what if it turned, had a little landing or something. Twelve feet one way, then twelve the other. It wouldn't be so bad. A temporary thing, until you are better."

"Something I could navigate more easily?" Michael considered this new suggestion. "Maybe. But it looks like you've got your hands full for now, anyway."

"It would not take long to make a ramp. We'd be glad to do it," Obie encouraged him.

"I'll mention it to Veronica."

"Let us know."

"I don't know why you think a ramp is going to help him so much," James said to Obie quietly at the mixer as they poured out the next batch of concrete.

"It's not the ramp. It's the decision *about* the ramp."

99

"But it's not any of our business."

"Don't say it—'*we are not on the island!*'"

"Well, we're *not*."

The driveway was about one-third finished when James' sons arrived after lunch. The addition of the young men made the rest of the work go quickly. When the children ran down the street from the bus at 3:30 the driveway was nearly completed.

"It's almost done!" Kevin was overjoyed.

"Can we write our names in it?" Lauren stood as close as she dared to the wet, gray, and tempting blank slate.

"Ask your mother first. It's fine with us," James told them.

Lauren ran in the house and was right back out. "She said okay, but not too obvious."

"Up there, then, by the house!" Kevin pointed.

"Here's a nail." James found a clean one from his toolbox in the truck. The children took their time carefully lettering their names by the garage door.

"Put Roger on a leash today, or keep him in the backyard," James told them. "We do not need puppy prints all over everything."

"Okay. Oh, and I asked my teacher about the science fair," Kevin reported to Obie. "She'll give extra credit to anyone who enters. Maybe I'll give it a try. I brought home a page that gives some suggestions for projects. Some of them are pretty boring. I'd like to do something really cool."

"Good! Look out now; here comes the last batch." Young James was guiding the heavy wheelbarrow over to the only empty space on the double driveway. Obie and James, shovels and trowels ready, turned at the sound of the BMW and Honda Civic racing down the street. Obie glanced at his brother, eyebrows raised. James simply shook his head.

The children left for baseball practice and Young James and John left for home as soon as the last square was smoothed. Obie and James took their time cleaning up, resting their sore muscles often. Seeing Sierra's boyfriend leave ninety minutes later, James called to Obie.

"Time for us to go, too. It's been a long day."

Sierra's mother turned into her driveway as Obie and James were pulling away from the curb.

"Do you think she knows the boy is over every day?" Obie watched the garage door go up and down.

"It's none of our business, Obie."

"I know. But the timing is interesting, isn't it?"

Saturday afternoon, Madigan heard the unmistakable noise of the two trucks as she snapped Roger's leash on him at the front door. The crew was unpacking their equipment to break up Liz and Frank's sidewalk as she passed them.

"Hey!" she called over to Obie.

He left his supervisory spot of Young James and John to walk over.

"Madigan and Roger! How are you this fine day?"

Madigan held her hand out to catch the raindrops. "Do you consider this a drizzle like we do here, or do you call it something else?"

"The same, more or less. I think it will stop soon, at least for a little while."

Standing at the end of Liz's driveway, Madigan admired the new surface. "The sports court came out nicely. The kids can't wait to play on it."

"Why are you still parking in front of your house? The concrete has set. You can drive on it now." James bent to pet Roger, who was jumping joyfully around both men.

"Down, Roger. Sit." Madigan gave a quick tug on the leash. "I checked out a book on basic dog training. I'm working on 'don't knock people over.'" She sighed. "It's the garage. Where once there was at least a little empty space in the middle for the car, now there's no room at all except a skinny path through my piles."

"If you need a truck to make dump runs, we can help you," James offered graciously. His kindness was met with a sharp look from Obie.

"Thanks. I might take you up on that later. Well, we're off to the park."

They watched her head to her car, then James turned to Obie. "Why are you giving me that look? You wouldn't be willing to make one trip to the dump for her?"

"She doesn't need two old men to help her move things. Let her find some new friends with trucks and strong backs. People who will give her the gift of their time."

"You are impossible!" James turned curtly back to the sidewalk. Young James and John worked on, unfazed by such exchanges between their father and uncle.


Once inside the gates of the dog park, Roger took off immediately. The drizzle had intensified and few people were in view. Madigan began walking slowly, hoping she might see the man with his golden retriever; however, there was no sign of them. She had a pleasant exchange with another young woman who had a four-month-old puppy from the pound, but then the rain started to come down more heavily, and she headed for her car.

As she backed out of her parking space, Pete pulled in with Sunny in an old Volvo. Madigan watched as he got out of his car, wondering if he would stay and jog in the rain. He took Sunny through the gate and began to run. Torn between wanting to go say hello and staying dry, she headed home. *Next week*, she thought. *Maybe I'll see him next week.*

Chapter Eleven

*(still) Saturday, March 31*

IT was difficult to tell whether it was their own sweat or the rain that had so soaked Obie and James as they labored to pull up the last of the Haffner's front walk, while Young James and John took the first load to the dump.

"Why does it always seem that the last pieces are the heaviest?" Obie objected to no one in particular.

"Because the boys work harder in the beginning to make nice little pieces. By the end they put one crack in it and think that they are done."

"They *are* done. Where have they gotten to?"

"The dump is slow on Saturdays, you know that. You are cranky today." James looked at his brother with some concern.

"My bones hurt. I'm going to rest." Obie created a seat in a dry spot under Madigan's tree and sat beneath its protective branches. James piled a few more concrete chunks in the wheelbarrow before coming to sit beside him.

"I don't think the rain is going to let up. I was hoping to finish this part today."

"I know. I think it's getting worse," Obie agreed.

The brothers sat in silence for a while. The breeze was beginning to strengthen, and the branches above them swayed in the wind. Two doors down, Veronica stomped out, shouting something over her shoulder before slamming the door and getting into Michael's car. She glanced at them without even a hello, then was gone in a whirl of spray from the street.

"I don't think things are good over there," Obie observed.

"No, I don't think so, either."

In a few minutes, Michael came out onto his front stoop, protected from the rain by the small roof above it. Looking around, he finally sighted them under the tree.

"There you are," he called loudly. "I didn't know what had become of you."

"We're resting," Obie responded.

"I wanted to talk to you about the ramp."

Michael watched as Obie struggled for a moment to get up off his seat, marvelling at the strength both men showed for their ages. Obie must be in his mid-sixties and James at least fifty-five. The rhythm of their work confounded him. They showed up on days that he would never expect them, like today in the rain, but were absent for days on end of better weather. Not that his own work pattern was anything to brag about now. Not at all.

Obie and James came up the steep steps onto the little porch with some effort. Michael motioned them inside.

"So," James began, "what are you thinking about my brother's idea?"

"Quite honestly, it would be a tremendous help. Getting in and out of the house a little more easily—"

"I do not mean to be rude when I ask this," Obie interrupted, "but your doctors, do they think you will be on crutches for a long time? Or might you get worse and need a wheelchair?"

The query startled Michael. "I'm not sure. We haven't really talked about it. Why?"

"I have been thinking. We could make you the temporary wooden ramp now. But maybe, once you know your recovery will be a good one, as I'm sure it will be, we could make you an elegant entry to your home. Low-rise steps, with a wide tread and planters overflowing with flowers on the sides, so that it would look very nice. It would not seem like, 'Oh, someone needs a ramp at this house.' It would be, 'Oh, what an elegant entrance that is!' Do you see what I'm saying?"

Michael felt his chest tighten in the odd way it did sometimes these days, the start of some small, inexplicable panic. Those had been Veronica's exact words when he'd brought up the idea of the wood ramp. *Everyone will see it and think a crippled person lives here! You shouldn't even need a ramp! You'd get better if you'd work harder at your exercises!* Then slam! And out the door. Obie was looking him steadily in the eye: Michael sensed Obie somehow already knew this. And that was his point, wasn't it? That a crippled person lives here. *And what am I going to do about that?*

"Let me think about it," Michael answered. "How soon would you need to know?"

James reassured him, "Take your time. We'll still be here working for a while. We have both sidewalks to do yet. Perhaps in another month you will know more?"

"I'll think about it," was all Michael said. But he knew already. And so did Obie.

The rain was coming down even harder.

"So we should start thinking about how we would do this thing, planter stairs. What made you think of that?" James paused in gathering his things.

106

"I don't know. It came into my head, that he needed something better than a wood ramp stuck on the front of his house."

"That wife of his. I don't know."

"What are we going to do?" Obie shrugged. "The driving lessons did not help so much as I had hoped."

"So let it be. It will work itself out." James dropped the truck's tailgate down with a bang.

"Can she not simply be happy that he's alive?"

"It's none of our business, Obie."

The downpour began in earnest, and they quickly grabbed the jackhammer and extension cord and threw them into the back of the truck, tossed a tarp over them, and hopped into the sanctuary of the cab.

"We have been lucky with the weather so far," James commented as they sat listening to the pounding rain.

A horn tooted behind them. James checked his side view mirror and observed Madigan pulling in. She got out and ran up to Obie's window with a struggling Roger tucked firmly in her arm, pulling her hood up to protect her head.

"Hey," she said as he rolled his window down.

"You're getting soaked."

"Looks like you got a little more done before it really started coming down."

"We had wanted to finish it all," James said.

"Do you want to come in for a cup of coffee or something? Maybe it will stop."

"You are kind, but we're both tired. Ask us another time, and we'll come in." Obie flashed his warmest smile.

"Okay. See you...whenever." At least she had learned that much.

"Good day, Madigan." Obie gave a wave as James began his truck-starting ritual. It always took three tries, and still Madigan often held her breath because it seemed impossible that a vehicle making such awful noises would actually spring to life. She stepped back as the truck pulled out slowly. Michael's front door opened, and he called to her.

"Hey, Madigan!" he beckoned her up to his porch.

"Hi, Michael." She put Roger down and walked over to his front steps, then on to the stoop's protection. "So, how's it going? Did you drive this week?"

"Do you want to come in?" Michael held the screen door open.

"We better not. Roger's soaked, and I'm not much better."

"Well, I did make it to therapy on my own, thanks to you. It's a tremendous help to be able to drive myself."

"I'm glad."

"Listen. Obie and James seemed tired today. Do you think they're okay?"

Madigan glanced back at the Haffner's. "They got part of the sidewalk pulled up. I've learned not to even try to figure out their work schedule. Somehow it gets done eventually, exactly when you think it never will. I mean, I *hope* it gets done. I'm still waiting for my sidewalk, obviously. But I'm happy with the driveway, and they fixed the drainage problems, *and* the garage door opener." She pulled her hood off and brushed her damp hair out of her eyes.

"I'd like your opinion about something. I'm having a lot of trouble with these front steps, and they offered to build me a temporary ramp. Then today Obie suggested making something more attractive: permanent steps out of concrete with planters along the sides. What do you think?"

"Concrete steps that go straight down to the yard?"

"With a wider stair tread, more room for my crutches, and less of a rise on each one to make it easier. With flower planters on the sides."

"Oh, I get it." She imagined the idea for a moment. "You know, that might be quite attractive. Especially if there was a way to match it to the style of your house. It could seem like it had always been there."

"I guess what I'm really asking is, do you think they can do it? It would be a big project. Veronica...." he let his sentence hang, embarrassed.

"I understand. When they first started my house, I didn't know what to think. Their schedule was impossible to predict, and it seemed like nothing ever got done. But then, suddenly, the driveway was finished. They've done everything they said they'd do... and more. Their work is impeccable. I trust them completely now. There's something about them that is—I don't know—peaceful. Once you've been around them, you can't imagine that they haven't always been part of your life. It's strange how they grow on you."

"That's good enough for me. Veronica's not going to go for the idea, so I wanted to be sure I was doing the right thing before the fighting starts."

"Is she working today?"

"No, she's has a match. We used to play a lot of mixed doubles, and I finally told her to find a new partner. There's no point in both of us being in bad moods from no exercise."

"Oh. Well, I hope your therapy gets you back playing soon."

Michael glanced down and shuffled his bad leg around a bit, then looked back at her. Madigan accidentally met his gaze, and was struck by the blueness of his eyes. Even with a scar on his face, he was one of the most attractive men she'd ever met. She averted her eyes quickly, sorry things seemed strained between him and his wife. Then she realized he'd been talking to her.

"—but I'm not sure it's going to happen. It's hard to admit, especially when everyone is trying to be so positive, but it might not ever be like it was before."

"I didn't realize that. I'm so sorry."

"When Veronica left today, the thought crossed my mind that running around a court is one more thing I'll probably never do again."

"You can't know that yet. You should—"

A large Cadillac pulling into the driveway beside Michael's house caught her attention. The driver honked twice and the woman in the passenger seat waved while they waited for their garage door to go up. Michael waved back.

"What's their name?" Madigan asked. "It's terrible to have lived here all these years and have never known my neighbors."

"That's Gene and Sophie Phillips. They've been to San Diego for the winter. They only spend half the year here, which is why you see them so little. When it gets to be spring up here, they return."

"Any kids?"

"All grown. The grandkids come around a little in the summer. But they're really by themselves most of the time. They've got that huge house for only the two of them. I keep wondering if they won't sell and move smaller at some point."

Madigan's damp clothing was making her chilly, and Roger had become impatient on the stoop. "Well, we've got to go. See you later."

"Thanks for the advice."

"I hope you're wrong about your leg, Michael. Don't give up too soon."

"I know. But there's this fine line between refusing to admit defeat and being realistic. I feel like I'm balancing on a precipice right now. I don't seem to have the energy for a marathon effort the way I used to."

Madigan instinctively reached out, touching his arm reassuringly. "There's plenty of time. I don't think it's a race. Day by day, and all that— right?"

Michael smiled. "Right. Thanks for the encouragement."

"Okay, then." Roger followed her down the steps. Michael watched the pair hop through the forming puddles for a moment before closing his door. *Day by day.*

But each day seemed endless, and tomorrow held no promise of being any better.

Chapter Twelve

*Tuesday, April 3*

"I thought you might like this idea better, is all," Michael said quietly, sitting at the kitchen table while Veronica stood across from him, her perfectly painted fingernails nearly drilling a hole in the table top as she punctuated her remarks.

"Michael, they don't know what they're doing! They're two old men. How long have they been here? Months! And what have they done? Practically nothing! It's a scam. Don't you get it?"

"I don't know how you can say that, Ronny." He looked at her sharply. "It's because of them that you learned to drive my car."

"I would have learned eventually. I was hoping you would improve a little faster. But since that isn't happening—"

"Then, what?" Michael finished for her. "So I'm slow to improve? What does that mean? What does that really mean to you, Veronica? Do you think I like being this way? That I'm doing it on purpose?"

Leaning back against the counter top and folding her arms across her chest, Veronica took a deep breath and stared straight into her husband's earnest blue eyes.

"To be honest? I don't think you're trying very hard, Michael. All you do is sit in that stupid chair all day watching out the window."

"I'm trying to pay the hospital bills and fill out the forms," Michael defended himself, keeping his voice even, despite the throbbing beginning in his chest.

"You're only going to therapy once a week, and I never see you practice your exercises at home."

Michael laughed. "Has it occurred to you that once a week is all that's covered now? I'm trying to stretch it for as long as I can. And I *do* my exercises at home. Excuse me that I don't do them in front of you every night. I didn't know that you would find leg lifts so fascinating."

Veronica dropped her arms and leaned against the table.

"Michael, you've changed so," she said beseechingly. "Where is that nothing-can-stop-me guy I married? The man who could build anything, do anything, the guy who never stopped moving all day long?"

"I don't know," he replied, slumping in resignation. "Maybe that guy is gone. There's every possibility that you're now married to a one-legged man with little future and no functioning skills who couldn't give a shit about anything except how long it's going to take to move from the kitchen to the bathroom."

"You need help, Michael," Veronica's voice softened a little for the first time that morning. "You need to see a counselor. You're depressed or something. You've got to snap out of this and get going. I can't live this way."

"Fortunately for you, you have a choice about it that I don't seem to have."

"See?" Veronica threw her hands up in despair. "Self-pity. It oozes out of you all day long. Pick up the phone and get an appointment with somebody!"

"Your compassion is overwhelming today, Ronny. Big tennis match tonight?"

"Screw you, Michael."

"That would be nice."

"I'll be home late." Veronica picked up her purse. "Don't wait up."

Working next door, Obie and James glanced over as the front door slammed. Veronica shot Obie such a withering glance he turned away.

"Why do I think she did not like the planter idea, either?" James waited until the car was down the street before speaking to his brother.

"That lady needs to find something else to slam. Their front door is going to fall off one of these days," Obie commented wryly.

"This is all because of you and the steps."

"Maybe. Maybe not."

The men made a neat pile of the chunks of the Haffner's sidewalk at the curb. After a steady rain the day before, this morning had dawned sunny and clear, and they hoped to finish the section.

"Morning!" Michael called from his front stoop.

"Good day, Michael. And how are you?" Obie asked optimistically.

"I'm sure you can guess my morning so far. But I've come to a decision. Let's do the concrete steps and planters. Can you give me an estimate, how much it would cost?"

"You should check with your insurance. With other house ramps we've built, they've picked up some of the modification cost."

"Okay, I'll ask. But how much do you think it might be?"

"You've always done construction, Michael?" Obie asked him.

"Yes, I understand the high costs of construction." Michael tried to keep the impatience from his voice.

"No, no, that's not what I meant. Your house is a mix of wood and stone. Have you ever done any stone work?"

"Me? No. I know a lot about framing and concrete…and design and plumbing…and electricity. But I don't know anything about stone."

"This is what we've been thinking." Obie carefully pulled a paper from the back pocket of his overalls. Unfolding it as he walked over to Michael, he handed it up to him almost shyly.

Michael regarded the sketch. There was his house, but with a striking new front porch approached by graceful, wide steps, bordered by planter boxes that rose up gradually to the front door.

"It's…it's stunning." Michael was overwhelmed.

Obie's eyes twinkled with pleasure.

"The question is the materials. It could be plain concrete, the cheapest, but not so good-looking. Although the flowers would tumble out of the planters and hide a lot of it. Or, it could be mostly concrete, but with a stone façade here on the front planter. That would be a little more expensive, and would look nicer from the street. Or it could be all stone. That would cost more but would look the best. Stone work is time consuming. Building stone walls, you know, you have to fit the pieces just so."

"Did you draw this, Obie?" Michael was clearly impressed.

"James is the one who can draw."

"It's amazing. It would add value to the house, especially with the new porch."

"It's too bad you can't set stone. If you could do some of the work, it would save considerable money for you."

Michael became thoughtful. "I could help with the concrete a little. And the framing. And I could figure out some lighting for it. Maybe you could teach me the stone work?"

"Perhaps a combination of materials." Obie turned to James, thinking aloud. "Mostly concrete, but with the big stones set in, like river rock. It would not be so hard to do. Or take as long."

"Have you ever made one like that?" Michael sounded uncertain.

"We made a circular planter in the middle of a driveway. Perhaps we could take you to see it."

"Okay. Then maybe if I try to help a bit—"

"Find out how much the insurance would pay. I think to do the porch, the ramp, and the planters, even with you helping, it will cost at least two thousand dollars."

"Okay. I'll go call right now and see what I can find out." Excitement tinged his voice in a way the brothers hadn't heard before. They could see him on the phone in his kitchen.

Obie smiled at James. "He's a little happier now, don't you think?"

"We'll see. But I don't know how he's going to be of any help, myself."

"You wait. He'll help."

They worked another half hour, then retired to Madigan's tree for lunch. Wordlessly, they ate their healthy, low-salt turkey sandwiches, accompanied by a sidebar of gooey delights from the grocery.

"One problem—" James finally ventured.

"How are we going to get him in and out of the house while we are working on the new steps?" Obie finished the thought for him.

"Exactly." James said.

"I've been thinking about that very thing. What if we make some temporary wood steps that go up to the side of the porch? Wide stairs instead of a ramp? Maybe eighteen inches, and then only six inches high, the way the news ones will be. What do you think?"

"I think you're right. Because a straight ramp for four feet of height would be all the way to the street, as Michael said. We could build it a little to the side, out of the way of the front work area. It's the only way, unless he is willing to move out or use the back steps."

They were still sitting beneath the tree, enjoying the sunshine when the children arrived home at 3:30. Lauren and Kevin tossed their backpacks in their front door, then raced to get Roger. Happily outside, the excited pooch jumped all over James and Obie.

"Hello, Roger." Obie pulled the bundle of wiggling energy onto his lap. "Do you still remember us?" The pup licked his face so much he finally put him back down. "I like the dog, but the kisses not so much," he chuckled to Kevin.

"Hey, guess what?" Kevin asked. "I brought home the entry form for the science fair. It sounds pretty cool, and you can win $100 for first place."

"Good! Have you decided on a project?"

"Not yet. Mom says I have to show it to Dad first. But I want to do something big. Like rockets."

"He wants to play with matches." Lauren plopped down next to Obie.

"I do not. I want to see how high I can get one to go."

"That sounds like a good project. And how about you, Lauren,"—Obie always said it "Lau-wren" in a drawn-out way that made the little girl smile—"will you do a project?"

"I don't think so. We don't do much science in my class."

"That shouldn't stop you. Don't you want to grow up to be a famous scientist like your papa? Now is a good time to start."

"I'll ask him. But he's too busy to help both of us."

"Hey, Obie, look what I can do!" Kevin bounced his basketball. "I can make a basket from here!" He launched the ball from the imaginary foul shot line. It hit hard on the backboard above the basket and came right back to him. "Well, yesterday I made one from here."

"Did not," Lauren observed. "You weren't that far out. You were right underneath the basket."

"Was not!"

"Were too!"

"Let me see that ball," Obie called, struggling to his feet and catching the ball in his big hands. He bounced it a few times. "Hmm. Nice bounce. All right, watch this." He walked over to where Kevin had been standing, bent down and dribbled the ball several times, lined up the shot and released. The ball flew through the air in a perfect arc and swished into the basket.

"Wow!" Kevin was nearly speechless. "Where did you learn to play?"

"On our island, there were not so many things to do growing up. One thing we did was to shoot baskets. See James over there? He was the best player when he was young, because he was the tallest of his friends. And he had a beautiful shot."

"Can you still do it?" Lauren peered at James expectantly.

James rose more agilely than his older brother had.

"Let me see the ball," he called to Kevin. He came to the edge of the court, dribbled several times, then launched a perfect three-pointer.

"Wow!" It was Lauren's turn to be astonished.

"Let's play!" Kevin said. "Me and Obie against you and James."

"We have work to do," James declined politely.

"Oh, please, just for a few minutes? We have to go to baseball soon," Lauren pleaded.

"You start," Kevin passed Lauren the ball.

"Do you know how to play?" James asked her.

"Kind of. I'll pass to you, and you shoot."

"Okay, let's go." James walked out onto the court. Lauren passed the ball in to him. Obie made a half-hearted attempt to block his brother, but James maneuvered two steps around him, then made a perfect lay-in.

"Two-zip," Lauren announced happily.

Kevin took the ball out. He threw it to Obie, who turned and sent in another perfect swish.

"Two-two," Kevin corrected.

"We should really let the children shoot," James said to Obie as Lauren passed him the ball again.

"Oh, no, that's okay," Lauren exclaimed earnestly. "You shoot today. I'm still learning."

Liz was inside the house, getting a snack ready, when the noise pulled her to the window. She was surprised to see Obie and James playing basketball to near perfection. Her children were beaming, calling out point after point.

Michael had also heard the activity. He stood on his front porch and watched, completely captivated, as the unusual foursome played, their laughter spilling up and down the street like a song.

Chapter Thirteen
*Saturday, April 7*

MADIGAN woke at seven-thirty, pulled on her running clothes, fed Roger, let him out, let him back in, then opened the front door to leave for her run. She was surprised to see a large, flat-bed truck with a load of wrapped lumber pulling slowly down the street. The driver stopped in front of her house and glanced at her for help.

*Oh, no. It's not for me. It couldn't possibly be for me.*

"I'm looking for 3509 Trail Run Road?" the driver yelled.

Madigan sighed with relief. "That's two doors down. With the van in the driveway."

"Thanks."

The truck pulled up, positioned itself, then the flat bed rose and the wrapped pallet slid onto the road with a tremendous crash.

*What can that possibly be for at Michael's?* Madigan wondered as she walked slowly in that direction.

"Madigan?" Veronica appeared on her stoop in a bathrobe. "What was that truck? What is that in the street? I don't have my contacts in."

"Hi, Veronica. It's a load of lumber. Two-by-fours and plywood sheets. Are you having some construction done?"

Veronica's back and a slammed door were the only answer.

*Well, that's an interesting start to the day.* Madigan got into her three-mile running stride, hopping onto the narrow, paved trail across the street that had been an old railroad line and was now a protected green space corridor. All facing the trail, the houses along her street enjoyed the forest as an extension of their urban space. When she came back past Michael's house, he was standing on his front stoop.

"Hi, Michael," she called, slowing to a cool-down walk.

"Hey, Madigan."

"Early Christmas present from a friend?" she motioned to the wood pile.

"From your friends, I think."

Madigan tilted her head quizzically.

"Obie and James."

*Oh, no.* "Really?" she tried to sound calm.

"You know what we were talking about before? I'm going to have them build it. Here," he opened the screen door and motioned for her to come up, "do you have a minute?" He disappeared inside his house returning with a piece of paper.

Madigan went up his steps, noting again how steep they were.

"Look." Michael moved onto the porch and handed her James's drawing.

Madigan took the sketch in her hands. It took a few seconds to find any words. "It's amazing, Michael. I mean, it's really gorgeous. It changes the whole appearance of your house."

"I know. I couldn't quite picture it when they first described it. I didn't think it could be anything like this."

Madigan tried to reconcile the picture with the pile of wood out front. "So it's made out of wood?"

"No, it's going to be concrete and stone. River rock. That's what I don't understand. That's a lot more wood than we'd need for framing."

"The truck driver had your address, so I don't think it's a mistake."

"Veronica had a fit when she saw it this morning. We didn't exactly get to completely discuss the whole thing. I'm sure she'll like this design better when it's finished than a wood ramp, but she doesn't really understand why I need anything at all."

Madigan contemplated the difficult situation. One day, you're married to a strong, active guy. The next day, everything has changed.

"How's your therapy going?" she tried something positive.

"I'm down to once a week. At the point where I can't show any improvement, the insurance company won't pay for it anymore. My doctor approved twenty more sessions, so I'm trying to stretch them out."

"Isn't there some kind of worker's compensation or disability that you can get?"

"Some. Although Veronica would be better off financially if I had actually died. Our current long-range financial outlook feels rather bleak."

"It's so unfair. Seems like the kind of thing those TV lawyers would sue for and get you a big settlement."

"That's what Veronica says. She wants me to sue my company, the scaffolding contractor, and the city. I can't sue the first two; I'm not sure about the city."

Madigan's head jerked up from admiring the sketch at the first mention of her employer.

"The city?"

"For failing to enforce the building and safety codes. The area around the site wasn't roped off properly. When I fell, I came down and landed on a car. A convertible, actually. I have the strut marks to prove it."

"Oh." Madigan's mind raced as she tried to think if she had seen any paperwork about the case…the potential case…the huge liability lawsuit that might come across her desk at any moment.

"The car helped break my fall. I keep trying to tell Veronica we'd be suing them for saving my life. She doesn't seem to get it."

"Oh." Madigan breathed a little easier.

"What do you do, Madigan?" It was the first time Michael had expressed interest in her.

"Funny you should ask. I'm in the city's accounting department. If you sue the city, I'll probably have to stop talking to you on the advice of our attorneys."

"You're kidding!" Michael laughed. "I didn't know you were with the city."

"I've recently been promoted to the head of the accounting department. My name would be underneath the treasurer's on your check for sixty billion dollars, or whatever we talk you into settling for. It might be closer to fifty-three dollars and ninety-five cents. The city's coffers are not exactly overflowing at the present time."

"Well, that settles it. I'm not suing the city," he smiled.

"Thank you. I'll mention to my boss how much money I saved him this morning. How did your accident happen, anyway?" Michael's look of distress instantly made her wish she hadn't asked. "I'm sorry, it's none of my business."

"It's all right. A couple bad things happened in succession." His hand unconsciously went to his face, his long fingers tracing the scar in a familiar movement. "Basically, I slipped on a wet board and slid right under the scaffolding rails. My harness should have held me, but it didn't." Michael tapped a crutch, punctuating his frustration. "I only needed to be on that side for a minute, and I guess I didn't pay attention. I can't remember any of it other than the first feeling of going over the edge. I remember thinking, *Oh, no, you dumb-shit!* and that's it. If it hadn't been for the car, I'd have been a blob on the concrete."

"I'm so sorry."

"It's okay. They didn't think I was going to live. So I'm supposed to be in that so-glad-I'm-alive glow of thankfulness." His voice was hard and sarcastic.

Words failed her. Cheerfulness on her part didn't seem to be what was called for. Maybe Veronica was right. Maybe Michael *was* depressed. Who wouldn't be after all that? She shifted her weight and handed back the picture of the house.

"Well, I'd better be going. I do like the planters, though. I can't wait to see how it turns out."

"Thanks...for listening and everything."

Roger met Madigan joyfully at her front door. "Hey, you," she said, giving him a good rub. "You ready to go see who's at the park today?"

Still damp from the overnight rain, the grass sparkled as the sun peeked through the clouds. The first thing Madigan noticed at the park was a large sign hooked on the fence, announcing a potluck dinner the next Saturday afternoon at four. That had some possibilities, she decided. Wandering through the play areas, she recognized a few of the regulars but didn't see Pete and Sunny. She finally found a few dry boards on a bench and sat down, letting Roger wander. He was getting much better at showing some manners to older dogs. She took a sip from her water bottle and enjoyed the sun on her face.

"Hi, Madigan!" a familiar voice broke through her reverie. Sue Downing, formerly of her own department, was walking toward her with a beagle waddling along behind.

"Hi, Sue."

"I didn't know you had a dog." Sue pulled a plastic bag from her pocket, spread it on the damp bench, and sat down. "Do you come here often? I haven't seen you before."

"I have a puppy. Let's see," she looked around the park, "there he is, rolling in the mud over there. Roger! Come here, boy! Come on! That's a good boy. Now sit." Roger arrived with a great amount of energy, but managed to sit, albeit, with his tail still thumping wildly. "Good sit. Good boy!" Madigan tossed him a treat.

"You named your dog after Roger Beck?" Sue's eyes grew big with merriment.

"It's kind of a long story. The dog arrived, Donald got fired, I was promoted—all on the same day. And Roger has always been nice to me."

"Did you tell him you named your dog after him?"

"Of course not!"

"Okay, it'll be my secret."

"What about you? Who's this?" Madigan bent over and extended her hand to the beagle to sniff.

"This is Sam. He's ten and slowing down. We've come here for our exercise ever since they opened the park. It's so relaxing. It amazes me how all the dogs get along."

"Do you know anything about that potluck sign on the gate?"

"Once a month there's a potluck. Real informal. Half the time, we don't have it because it's raining. A couple of people set up card tables to hold the food, and everyone eats standing up. All the dogs circle around waiting for you to drop something. It's about the only time a bit of a dogfight ever breaks out, because of the food. But it's lots of fun. You kind of get a chance to get caught up on your friends and what they're doing, and of course on the health of all the older dogs. We trade a lot of dog stories."

"There's a whole dog world that I never knew existed before I had Roger."

125

"And this is only the pet group. There's the show people, and the guide dogs, and the whole humane society group. It's pretty cool."

Another young woman with a huge German shepherd approached them.

"Madigan, this is my friend, Bethany," Sue made introductions. "Bethany, this is Madigan Gardner, my boss in accounting before I changed departments."

"Oh, hi," Bethany held out her hand. "Nice to meet you. I've heard a lot about you."

"I can only imagine. We had a pretty grim six months there at the end. I keep trying to entice Sue back from environmental resources, but she won't come."

"Bethany's a buyer for the Fairview group of department stores. We grew up together."

"A buyer? I wonder if you know my neighbor. She works for Larsson's, and her name is Veronica? Tall, pretty, blond hair—"

"Veronica Stevens? Sure, I know her. Too bad about her husband having that terrible accident. And now their marriage is in serious trouble. She thinks they might split up. It's really a shame."

Madigan choked on the sip of water she was drinking. "Veronica said they might split up?" She wiped the water from her chin with the back of her hand.

Bethany looked concerned. "I hope I haven't betrayed a confidence. Veronica talks about it frequently, that her husband is depressed and won't go out of the house. She's tried to get him help, but he refuses. And he won't go to therapy, and he won't try to get a new job. He won't sue anyone to get some financial help. She doesn't seem to know what to do."

"Oh." Madigan digested this news.

"I've got to go." Sue stood. "Why don't you come to the potluck next Saturday? It's lots of fun. Roger will be the hit of the party. Everyone loves the puppies."

126

"Thanks. I'll think about it."

Madigan took one more cruise around the park, then snapped the leash on Roger and headed home at noon. Obie and James were seated beneath her tree eating lunch as she pulled in behind their truck.

"I'm going to start charging you guys rent," she said good-naturedly as she came up to them. She held Roger close because Obie's lunch box was open on the ground.

"Good day, Madigan. And how are you this fine day?" Obie greeted her as he moved his chicken wings out of reach.

"What's with all the wood?" she nodded toward Michael's.

"We're about to start something fine down there. *Very* fine. We are building him steps with planters."

"He showed me the picture this morning. It's *so* attractive! But I don't get the wood part."

"That's only temporary," James joined the conversation. "We need to make some steps up the side so that he can get up and down while we're working on the front porch, the planters, and the stairs. It won't be so nice to look at, but it will be easier for him than those steep steps he has now."

"He does have a hard time on those steps," Madigan agreed. "I've watched him sometimes, and I worry he's going to tumble right off the top. But you haven't forgotten our sidewalks?"

"Of course not. We'll be doing them soon," Obie reassured her. "Yours and the children's, we want to do them together. We need to frame up their sidewalk. But first, we want to make these steps for Michael, because it's important for him to be able to get in and out more easily. Don't you agree?"

"How could I possibly say no to that?" Madigan conceded.

"Uh-oh." James looked across the lawns toward Michael's. "The wife is back home."

Madigan noticed that both men got instantly busy with their lunches. Veronica parked, then stomped across the lawns to stand in front of the group, hands on her hips.

"Hi, Veronica," Madigan said cheerfully, trying to set a positive tone.

Veronica barely acknowledged her greeting. She addressed Obie and James coolly in a steel-edged voice.

"Now listen, and listen carefully. I want this job done, and I want it done now. You're not going to sit around here doing nothing like you have on these other jobs. This is a big waste of money, as far as I'm concerned. So it had better be done right. And it had better be done fast." With that she stalked back to her own house, marched up the stairs and in the door. Obie and James waited for the slam, and got it.

"Does she want it done right, or does she want it done fast? You cannot have both," Obie said, shaking his head.

"I think you two have bitten off more than you can chew with that one," Madigan observed. "I'm not sure Veronica functions on island time. She's sort of on some kind of hyper-speed."

"And Michael, what kind of time is he working on?" Obie asked.

Madigan shrugged in answer. "I'll let you guys finish your lunch in peace so you can get started. Good luck." *And you'll be needing more than luck to escape with your heads intact*, she thought as she tugged Roger into the house.

Chapter Fourteen

*Sunday, April 8*

DESPITE her lovely new driveway, Madigan was still parking her car on the street. She resolved to make at least a minimal effort in the garage so she might park inside again.

She fed Roger, procrastinated over her coffee and paper, then slowly dressed in some old jeans and a work shirt. She opened the door from the kitchen to the garage, trying to maintain her dwindling sense of enthusiasm. In two months, she had barely made a dent in the mess, and had, in fact, simply spread out what was once vertical walls of boxes into shorter stacks over the entire area, with a pile for her brother to look at, a pile to go to the dump, a pile she didn't know what to do with, and almost half the boxes which she hadn't yet touched. She fought a desperate urge to take Roger for a walk.

*One hour. Make yourself work for one hour.*

She approached a stack of unopened boxes, none giving any hint what might be inside. She pulled off the top one. Not too heavy. Folding back the flaps revealed old tarps and rags. *Oh, great, I've found their garage.* She pulled out one tarp that was still in good condition, then put the rest in the dump pile. The next box weighed much more and rattled metallically: her father's tools. Not having

129

many tools herself, and knowing her brother already had a complete workshop, she put that box in the keep pile. Two more boxes of tools followed. Too many to keep, and no time to dig through. She started a new stack: "sort later." The next box also jangled. Incredulous that one person could have so many tools, she discovered instead that it was her father's gardening implements: four sizes of trowels, gloves with dirt still on them, a weeding fork, a straight weed digger, several pruning shears, and finally a bulb planter. She held the gardening gloves tenderly and thought of her father's hands. How often had she sat in the backyard of their house reading while he worked in his garden? She slid her left hand into a glove, thinking she might actually be able to feel him, and wondered when was the last time he'd worked in the yard before the accident. Picking off some dried mud and examining it on her fingertips, she crumbled it and let it fall to the floor. *Oh, Dad. How I miss you.* With a sigh, she pulled the glove off and carried the box to the keep pile. In the cleaned out garage, there would be a neat and tidy gardening section for these tools and her own small trowel, clippers and gloves, which now sat forlornly in a bucket in the corner.

*That's five more boxes done.* She looked around the garage again and tried to force herself to stay longer. But it hurt too much. *How can it be five years when it still hurts this much?*

## Chapter Fifteen

*Monday, April 9*

J AMES lifted their circular saw out of the back of the truck while Obie grabbed the other tools in the early morning light. They stood on the sidewalk in front of Michael's house for a long time, studying and discussing.

Veronica departed, sending a withering glance their direction. The children walked past them to the school bus, with Liz leaving shortly after. Michael spotted them, and came out on his front porch.

"Good morning," he called pleasantly. "I wondered what you were doing. I couldn't hear anything after the truck arrived."

"Good day, Michael. And how are you this fine day?" Obie's exuberance filled the space between them.

"As good as can be expected…living with a rather irritable spouse."

"Are you having second thoughts about this?" Obie asked with concern. "It would be a good time to stop us, before we get started today."

"No, I want to do it. Perhaps once Veronica sees it taking shape…."

"The first thing is to put up some temporary stairs for you. That's what we are talking about." Obie walked up toward the house a little way, to the left of the old steps. "They would start up at the side edge of your little stoop, and then come straight out to here." He walked backwards about halfway down the lawn. "Could you manage that? They will be wider steps and much less steep."

"That would be fine. Then I can go right across to the car."

"All right, then. We'll begin. You are going to see a lot of work done today. Where can we plug in our extension cords?"

"I think the garage outlets would be the closest. Come in through the house and you can go down and open the garage door."

They set up the sawhorses to make a work space, laid out some two-by-fours to define the area, and went to work. Michael couldn't see them from his usual spot at the kitchen table, so he spent the morning walking back and forth to the living room window. By noon, the basic stairs had been built. He stuck his head out the door as they were stopping for lunch.

"Wow! That's amazing."

"Wood is easy. Now look here." Obie walked up to the old front steps and pointed. "We will have to take off the wrought iron porch railing on this side to connect the temporary steps to your stoop. But it will have to come off anyway when we widen the porch."

"That's fine. I can't believe you're almost done."

"No, we still have the railings to do. And it is temporary, remember. It's not built to last forever."

"I can't wait to try it. Come get me when you're finished."

"We'll stop to eat now."

"Would you like to come inside?"

"No, I think we will sit under Madigan's tree. It's peaceful there."

James looked approvingly at the steps they had created as he spread his lunch on his lap.

"Looks good. Fits just right," he said as his brother joined him.

"Only the rails to finish." Obie sat down carefully.

Michael watched them from his spot in the kitchen, sitting under the tree, eating and talking. He didn't know why he was so excited about the new stairs. Certainly, getting into the house would be easier, and getting out, too. He would not have that fearful moment at the top of the old steps when he always felt he was about to fall. There was something about the top step, as he placed his crutches down one and trusted them to hold him as he leaned forward to get his leg to clear, that moment when he felt he was going to pitch into space and fall. Fall with no control, as in the accident. He pulled his thoughts back to the papers before him. Yes, the new entrance would help a lot.

Obie and James were still sitting under the tree at three-thirty when Liz pulled into her driveway and the children arrived breathless a few minutes later, racing from the bus.

"Wow!" Kevin stopped, admiring the morning's work. "Cool. Can I skateboard down it?" he yelled.

"You would have to ask Mr. Stevens about that," James replied.

"I'll get Roger," Lauren told her brother as he wandered over to Obie and James.

"And how was your day at school?" Obie asked him.

"Pretty good. And I'm going to start my science experiment today."

"Oh? You and your father have decided on a good one?"

"Not exactly. He's still trying to find something for me at work. But I thought of one to do. I can use some stuff we already have."

"Hmmm," Obie paused. "Do you not want to have your father's help?"

"Oh, he can help. But I'm doing some test runs. You know, it might take a couple of tries before I can get it to work."

Lauren arrived with Roger.

133

"Not so fast, you!" Obie cried as he stood to avoid the pup's kisses.

"He sure loves you," Lauren noted.

"Will you take care of Roger today?" Kevin asked her. "I want to start on my project."

"Sure. You better hurry. There's only half-an-hour before baseball."

Lauren took the pup for a short walk down the street, then came back and disappeared with him behind her house. Obie and James returned to Michael's. With some effort, they unbolted the old wrought iron railing and finished the new steps to fit snugly against the side edge of Michael's front stoop. When this was secure, they began to measure for the railings.

Seconds later, the sound of an explosion tore through the air, followed by Kevin's screams, Lauren's cry for help, and Roger barking. Lauren came racing to them.

"Help! Kevin's hurt," she gasped.

As Obie moved toward her backyard, he glanced in Michael's kitchen window. Michael already had the phone to his ear and nodded to Obie's questioning look.

"There's a fire!" Lauren panted.

James backtracked to his truck and pulled out a small fire extinguisher.

In the backyard, Liz was on her knees beside the unmoving Kevin, her hands splattered with blood as she pressed above his eye. A rocket part sparked in the grass and flames had erupted beside it.

"Please, help me," Liz cried as Obie fell awkwardly to his knees beside her. "It's his eye—"

"Michael has called for help." Obie tried to determine the exact injury, but there was so much blood it was impossible. "We must stop the bleeding. Quickly—we need something to hold on it."

"Maybe this." In one fast motion, Liz pulled off her white t-shirt, and Obie placed it over the wound.

"I'll hold the pressure, you get some towels."

Liz ran into the house and was right back. Obie took the clean layer of towels and held them atop the blood-soaked shirt with one hand. His other hand lay lightly on Kevin's chest, measuring its rise and fall.

"Kevin! Can you hear me? Kevin!" On her knees by his head again, Liz frantically called his name. She looked at Lauren, standing at Kevin's feet, her face a pasty white. "What was he doing?" their mother asked.

James emptied his extinguisher on the two small fires, but another was growing in the brush at the back of the yard.

"Do you have a hose?" he called to Liz.

"On the side of the house. By Michael's. It should reach. Lauren —what was he *doing*?"

"He wanted to make a rocket," she burst into tears.

Kevin's leg moved a little, and he began to moan.

"Kevin! Oh, thank God."

Obie looked around the yard as he continued to apply pressure. "Do you keep gasoline in your garage?"

"For the mower." Liz touched Kevin's shoulder gently.

They could hear the sirens coming closer, now out front. Then Michael's voice, directing them. Two firefighters came around the house into the backyard.

"What happened?" the first asked, plopping down his medical kit.

"He was making a rocket, I think," Liz replied.

"It's his eye," Obie indicated. "He has begun to move a little." He dropped his voice, "I am worried about gasoline that may be sprayed around the yard. I do not see where the can of gas is that he was using."

135

"Right," the firefighter agreed. "We need to move him to the front yard," he called to the other firefighter. "Bring the board!"

The siren of a second truck fell silent as it pulled up out front.

Two more responders arrived, the board was brought around, and a neck brace fitted on Kevin. One responder took over for Obie, and then Kevin was carefully slipped onto the board. A fifth responder came through with a hose and took over for James.

A medic unit pulled alongside the two fire trucks as the group came around the house carrying Kevin.

"Face wound for sure. May have an eye injury," the first firefighter relayed to the medics.

"Okay, we've got it." The EMTs took over, checking Kevin's vitals quickly.

"Mom?" Kevin spoke, moving his head against the restraining collar. "Mom?"

"Right here." Liz tried to stay close without being in the way.

"Don't move, son. Hold real still now. Can you tell me your name?"

"Kevin."

"Good. You're doing real good, Kevin. We're going to get you straight to the hospital."

"He's ready for transport," the other medic said. "Let's go."

"All right, here we go." Two firefighters helped load Kevin into the ambulance. Liz looked around wildly for Lauren, who had taken refuge beside Obie.

"Go with him," Obie said to Liz. "We'll stay with Lauren until you return."

Liz mouthed, "Thank you," and climbed into the back of the ambulance.

The entire event had taken no more than fifteen minutes. Obie and James stood with Lauren, watching the medic unit disappear down the street, siren on as it approached the intersection at the corner. The first firefighter looked at them carefully; both older men seemed visibly shaken.

"Are you two all right?" he asked as Obie attempted to wipe the blood from his hands.

"Yes…it happened so fast," James said.

"If it's his eye, then the quicker they get him to the hospital, the better the chances of saving his sight."

"Is this yours?" A firefighter held up James' extinguisher. James nodded as Michael joined them, coming down to the yard on the new steps.

"Thank you for calling so quickly," Obie said to him.

"Is it bad, do you think?"

"There was a lot of blood," James answered, "and the injury was close to his eye. Could you see what happened?"

Michael shook his head. "I can't see their whole yard because of the fence. So I don't know what he was using as a propellant. But he carried the rocket toward the back part of the yard, got the second match to light, and then the whole thing exploded."

Obie knew he should sit down. He could feel the dizziness that annoyed him so.

"Sit on these steps, sir, and let me check you," the first firefighter was speaking to him.

"I'll be all right. I'm an old man with too much excitement. I'll be fine. I feel bad about the boy, is all," Obie objected, nevertheless he took a seat on Haffner's steps. Lauren nestled beside his great bulk.

"You are all right, little Lauren? You were not hurt back there?" Obie took her small hand in his and looked at it. She shook her head no and snuggled closer, pulling Roger near.

"Your blood pressure's a little high," the firefighter released the cuff on Obie's arm, "but that's not unusual after such excitement. Your breathing seems better now. Do you have any chest pain?"

"No."

"Any underlying medical conditions?"

"No." None that he was going to mention here.

"He has blood pressure medicine at home," James put in, "that he takes sometimes." Obie shot him a dark glare.

"Feeling dizzy?" the firefighter looked at Obie's face carefully.

"No, I'm fine. I feel better now."

"I'll take your pressure again before we go."

"Let's take Roger home, then we'll go inside and I'll make Obie a cup of tea," James spoke to Lauren who nodded. A firefighter appeared from behind the house, holding a gasoline can.

"I found it. It was back by the trees. At least he knew enough to keep the can away from the matches."

The final responder dragged his hose from the backyard.

"Everything's cooled down back there." He glanced at Obie sitting on the steps. "You're okay?"

They all waited while Obie's attendant took a new reading, then nodded okay.

"I'll keep an eye on him," Michael reassured them.

The final responder, beginning to load the hose on the engine, glanced at Michael and then took another look.

"You look familiar."

"He is a famous person," Obie piped up from the steps, happy to divert attention from himself. "He has almost risen from the dead. He's the man who fell three stories off the new building downtown last Thanksgiving."

"Oh, yeah! Sure. I didn't know you lived here. You were the talk of every station house in the city."

"Really?"

"I told you you were famous," Obie mumbled, wiping the perspiration that still came from his forehead with a clean corner of the towel he held.

"That was a spectacular fall. So how are you doing? You're looking good."

Embarrassment flooded Michael at this unexpected interest in his well-being.

"Hey, guys," the firefighter called to his partners before Michael had a chance to answer. "Guess who this is. That November 'save' on the convertible. Remember?" The others looked over with interest. "I'm sure you know how lucky you are to have survived."

"That's what I've been told. I can't remember much."

"My friend was one of the first responders to the scene. He works downtown at Fire Station 4. He still talks about it. Wait till I tell him I saw you—up, around, and looking good."

*Up, around, and looking good?* It seemed such a foreign concept Michael could hardly fathom it. He tapped his crutches in awkward discomfort.

"Okay, we're done here." Obie's attendant picked up his kit. "You call us back if you start feeling any chest pain, arm discomfort, dizziness...any of it, okay? We'll get the extinguisher refilled for you and drop it back off."

"That's not necessary, but thank you." James returned with Lauren after taking Roger home.

Lauren watched as three firefighters went to each truck. She waved as the engines started up and the trucks pulled off down the street.

"They were nice, weren't they?" she said to Obie.

"Very nice. I'm glad the station is nearby." He looked at Michael. "I don't think we're going to get the handrails on today."

"Don't worry about it. See how easily I used it just as it is."

Obie stood up slowly. "Lauren, I guess we should go in and wait for your momma to call. Thank you again for your help, Michael."

"If you need anything else, you know where to find me."

Lauren led the way into the house's light-filled kitchen.

"Where does your mother keep the tea?" James asked. "I think a strong cup would be good for Obie and me." Obie sat at the kitchen table and rubbed his face with his hands. James filled the tea kettle and readied one mug for each of them. "What about you, Lauren? What kind of snack would your mother be making for you? And is there someone we should call? Someone about your baseball?"

"Well, I guess we better call Dad." She went over to the phone.

"How are you feeling?" James asked his brother quietly. "You had me worried out there."

"It's nothing. A cup of tea will help. I'm afraid for Kevin. I couldn't be sure about the wound. It might be bad."

"Wait until we hear something."

Lauren came back to the table. "Dad's lab said he already knew about it and he's gone to the hospital. I guess Mom will call everyone who needs to know."

"All right then, how about a glass of milk for you? What else would you like? And what do you usually do on a day without baseball?"

"Watch TV. Or start my homework. We have to read for twenty minutes every day. My mom signs a chart." She sat down at the table and put her hand on Obie's arm. "Are you feeling okay?"

Obie covered her hand with his. "Thank you, Lauren. I will feel much better after a cup of tea and when we hear about your brother. And how about you? You should not worry. They have good hospitals here."

"The blood scared me. And the way he screamed. He was so happy about making his secret rocket. He wanted to surprise Dad and have it all working and everything. And he's always liked stuff with fire." She was quiet for a minute. "I knew he shouldn't have had the matches. I should have told Mom."

"We are lucky, Lauren. We are lucky your mother was home and that the firefighters came so quickly. It will be all right." Obie patted her hand. James set a cup of steaming tea down before him. Lauren got herself a cup of juice and brought a package of cookies to the table. They sat quietly for a while before Lauren went to the living room. Obie and James remained at the table, the babble of the TV a background for their own thoughts.

There was a loud knock on the front door. Lauren was looking through the window as James came from the kitchen.

"It's Madigan!" Lauren called in surprise, opening the door and collapsing against her neighbor.

"Hello, Lauren." Madigan hugged her warmly. "Hey, James." When Lauren finally released her, Madigan followed them to the kitchen and greeted Obie. "Liz called me at work and asked me to come over. I left right away. Have you had any word yet?"

"No."

"They had gotten to the hospital and were taking him up. I wasn't sure if she meant up to surgery, or maybe to the floor where the eye specialists are. Anyway. What happened?"

Obie stared into his tea as Lauren related the story. Madigan slid into the chair beside Obie and touched his sleeve.

"Liz says you saved him, Obie. She doesn't know what she would have done if you and James hadn't been here. And Michael calling 9-1-1 so fast. She said the blood overwhelmed her."

Obie didn't answer, and Madigan look questioningly at James.

"It was the science experiment," James explained. "He is feeling bad because it was his idea."

"But, Obie, accidents happen all the time."

"Yeah, Obie." It was the first time Lauren had ever addressed him by name. "Kevin gets hurt a lot. 9-1-1 has been to our house a lot of times."

"Oh, really?" Obie clearly did not believe this.

141

"Honest. At our old house, he fell out of a tree in the backyard and broke his arm. I think he was six. 9-1-1 came. Once he tried to build a skate ramp, and he hit his finger with a hammer so hard we had to take him to the emergency room. And then Mom always tells about how, when I was a baby, he locked himself in the bathroom and couldn't get out, and she had to have the firemen come put up the ladder and climb in the window. Really, you don't know him very well."

Obie had to smile. "Thank you for that, Lauren. I guess there is some comfort there."

The phone rang and Lauren jumped to answer it. "Oh, hi, Mom. Yes, she just got here. Yeah, they're still here, too. Okay." She held the phone out towards Madigan. "She wants to talk to you."

Madigan got up and took the phone. Obie watched her face anxiously. "Oh, that's good." Madigan gave them all a thumbs up sign. "That's great. Okay, yeah, we're fine. No, stay as long as you like. I can be here. Okay, here he is." She handed the phone to Obie.

His hand shook a little as put the phone to his ear. He had been praying with his whole body for this boy, ever since he first saw him lying on the ground. Could it really be good news?

"Hello?" he couldn't keep the hope from his voice. "Oh, that's good news. When I first saw it, I couldn't tell, it was so close to his eye. But I was hoping it was above. All right then, we will see you tomorrow. Tell Kevin we will be thinking of him. Good day, Liz."

He handed the phone back to Lauren, who disappeared around the corner with it to talk to her mother. Obie smiled broadly at his brother.

"Good news, James! Good news. The eye is saved. It's a big cut, right above, so close! Seventeen stitches! Oh, we are lucky. We must tell Michael. Do you have his phone number, Madigan?"

"No—"

"I'll go tell him." He pulled himself out of the chair and headed quickly for the front door.

Madigan noted how his whole demeanor had brightened. "He was really worried, wasn't he?" she asked James.

"On the island, accidents can be serious. There is a little clinic, but nothing like you have here. Always a time for much worry and prayer. And rejoicing when things work out. Are they coming home tonight?"

"Liz wasn't sure. They'll keep Kevin a few more hours at least. But I'll stay with Lauren, you can go whenever you need to."

Obie used the wobbly iron handrail to haul his sore body up Michael's concrete steps, wishing he and James had gotten the railing on the less-steep wooden ones. Michael opened his door expectantly.

"So?"

"It's good news, Michael. The rocket piece hit right above his eye. Seventeen stitches! But no eye damage. He will be home tonight, perhaps!"

"That's great news." Michael's relief was obvious.

"We were lucky this time, Michael," Obie's voice dropped. "It could have been bad, very, very bad. Half-an-inch, he could have lost his eye."

"It looked terrible. I...I...," Michael faltered for a moment. "I was thinking that I should have yelled out to him or something. I didn't see what he was doing until he struck the first match. The wind blew it out before the fuse lit. But then, the second match caught, and it happened like that," he snapped his fingers forcefully.

Obie smiled. "You are the third person with regrets today. Four, counting Kevin! But we should give thanks and be happy. This is a good day."

"You're right."

Obie glanced down at Michael's leg brace.

143

"Were you surprised that you are famous among the firefighters?"

"Well, yeah. I had no idea. How did he recognize me?"

"Your picture was in the paper several times. You haven't seen the articles?"

"No. I was out of it for quite a while. Veronica was staying at the hospital with me. She might not have seen it herself."

Obie looked at him sincerely.

"You are a miracle, Michael. Don't forget that." Then he gestured toward Kevin's house. "Now I know two people who are miracles! And they live beside each other. How funny is that?"

Michael didn't know what to say. So many strangers aware of his accident seemed unsettling, somehow. Maybe he would go look up the newspaper articles in the library one day.

The screen door opened and Veronica entered, looking coldly at Obie, whose backward retreat to the kitchen did not spare him her wrath.

"Those steps out there are the ugliest things I've ever seen."

"Veronica, it's not really the time—" Michael started.

"Oh, it's all right," Obie replied, glancing out the window and appreciating Michael's view of the street. Nothing could deflate his good mood, and he addressed Veronica cheerfully. "You are right, it's not pretty, but, it will work. And soon you will have a wider porch, safer stairs, and new planters overflowing with flowers. You'll like the end result. Sometimes it takes a bit of ugly to get to the beautiful part."

"You two certainly specialize in ugly. When are you going to finish that sidewalk at Madigan's? It's been torn up forever."

"We wanted to get the steps in first, to make things easier for Michael."

"Oh, yes, let's all make things easier for Michael." She turned on her heel and headed for the back of the house.

"I'm sorry, Obie," Michael apologized. "It's not going well here."

"Don't let her spoil our good ending to the day," Obie said conspiratorially. "Go over to Lauren's and give her a hug. You should be happy. Because of you, help got here fast. Kevin's eye is saved. That's the important thing for today." With that, he let himself out the door.

Michael stood in the hallway a few minutes, trying to decide what to do. Veronica brushed past him, now changed into tennis clothes.

"That was totally uncalled for, Ronny. I don't know why you feel you have the right to be rude to him," Michael said to her back, following her to the kitchen.

"Because he's a scam artist who has you under his spell. And I won't have anything to do with it."

"He helped save Kevin today. There was an accident and the poor kid nearly lost his eye."

"Yeah?" Veronica opened the refrigerator door and grabbed a chilled water bottle.

"He was trying to set off a rocket and it exploded."

"We're probably lucky it didn't set our roof on fire."

"When did you become so. . . unkind?" Michael examined the tight corners and tiny lines on his wife's face. "A little boy almost lost his sight today, and you only care about our roof?"

"I'm supposed to be sorry he didn't know enough not to be playing with matches?"

"He's a kid. It was an accident."

"There *are* no accidents," she said it so quickly and venomously, it was a moment before they could both recover. "I mean—"

"No," Michael said slowly, "I think that's exactly what you do mean. 'There *are* no accidents.' You think I could have prevented mine somehow. What, if I'd been smarter, maybe? Or more careful? What is it exactly that you think I didn't do?"

"Nothing, Michael. Nothing."

145

But her outburst dangled before them, filled with four months of hurt. Michael suddenly knew that this was right, that underneath it all, she thought the accident was his fault.

"I'd like to know what you think I didn't do?" he asked again quietly.

"I think you weren't careful and you weren't concentrating," Veronica spoke her words slowly. "I think that you were fooling around, maybe telling a joke. I think that you didn't look where you tied off. You were talking. Josh said you were talking to him, then you stepped on the board and that was it."

"Well," Michael paused. "You're right. I can't exactly remember, but I was probably doing all those things. And even worse, I didn't report the missing toe board to the supervisor when I saw it first thing that morning, and I didn't look at the board I tied off on. I only had one quick thing to do on that side. I was anxious to get started, and I *was* talking to Josh."

Veronica made no reply. Finally she picked up her athletic bag.

"I'm going to the club. I'll be home late." And she slipped out the door.

*I guess that about wraps it up,* Michael thought as he watched her back the car out of the driveway. Next door, Obie and James were leaving, too. Madigan stood on the front steps talking to them, Lauren leaning against her. Obie turned and saw him at the window, and flashed him a big smile. Michael gave a small nod.

*Why doesn't it feel very good to be a miracle?*

Chapter Sixteen

*Tuesday, April 10*

OBIE and James arrived around noon. James carried the long extension cord up and knocked on Michael's door, then disappeared into the house and came out through the garage. Plugging in the saw, they began to make the handrails for the wood steps. At the first sound of the saw starting up, Liz and Kevin appeared from next door.

"Hey!" Kevin yelled.

Obie waved. "Good day, Kevin! And how are you this fine day? You're looking quite a bit like a wounded pirate! When did you get home?"

"Late last night."

Liz came up to Obie and gave him a hug. "Thank you," she said quietly. "Thank you for everything." She pulled away and hugged James, also, her eyes welling with tears. "The medic in the ambulance said if we hadn't acted so quickly...stopping the bleeding and keeping out the dirt...it was the best thing. It was as close as it could be."

*Thank you, God, for these our blessings,* Obie thought automatically. "So you are home today recovering?" he asked Kevin.

"I have to stay quiet for a few days. I wanted to go to school, but Mom didn't trust me not to go play at recess."

"That's all he needs, is to have it hit with a ball or something."

"And what did your papa say? I see his car is still home?"

"He's pretty mad at me for being so stupid. But, I guess he understood I was anxious to get the project going. He stayed this morning so we could talk about it."

"It's not the first time I've had to call 9-1-1," Liz said. "Kevin has a way of getting himself into some trouble. But this was the worst, by far. And hopefully, the last. I think we've been able to make that clear to him this morning."

"Lauren was telling us something like that—" Obie stopped as Frank came out of the house.

"I'm off," he called to Liz and Kevin as he headed for his car, still parked on the street. Then he stopped and came over to Michael's yard, his hand extended to Obie and then James. "Thank you. Thank you so much for your help yesterday. And for taking care of Lauren. And for the sports court. I haven't had a chance to tell you how professional it looks."

"You are most welcome. The children have been wetting it down nicely, and it's two weeks today since we poured it, so you can drive on it now. But don't park on it and drip oil. It's porous at the start."

"Okay." He kissed Liz. "I'll try to be home for dinner." Giving Kevin a gentle tussle to his hair, he drove off with a small wave.

"It scared him," Liz said, indicating her husband's retreating car. "For a scientist, to protect your eyes, that's everything—the most basic rule. He was furious at Kevin, and then so mad at himself because he'd been promising to help, but then hadn't. He had hours to think at the hospital last night, and I guess, maybe he realizes how little time he has with the kids."

"It's important work that he does," Obie stated simply.

"It is. But he's got to find more balance. Other people can do some of it, *should* be doing some of it. We'll see. It's easy to say you're going to change your ways right after a crisis." Liz turned her attention to the board at Obie's feet. "What are you working on today?"

"We're making handrails for Michael's wood steps. Then we will begin the front of his house. Have you seen the design?"

"No. You're changing these awful steps, I assume?"

"Yes, a wider tread and less high, with planters and a little bit more of a porch."

"That sounds much more practical. Now, what about my sidewalk? And I owe you money."

"We'll take your money any time now. And the sidewalk, we want to wait to pour it together with Madigan's. It will look the nicest that way. All the concrete will have the same color and texture because it's done on the same day with the same conditions."

Liz glanced at the uneven sidewalk in front of Michael's house. "What about his? Are you going to talk him into doing it, too?"

"We haven't mentioned that yet. The steps are a big project, so we want to get them started. The wife," Obie nodded toward the house, "she's not too happy with us. We're anxious to show her what a good job we can do. How much better it will make things for Michael. Maybe that will help."

"Good luck. I've never heard that front door slam as much as I have in the last month. I wondered what was going on."

"It's none of our business," James put in as he picked up the rail Obie had cut. "Our job is to make the new entrance."

"Yes, but we hope it will help." Obie took the board back from his brother in a small show of one-upmanship.

Liz smiled, amused by the interplay between the siblings.

"How many years apart are you in age?" she asked James.

"Ten years." James relinquished the board to his elder. "He's the oldest in the family. I'm second to last, our sister is the baby. Obie wants to be the boss. But here in America," James smiled a big grin, "being the oldest does not matter. Even the youngest brother can own the business and be the boss."

"I just let him *think* he's the boss," Obie confided to Liz as he handed back the first board and picked up another to cut. "All the good ideas are mine."

After finishing the rails, Obie knocked on Michael's door, updating him on Kevin and double-checking the fit of the new wood steps and railings.

"It's time to take off the old steps. Is it all right to do that today? You can make do with the wood steps, now?"

"They're perfect. I don't dread going out as much. I never realized some of the difficulty was the stupid steps. Yes, take them off, get rid of them. I'm ready."

"It's going to be loud for a while."

"That's all right."

By five o'clock the remnants of the old steps were piled by the street. Obie and James had placed plastic fencing across the gap so no one would fall off the front of the stoop.

"Tomorrow the real fun begins," Obie said, wiping his brow.

"I'm getting excited to see how it will look when we're finished," James nodded. "Maybe I'll have to admit this was one of your better ideas."

"Uh, oh." Obie turned at the sound of a car in the driveway. "We didn't leave soon enough."

"Where are the steps?" Incredulous, Veronica jumped out of her car. "What have you done?"

Obie spoke first. "We're preparing the way for the lovely new entrance to your home."

Veronica took the wood steps two at a time, slamming the front door behind her.

"Good day to you, too," James said. "Time for us to be going, Obie."

"I told you 'no.' I distinctly told you not to do this, Michael. What is wrong with you? That wood thing is bad enough. Now they've ruined the house. We don't have the money for this."

"I'd appreciate it if you would lower your voice so the entire street doesn't hear our conversation." Michael was seated at the kitchen table, the window open beside him.

"I don't care what they hear," Veronica shouted even louder. "We'll be the laughing stock of the neighborhood. I can't *believe* you would go ahead with this." She paced back and forth across the kitchen, angry frustration in every stomp of her heels.

"I guess I feel it's really important. I have to be able to get in and out of the house more easily."

"For what? For your therapy? For your job interviews? Where are you *going* all of a sudden, Michael?"

"I want to be able to get in and out more easily. Why is that so hard to understand?"

"What I understand is that nothing *I* think or say is important to you, but two old men can extract thousands of dollars from you with a simple smile and handshake."

"Ronny. Let's not fight. Please. I'm willing to go see a counselor if you'll come, too. Maybe we can get back to the way we used to be. I don't want it to be like this."

"*I* don't need counseling. *I'm* not the one sitting inside all day."

"Right. You have a life. You have our old life. I'm not sure that any amount of therapy is going to get me back there, physical therapy

151

or otherwise. I'll try. You know I want it to be like when we got married. But I can't promise you I can do it. This has been a big loss —for both of us. But you know how much I love you."

"I've been talking to Daddy."

"Oh, here we go." Michael flipped the pencil he'd been holding onto the table.

"He thinks it would be a good idea if you moved out for a while."

"You're joking." It was Michael's turn to be incredulous.

"A trial separation."

"I'm not moving out."

"But it's my house. My parents gave us the down payment."

"After we got married. Community property state. You're out of luck. If you want out of the marriage, you leave. I can't make you stay, but I'm not making it easy for you."

"Fine. You stay in the house. I'll move in with a friend for a while."

"And who would that be? Hank?"

"You are so hateful to assume he's more than my tennis partner!"

"My legs are hurt, Veronica. I'm not blind and deaf. How many times do you think he calls here when you're not home? He's not the smartest guy to be getting involved with, I gotta tell you. I'm a little offended you didn't go for someone brighter."

"Just what my father said about you."

"Well, then he's *really* gonna love Hank."

"I'm out of here. I'll be back for my things."

"Ronny, wait—" he was speaking to her back, sorry he had brought up Hank. He heard his car squeal out of the driveway, and saw the edge of it as Veronica pulled away.

Obie and James had gone; the street was quiet. Michael sat and watched as Lauren came home from baseball, followed soon after by her father from work. Later, Madigan's car pulled up. She went in with her briefcase, then came out fifteen minutes later in casual clothes with Roger on his leash.

Michael was still sitting at the window when they returned from their walk. He noticed it was staying light longer now. He remained at the table, watching the sunlight turn to dusk, unable to bring himself to do anything else.

Chapter Seventeen
*Wednesday, April 11*

T HE banging on his front door reverberated unpleasantly in Michael's head. Not yet dressed and still unshaven, he glanced out the window and saw James' truck. He opened the front door to the radiance of Obie's cheerful abundance.

"Good day, Michael! And how are you, this fine day?"

"Not the best night. I'm just getting up," Michael mumbled, feeling as if Obie's eyes looked straight through him and already knew every dark thought that had haunted his night's sleep.

"Today we'll start the framing. Will you come look at it?"

"Sure." He rubbed his stubble and felt the raised line of his scar. "Give me a couple minutes."

"May James come through?"

"Yeah, sure." He turned away and headed to the bedroom.

"He doesn't look too good today," James said quietly on his way in.

"We'll see what some fresh air will do."

Obie sorted the wood pieces, then watched Michael come easily down the new steps thirty minutes later.

"So, Michael. You said you were a great framer, no? We may need your help later. Do you still have a carpenter's apron?"

"I don't know what happened to it after the accident. My friends probably brought it over, back when they visited occasionally. Maybe Ronny put it in the garage."

The three men spent the next hour discussing how wide to make the new wood porch, the exact positioning of the new stairs, and how wide the planters should be. They marked all this out in the yard with stakes and guide strings. By the end of the hour, Michael could actually imagine what it would look like.

"Do we need to pour new footings for the porch?" he asked.

"No, but we will for the steps and planters. That's the next thing to do, digging the footings."

James went to his truck and got out the shovels. Michael sat on a bucket and watched as James and Obie dug up the lawn. At three-thirty, Liz drove down the street and into her garage, followed a few minutes later by Lauren and Kevin, racing home from the bus stop.

"Wow!" Lauren said, stopping to look at the layout.

"Cool!" Kevin agreed.

"And how did your friends like the pirate look?" Obie asked him.

"Nobody said much, but the teacher made me explain how it happened in front of the whole class. I had to tell what I shouldn't have done, and especially the part about the matches and not having the safety glasses on. That was really dumb. We've got three pairs in the basement. I don't know why I didn't use them."

"Well, now you'll remember. And gasoline is only for the mower, right?"

"Yeah. Dad went over that a few times, too. Don't worry, I learned my lesson this time."

"He's not allowed any TV for two weeks," Lauren added.

"Mind your own business," Kevin retorted, taking a swipe at her. Lauren deftly jumped sideways.

"I'm going to get Roger," she called, running into the house for the key.

The Cadillac pulled into the driveway beside Michael's and stopped before entering the garage. The older couple got out, and the driver looked with interest at the work going on in Michael's yard.

"Hello, Michael," he called over.

"Hi, Gene, Sophie. Welcome back!" He made his way over to their car.

Sophie got out, her head buried in the front seat as she grabbed packages.

"Goodness!" she exclaimed, seeing Michael for the first time, standing before her with his crutches. "What happened?"

"An accident in November. That new, big building on the corner of 5th and Sitka? I took a fall from the third floor. Pretty bad. I'm still laid up after all this time."

"Did you hear that, Gene? We had no idea. We saw the workmen here, but we didn't realize you'd been hurt. I guess we haven't seen you outside since we've been home."

With silver gray hair and the light tan of those who travel south for the winter, but remember to wear a hat, Gene came around the car and extended his hand. "No harness?"

Michael tried to fight the sudden lurch his stomach took whenever he had to explain the accident. As a contractor, Gene would understand the infinite number of opportunities for disaster on scaffolding.

"No, my harness was on. One minute I was talking to my friend, the next I had slipped on a wet board. There wasn't a toe board so I went under the rails, then the board I tied off on split. I had only needed to be there for a minute, I didn't look carefully where I was tying off." Gene's questioning look showed he was visualizing it. "I didn't see anything wrong with the board, but there must have been a knot on the back. The great irony is that I fell mostly feet first onto a convertible that shouldn't even have been there. Went right through

156

the top and broke all the canvas supports and landed on the seats. Somewhat crumpled…but alive. My legs took the worst of it."

"Michael, that's terrible. I'm so sorry we didn't hear about it earlier. And how is Veronica doing through all this?" Sophie was visibly upset.

"It's been a rough couple of months. Harder on her than me, maybe."

"I'm going to make you two a dinner or something right away."

"Thanks, Sophie, it's all right. I'm doing much better now."

"What's all this?" Gene nodded toward Michael's front yard where Obie and James had continued to work.

"Come on. Let me introduce you. These gentlemen are friends of Madigan's. You know, the woman who lives two doors down? They re-did her driveway for her, then did the sports court for the Haffners. They're going to do the sidewalks, too. When they saw what a tough time I had on the front steps, they came up with a plan for a new entrance with concrete steps and planters that will go up to the front door. The sketch is inside, would you like to see it?"

"I would. And you're extending the stoop into a bit of a porch, I see."

"Right. And the wood steps are temporary, of course."

Sophie took in the wide, easy-step wood stairs and Michael with concern. "Do you think you might not get walking again, Michael? What do your doctors say?"

"Too soon to tell. My left leg has improved enough for me to bear weight on it, but the right leg was pretty badly mangled. They've reconstructed everything they can, but I don't have much movement in the knee."

"I'm *so* sorry. Let me go put these packages inside, then we'll come see the design and meet your workers."

Michael smiled to himself. Now *this* was going to be interesting. Their home was the first house built on the block, forty years ago.

Situated in the middle of a double lot, they had remodeled the place bit by bit, until it was a stand-out, far surpassing the other modest homes around it. Prosperous and steady business had allowed Gene to semi-retire several years early. The couple went to San Diego right after Christmas each year and didn't return until the beginning of April. Still tall and attractive at seventy-two, Gene checked in at his office every day while home, golfed three times a week without fail, and took pride in the looks of his house and car.

Michael studied James and Obie. Obie was ten years younger, at least, but looked older than Gene. Their building methods could not be more opposite. Gene was a meticulous follower of blueprints. Except for the sketch of the ramp, Michael had yet to see Obie and James write anything down, or even measure a board, for that matter. They simply looked, studied, cut, nailed, and poured, and somehow everything fit. Oh, yes, this was going to be interesting.

Michael returned to Obie and James, explaining, "My neighbor returned from San Diego. He's a builder. I invited him over to see the drawing."

"That's good. Perhaps he will have some advice."

"He's an extremely nice person." Michael admired how Obie showed no hint of defensiveness. "You won't have to worry about him getting in the way or anything."

"We wouldn't worry about that," Obie replied cheerfully. "We'd like to know if he can swing a hammer or mix concrete. James' sons are busy this week. They will not be as helpful as we had hoped."

"Oh." Now the worry was in Michael's voice.

"Don't be concerned, Michael. We'll get the stairs done for you."

A few minutes later Gene arrived in work clothes, and Michael introduced the brothers.

"Where are you from originally, if it's not impolite to ask?" Gene smiled at Obie.

"We are from a small island near Tonga in Polynesia, the south Pacific Ocean."

"I thought so. I once had a small crew of men, they might have been from Tonga, I don't remember now. They knew how to do everything. The biggest problem was convincing them to measure before cutting. I swear they could look at a length and cut it exactly. But of course, in contracted work, I had to convince them to do it my way. They didn't like it, and they left after a few months to work on their own. But they were wonderful builders."

"Many people from the islands are skilled with their hands," Obie commented.

"And," Gene seemed to be remembering as he talked, "it did seem as if there were some difficulties over the work day. Their pace was a little different. It caused some friction with the other crews."

Michael could hardly contain his smile. *Oh, yes, the work pace.* He imagined how an island crew, with its three-hour lunch break, would have difficulty with an American crew that punched the clock to the minute.

"Let's see what you're doing here," Gene murmured and looked with interest at the layout before him. Michael ascended the wood steps to get the drawing, but Gene's attention was captured by James and Obie as they waved broadly and pointed to describe the project. James walked through the site, showing how the stairs would come down gradually and what the width of the planters would be, while Gene listened intently. By the time Michael got back with the drawing, his neighbor barely glanced at it.

"Yes, Michael, I can see exactly what you're thinking here. Excellent plan, it adds value to the house, and will be much more attractive than those old steps. I told the man who built this house that those stairs were no good, but he was in a hurry to finish. They weren't even up to code—way too steep, but he wouldn't listen. And

159

back then, no one checked too much on the last finishing work. No, this will be excellent."

The unexpected and exuberant praise rang welcomely in Obie's head. He had not been sure if Michael might still have some reservations about the project, what with his wife being so disagreeable and all. But now he could tell that Michael was more at ease, with this positive opinion of his neighbor's to reassure him. What a good day it had turned out to be!

Michael and Gene talked a bit while Obie and James finished digging. At five o'clock, Sophie showed up with a tray of sandwiches and four cups of steaming coffee.

"Please, have something," she said to all of them. "You've been working so hard. What time will Veronica be home, Michael? Perhaps you two would like to come for dinner? I've got plenty."

"She's working late tonight," Michael replied as Obie and James exchanged a small look with each other. "But thanks, I'll take a rain check."

Gene disappeared around the side of his house and came back carrying five sturdy lawn chairs.

Michael shared the picture from his pocket with Sophie while they were eating.

"I love what you're doing on the street," she said to Obie and James between mouthfuls.

"Tomorrow," Obie began, "you may hear a big truck first thing in the morning. The stones are coming, and they seem to deliver early on your street. And the fill. The fill is coming, too."

"The stones?" Michael's brow furrowed in consternation.

"The river rock. For the planters. Don't worry. You'll see. It will all work out."

"But are we that close to doing the planters?"

160

"Better to have the materials here at hand, so they are ready when we are ready, than to be standing around waiting for the truck to come."

This seemed to make sense, in an Obie kind of way.

"It might be a little noisy when they dump the load," Obie said, wiping an errant dribble of Sophie's tuna fish sandwich from his chin.

Chapter Eighteen
*Thursday, April 12*

**M**ADIGAN shot straight up in bed. The house shook with noise and vibration, and she wondered if it was an earthquake. Roger whimpered beside her. Looking at the clock as she ran to the window, she had a sudden suspicion that the earthquake was man-made, because now the rumble had ceased and the only noise was truck-like. It was six-thirty, and the view out the window was of a large dump truck returning its bed to the normal position. Behind it, in front of Michael's and spilling into the street, was a load of good-sized stones.

"Oh—my—gosh!" Madigan had thought she could no longer be surprised by anything James and Obie did, but she was aghast at the size of the mound. As she looked, she wondered why only the van, and not Michael's Toyota, was in the driveway.

"What are they ever going to do with all that rock?" she said aloud to Roger as another truck pulled up, maneuvered to a spot near the stairs but away from the rocks, and dumped a load of sand and gravel.

Tearing herself away from the scene, Madigan prepared for work. When she left home at seven-thirty, nothing was moving on the street, but when she returned home ten hours later, the old truck was parked in front of her house, as usual, and Obie and James were at Michael's.

Briefcase still in hand, Madigan wandered over to say hello.

"We're soon going to run out of parking spaces on the street because of you two," she said good-naturedly to Obie. "What possessed you to have all that rock dumped?"

"Good day, Madigan! And how are you this fine day?"

"Now that I've recovered from my early morning heart attack, thinking we were having an earthquake, quite well, thank you. And you?"

"It has been a fine day for us. Look how far along we are."

Madigan admired the scene. Though unsure what all the stakes, string, and beginning framework meant, she could definitely tell by the dug-up yard that the work was moving ahead. Michael came to the front door and was headed out, but the phone rang and he disappeared back inside.

"It's looking great. You're really making some progress." She glanced back up at the door to be sure Michael was out of earshot. "So what does Veronica have to say about all this?"

"We have not seen her for several days." Obie ran his hand through his grizzled hair. "We're afraid things are not good in that regard."

"I noticed only the van was here this morning, and his Toyota was gone last night, too, when I went to bed. I wondered if they were having car trouble, but then, why wouldn't she just drive the van?"

"I don't know. He doesn't speak of her at all. Yesterday, the neighbor over there, Sophie...do you know her? Very nice. She invited Michael and his wife for dinner, but Michael said she would be working late. But she has never worked late. All this time, she has always come home, changed her clothes, and then gone out again. I don't know what has happened." He shook his head in concern.

163

"Maybe she's out of town. Let's not worry yet." Madigan turned her attention to James. "Hey, James. I hope your sons are coming to help with this rock. How are you ever going to move it all?"

"Piece by piece, Madigan, piece by piece. That's where the art comes in. Each stone has to be chosen to fit just right for the planters. You'll see. Like a puzzle. It will all go together."

Madigan seemed unconvinced. "I'm going to change and walk Roger. Did the kids take him out today?"

"Oh, yes. They're very faithful about it," Obie responded.

After changing clothes, leashing her excited pup, and heading out the door, Madigan noticed the Toyota turning at the corner. In seconds, Veronica had pulled into her driveway in a rush. Heading up the wood stairs without a word to James and Obie, she disappeared into the house. Madigan hesitated, then continued in the opposite direction with Roger. When she came back past Michael's house thirty minutes later, Veronica was shoving suitcases into the Toyota, and Obie and James were sitting under Madigan's tree.

Veronica didn't speak, and Madigan couldn't come up with the proper greeting for the circumstances. So she continued home. She dropped the leash, and Roger ran to Obie. Madigan settled on her bottom step.

"So what's up?"

"She has taken out several large suitcases. That's all we know."

"No sign of Michael?"

"No."

"How do you think he's doing…with his leg and all?"

"He says he has gone out every morning." James looked at Obie and shrugged. "And the car is always in a little different spot in the driveway. He has helped us a bit each day. But I don't know about this," he indicated Veronica's packing.

"We thought we might sit over here a while longer before going back for our tools," Obie explained a bit sheepishly.

164

"Good plan, Obie," Madigan smiled. "*I* even went the other way around the block to avoid her."

"There she goes," James pointed.

Madigan turned and watched the small car back out of the driveway and zoom down the street.

"Now what? Do you think we should go check on Michael? But I don't want to be a busybody."

"We'll say goodbye and see how he's doing. He's probably sitting in his kitchen window."

From her steps, Madigan watched Obie stick his head in Michael's front door, while James closed up the garage. She met them at their truck.

"Go see him," Obie said to her as he pulled himself gingerly into the front seat, the tension setting off his back pain. "He needs some good company right now."

Madigan returned Roger to the house and walked to Michael's. The truck had finally started and was halfway down the street. Obie's hand came out the window in that slow wave she had learned to love. She raised her hand in a fond goodbye.

"Hey, anyone home?" she called at Michael's front door.

"Come on in, Madigan." Michael's voice sounded dull and lifeless.

"It's looking good out front," Madigan said brightly as she entered the room. She was struck by the dirty dishes lined up by the sink, and the general state of decline in the house since she had last been inside. Michael sat at the table, a beer in hand. Madigan had never seen him drink before.

"Well, Madigan. You have witnessed the end of my marriage."

"Oh, Michael, I'm so sorry."

"She moved out Tuesday night, but she didn't take anything. I was hoping she'd think it over and come back. She came back all right—for her stuff. I'm surprised so much fit in my car. Certainly opens up some closet space."

"Gosh, Michael. Maybe it will still work out. Give her some time."

Michael shook his head. "No, I knew it was coming. She's pretty young, you know, only twenty-three. I'm six years older. We got married when she was twenty-one, right out of school. We came from different backgrounds, but our lives revolved around our sports. I know she loved me, but she's an active person. The accident changed too much."

"Everyone's at risk for an accident," Madigan attempted feebly. "You could have had a car accident or been hit by a bus."

"No, no, you don't understand." Michael rubbed his hand through his hair. "It's not the accident that bothered her. It's me... because it was my fault." The fingers of his right hand came to rest on his scar.

"How could it have been your fault?"

"I wasn't paying attention. It had been a great day. We'd come back from lunch break. The rain had stopped, and I was talking to my buddy. I'd noticed the missing toe boards in the morning—" he stopped when Madigan got a quizzical look on her face. "The toe board on scaffolding makes an edge along the boards you stand on. If you slip, your foot should hit that and stop you. Somebody had messed up on the third floor scaffolding and that section didn't have any toe boards. I don't know; it seemed like such a little thing, but I should have reported it to the super. But things like that are missing all the time."

"So when you slipped, you didn't stop. But your harness?"

"I had pretty good momentum going over the edge. I slid feet first right under the railing. The harness would have held, but the board I'd tied off on broke."

"Oh, Michael!"

166

"I should have looked more carefully where I tied off. There must have been a knot right there so it was a weak spot. I'm usually cautious, especially if I'm up high. But three floors doesn't seem so high, you know?" He took another long drink of his beer. "I'd give anything to have those five minutes back after lunch that day. Anything."

"So, so sorry," she murmured, unable to meet his eyes. The admission to his part in the event leading to his break-up with Veronica made him seem like such a nice man, not blaming his door-slamming wife at all. What a nice guy.

"Hey, I'm being impolite. Want a beer? I think there's a cold one left in the fridge."

Madigan noticed the four empty bottles lined up along the sink edge.

"No, thanks. And if I were you, I'd quit pretty soon. You don't want to be home with a hangover tomorrow with James and Obie pounding away out front." She shot him a knowing smile.

"You are right," he was close to slurring his words. "You are absolutely, positively right." He put his bottle down loudly on the table.

"Is there anything I can do? Bring you some dinner?"

"Nope, no, no thank you. I'm a big boy, as I was informed rather rudely by my soon-to-be ex-wife. I'm a big boy, and I should know how to take care of myself. But I thank you kindly." He gave her a bit of a lop-sided grin, but there were tears close behind. He picked up the bottle again and swirled the rest of the beer around. "I really loved her, you know?" he said quietly.

Madigan put her hand on his arm. "I'm so sorry, Michael. Do you want me to check on you later?"

He pulled his arm away and wiped his eye with the back of his hand. "Don't bother. I'm a mess, I know. I'm going to call it a day and go to bed. Start over again in the morning. Like you said—a whole new day."

Madigan didn't think she had ever said that, but she stood to go.

"See you tomorrow, Michael. I'm really, really sorry. Don't give up hope. It might work out."

"You don't know her daddy. It's over. He didn't like me much from the start, but I kept his daughter happy, so he put up with me. But now...no, there's no hope. No hope at all."

Chapter Nineteen
*Friday, April 13*

WHEN they arrived after lunch the next day, Obie and James could see no sign that Michael had yet been outside. Nor was he sitting in the kitchen window. Obie knocked on his front door —nothing. He knocked a little louder. Still no response. On the third try, he heard movement inside. Michael finally opened the door, unshaven, still in his boxers and t-shirt, and squinted at the cloudy daylight.

"Good day, Michael. And how are you this fine day?" Obie asked with his usual cheer.

"Hey, Obie." Michael looked as if even speaking hurt. "Tell James to come on through. I don't think I can help you today."

"That's too bad. We wanted you to advise us on the design of the stones. There are so many different hues out there, we want to put the best where they'll be seen."

"I don't care, Obie," Michael mumbled, closing his eyes against the light. "Do it however you want."

"You are not feeling well, Michael," Obie spoke softly to him. "Go back to bed. We'll try to work quietly."

"Yeah, I'm going to do that." He made his way gingerly down the hallway, seeming to wince with every movement of his crutches.

"He's not good today?" James asked as the brothers began to set up their work area.

"No, not good today at all. The beer, perhaps."

They had been working for an hour when Gene and Sophie pulled in next door.

"Hi. Where's Michael?" Gene called.

"Not feeling well," Obie answered.

"Do you need help? I'd be glad to come over."

"Thank you. We can always use more hands." Obie smiled welcomingly.

"Don't let him try to take over." Sophie wagged her finger sternly. "It's hard for him to remember that not every project is his."

"Oh, this is not that type of project," Obie reassured her. "Many cooks can only help this soup."

"All right, but don't say I didn't warn you," she grinned. "I'll bring you coffee later."

Gene changed his clothes and was back out quickly.

"Now, what can I do?"

"We need to find the best stones," Obie told him. "The ones that will look the nicest for the front of the planters. With the best color for the house, like this." He held up medium-sized one with a bluish-gray sheen. "And organize the stones a bit by size."

"Yes, I see what you mean. I'll pick through the pile and set some aside."

"Thank you. That would be a big help."

They worked for another hour, framing a section then carting up the fill mix. As Sophie arrived with a steaming cup of coffee for each of them, a spotless green gardener's truck pulled up, rakes and hoes neatly standing at attention along the sideboard of the truck bed.

"Oh, here's Phil," Sophie said happily.

A man in his sixties descended, looking at the huge pile of stones and Gene's smaller pile beside it.

170

"Welcome back," he said, waving to Sophie and putting his hand out to Gene. "What's going on here?"

Gene made introductions and explained about Michael and the entrance.

"I wondered about these owners," Phil said. "I used to see them coming and going when we were working here late in the fall, but it's been months since I've seen anyone outside. No wonder. I remember that accident. It's a miracle he lived. Say, that's nice work you've done on the other houses," he addressed James and Obie, gesturing down the street.

"Thank you," Obie replied humbly. "And we have admired the fine landscaping on the gardens," he nodded toward Gene and Sophie's immaculately groomed yard and flower beds.

"I'll be looking forward to seeing your project when it's finished."

The passenger door opened and a younger man resembling Phil but with darker hair hopped out of the cab, shoving his cell phone into his pocket.

"Did you know my son came back to work for me this winter?" Phil announced to Gene and Sophie. "Greg! Come say hello."

"Gregory! It's been a long time since we've seen you." Sophie embraced him, then introduced Obie and James.

"Have you always lived in town?" Obie asked in a friendly way.

"No, I've been out of state for several years," the son answered.

"What has brought you back to all this rain?" Obie inquired again, all innocence.

"I thought you and Sheila were living in Michigan?" Sophie interrupted. "I don't think we've seen you since the wedding. It must be nearly five years now. Oh," she gushed to Obie, "you should have seen it. In Phil's backyard, in August. The flowers were breathtaking."

"Sheila and I split up last summer," Greg was finally able to insert the news.

171

"Oh, no. I'm sorry to hear that." Sophie was stricken. "You seemed so happy."

"I stayed in Michigan for a while...." Greg didn't get into the cause of the divorce—his neighbor and now ex-friend. "But I never liked it as much as Sheila did. So I came home and started working for Dad until I could find something else."

"We must get back to work," Obie said, politely averting his eyes. "We'll see you again, I'm sure."

"Right. I need to get started, too."

"I'll be back in a minute," Gene told James. He and Phil wandered over to his yard and began going around the perimeter beds, their seriousness resembling that of doctors on morning rounds.

"What do you know?" Obie said quietly to James. "An unmarried man with a truck suddenly appears."

James hammered a two-by-four into place with more vehemence than needed. "Let us mind our own business, for once, Obie! Look what happened with the science experiment!"

"I'm not saying we should do anything. Just that here we have a man with a truck," he shrugged his shoulders, "and three doors down there is a woman who needs a truck. That's all."

"You are impossible! Will you never learn?" James continued driving nails, but Obie leaned on his shovel and studied Greg pulling his lawnmower off the truck gate and getting ready to mow. It was too soon to tell, of course, what kind of man this Greg might be. But sometimes things had a way of working out.

Chapter Twenty

*Saturday, April 14*

**M**ADIGAN woke up with a burst of energy. She pulled on her running clothes, though a light sprinkle hid the promised sunshine. The temperature was perfect, the coolness in the breeze a welcome balance to the sweat beading on her face at the end of the three miles. After a shower and feeding Roger, she clipped him to his leash. Today was the potluck at the dog park. *What would be the best thing to bring?* she mused as she walked. Her friend Sue had said everyone ate standing up, so it needed to be finger food of some sort. *Little hot dogs rolled up in biscuits?* Always a favorite. *Mini-sandwiches with crusts cut off? Oh, what is appropriate for a dog party?* She finally decided to take the easy way out. Armed with soft round rolls, cheese, and turkey from a quick trip to the store, she made a plateful of tiny sandwiches. She covered them and put them in her refrigerator, regarding them with satisfaction. *They look nice on the plate, anyway.*

Next she straightened the house, hitting only the worst spots, marveling at how much less perfectionistic she'd become lately. Out in the yard, there was no sign of anyone at Michael's. Obie and James seemed to have accomplished quite a bit, compared to their usual pace. The older neighbor of Michael's had been helping a lot.

At 3:30, Madigan gathered up her dinner offering and headed for the party with Roger. A few people had started to set up card tables when they arrived at the park. Madigan pitched in to help while Roger romped with the other dogs. She kept an eye out for the man with the retriever, but didn't see him.

Her friend Sue arrived a little after five with her beagle, accompanied by Bethany with the big German shepherd.

"It's such a shame about your neighbors," Bethany started after the hellos. "I heard it got so bad Veronica had to move out."

"I did notice Veronica hasn't been around much this week." Madigan kept her face blank.

"She said it's been terrible. I guess her husband has been having these rages, and she doesn't know what to do. She asked him to move out, and he wouldn't, so she had to. It's awful."

"Michael? Having rages?" Madigan maintained her composure with some difficulty considering the absurdity of the statement.

"Veronica is such a sweet person," Bethany oozed, oblivious to Madigan's emerging expression of disbelief. "She's distraught that she can't save the marriage. She's terribly worried about finances. She thinks they'll lose the house with him not working. Her dad's an attorney. I think he's trying to help her get out of it."

"I don't know much about it," Madigan stammered. *Such a "sweet" person? Are we talking about the Veronica on my street?*

"So, how's the pup?" Sue asked, looking around for Roger.

"He's great." Madigan was relieved to change the subject. "Growing fast. I never knew having a dog could be so enjoyable. He's over there under that tree. It must remind him of home."

Sue introduced Madigan to a few other people as they helped set out the food on the tables. Madigan kept looking for the man with the retriever, but didn't see him. She noticed a group of people standing around a young couple with another beautiful golden. She wandered to the edge of the conversation.

"We don't know what to do," the woman was saying. "No one can take him for us, and we can't take him with us. I don't want to have to give him up forever."

"What's going on?" Madigan whispered when Sue came up beside her at the back edge of the group.

"That's Art and Kristen. They're headed for an archeological dig in Israel for five months. They're trying to find a last minute placement for their dog—something happened with their original plan. He's a nice boy. But everyone in this group is sort of maxed out on dogs, and it runs right through summer vacation. Most of these people take their pooches along, and traveling with a second big dog is more than people want to take on. She needs to find someone who's going to be home for the summer, pretty much."

Madigan looked at the dog lying calmly at Kristen's feet. She *did* know someone who was home a lot, wouldn't be traveling, and needed companionship. *But Michael might not even like dogs.* Then she thought how Obie had brought Roger into her life. He had plunked Roger into her lap and that was all it took.

Madigan made her way to the front and introduced herself to the couple as a friend of Sue's. She explained about Michael and offered to inquire.

The young woman brightened. "I never thought it would be so hard to find a place for him. We thought we were going to be able to leave him with the family staying at our house. But their daughter has come up with animal allergies, big time, and they can't do it. We've only got two weeks, and I'm getting desperate to know he'll be in a good place."

"We won't give him to just anyone, though," Art interrupted. "We'd have to meet your friend, to see if Shiloh likes him, to see if it would work out."

"But he's a wonderful dog. We'll pay for all his food, his vet bills, everything," Kristen added. "The biggest problem is that no one wants to keep him five months and then have to give him back."

"Of course." Madigan was sympathetic in a way she could not have fathomed two months earlier. "Why don't you give me your phone number? I'll ask my friend tonight, then I'll call you."

"Thank you so much." Kristen pulled out a piece of paper and scribbled a number on it.

"I can't make any promises, but I'll be glad to check."

The rest of the potluck was quite fun. Madigan admired the easy way Sue introduced her to new people. But Bethany's comments about Michael were still rolling around the back of her head. *Michael having rages? What could that be about?*

It was seven o'clock when she got home. She put Roger on his leash and walked over to Michael's, enjoying how Roger boldly leaped up the new wood steps. It took a few moments for Michael to appear at the door.

"Hi, Madigan. Come on in." He held the screen door open for her. "Hey, Roger," he bent down and patted Roger's head, "how are you doing?" The puppy immediately flipped onto his back for a tummy rub.

"Things are looking good out there, Michael. I love the look of that stone."

"Gene, next door, has been pulling stones out of the pile all week. It's going to be a work of art. I hope he doesn't send me a bill."

"I'd like to meet him. Nothing like a group project to get everyone out and about, I guess."

"Right. What can I do for you? You want to come sit in the kitchen?"

"Do you like dogs, Michael? Have you ever had one?" Madigan had decided to come right to the point.

"Why, are you tired of Roger already?"

"Oh, no, not at all. I was only wondering."

"I do like dogs. My family always had one growing up. With Veronica and me both working, we never looked into getting one. She wasn't much of a pet person, anyway. Why?"

"Today there was a couple at the dog park I go to every week. They have a beautiful golden retriever, a male, and they're going to Israel for five months on a research project. They leave in two weeks. The family that is going to stay in their house was supposed to keep the dog, but now they can't. So this couple is desperate to find a placement while they're away. They'll pay all the costs. For some reason, I thought of you. Some company right now might…" Madigan began to falter, realizing she was treading into Veronica territory.

"It's okay to talk about it, Madigan. Veronica has announced her intention to file for divorce. I've already heard from her lawyer, and she's only been out of the house for two days. I knew it was coming, and you probably did, too. It would be hard to ignore the slamming door."

"I'm so sorry how this has turned out for you," Madigan looked at him sympathetically.

"About the dog…" Michael changed the subject, but his voice was choked up. "I hadn't thought about a dog, but I suppose it might be a good way to see if I want one. But I wouldn't be able to walk it. And what if I have to give up the house?"

"You'll have to tell them that. I could take him to the dog park with me when I go. Maybe Kevin and Lauren would walk him for you when they take Roger out. If something bad really happens, maybe I could find someone else to take him."

"Okay, I'll give it a try, I guess." Michael leaned back against the wall.

"Great. I'll give them your number. I'm sure they'll contact you right away." Madigan observed Michael's face closely. "So how are you doing, really? How's therapy?"

Michael seemed surprised at her sudden, specific, interest.

"I'm good."

Madigan was still staring at him.

"Oh," he thought he understood. "You mean the other night? When Veronica left? I know I was drinking too much. I rarely do that, don't worry."

"No, I was only wondering…if things are okay, that's all." Madigan knew she was making a mess of it.

"What is it, Madigan?" Michael tried to read what was on her mind, but her eyes wouldn't meet his. "I know you're trying to get at something. Just say it." His fingers came up and rubbed his face while he waited.

Madigan sighed at the thought of this young guy about to be totally screwed by his wife, his father-in-law, and the divorce lawyer.

"This is hard, Michael," she began slowly, "but I met someone at the dog park who knows Veronica from work. She's a buyer for another department store, but she sees Veronica fairly often. The description she gave of your situation isn't anything close to what I've observed. It worried me a little."

"What did she say?"

"That Veronica thinks you're depressed and won't get help. That you won't go to therapy. That you're having…anger management problems?" Her voice rose in uncertainty.

Michael looked at her with disbelief.

"Me? *Me*, having anger management problems? Are you joking?"

"I know. I was surprised myself. I didn't know what to say."

Michael headed for the kitchen, and Madigan could see she had upset him.

"I'm sorry, Michael," she followed him. "I shouldn't have said anything."

Michael sat heavily into his chair. "She must be trying to build a case. Odd, because it's a community property state, with no-fault divorce. It's not like she has to prove anything. Unless she wants something," his voice trailed off. "Oh, of course. She wants the house. That's got to be it. Well, thanks for the heads up."

"Look, Michael, no one wants to get involved in your personal life, but it's pretty obvious to anyone living on the street that you're not the one with the anger management issues."

"Thanks. Shall I have my attorney call you all to speak in my behalf? Can't you see Obie on the witness stand?"

Madigan smiled at the thought. "And having a devoted dog at your feet could only help with the sympathy vote. I'll go get started on my part of your defense."

"Thanks for stopping," Michael said sincerely. "I wasn't going to contest the divorce, but I guess I better get a good attorney to protect myself."

"Good idea. And keep a lid on that temper, okay?"

"Right. No more door slamming for me."

Madigan was glad they could joke about it. She was pleased that she had even been able to broach the topic with him. But he deserved better. She glanced at the pile of stones as she went home. He deserved so much better.

Chapter Twenty-One
*Sunday, April 15, Easter Sunday*

O BIE relaxed in his chair in the backyard, eyes closed. He was tired today. The Easter service had been crowded and long, followed by an especially filling, mid-day meal. Usually he would tend to his flowers before resting, but today exhaustion pulled at every weary muscle. It had been a long week at Michael's. They were trying to finish the job more quickly than usual. The neighbor Gene was a big help, but it was tiring work. Moving the sand and gravel was hard on his back, even with the wheelbarrow only half full. Obie did not want to admit how difficult it was for him to work every day with no rest.

He felt the sun on the bare skin of his face and hands, then the beginning warmth as it seeped through his clothes. He listened to Lilly's voice in the kitchen, to the young girls' calls in the front yard as they played, to the noises of the street and neighborhood beyond. He tried to imagine all the noises gone and replaced by those of the ocean, the sweet sound of waves rising and falling, their gentle lap on the sand on a quiet day. Obie yearned for the feel of the warm sand under his hand. But mostly he yearned for the comfort of his wife.

*Keep me going, Lord, please. Keep me going. Let me be a help to my brother. Let us finish the stairs easily for Michael. Keep my loved ones safe from harm, let us live to praise you on the morrow. Thank you, Lord, for these my blessings.*

Obie's tiredness overwhelmed him as he thought through the names of his family in his prayer. The sun beat down, and still he prayed, until his breathing was a slow, steady rhythm, and his thoughts had stilled. *Keep me going, Lord,* was his last thought before he was fast asleep.

Chapter Twenty-Two

*Monday, April 16*

G ENE woke slowly. He sat on the side of the bed, trying to summon the energy to get going. Sophie was coming out of their master bath when she saw him sitting so oddly. It was unusual for him; most mornings he was up bright and early with a bounce in his step, anxious to start on the day before she was even awake.

"What's wrong, Gene? Are you not feeling well today?"

"A little tired, I guess."

"Are you sure?" She came over closer so she could look at him carefully. The man had not had a sick day in his life. Barely even a cold, and never anything that had kept him in bed for a day. She put her hand on his forehead, then slid it lovingly down his cheek and let it rest there for a second.

"No fever."

"It's nothing." He stood up and went into the bathroom. "I must be getting old if a few rocks slow me down this much."

"You should be careful what you lift out there. Aren't there any younger men on their crew to help?" Sophie called after him.

"James' sons are going to be by one of these days. And I don't have to help," he spoke louder now as he started the water running at the sink. "Quite frankly, I'm enjoying it. I've always liked laying stone."

"I know. But I don't want you to hurt yourself." She watched as he got out his toothbrush, then she headed downstairs to make breakfast.

Gene shaved, showered, and joined his wife. Taking his place in the breakfast nook, he separated the morning paper into the sections they each liked to read first, and placed hers beside her juice. He observed the backyard. Their gardens were a colorful contrast to the dreariness of the overcast day.

"Are James and Obie coming today?" Sophie asked as she brought over their eggs.

"Yes, I think so. They seem quite determined to get the stairs done this week. I'm trying to talk them into ordering a truck instead of mixing all of it by hand."

"But look at the other driveways...they seemed to manage those quite well."

"I know, but this is a lot of concrete to pour. Well, I don't want to interfere."

Sophie smiled. "From what I've seen, I think they would let you make whatever suggestions you wanted to make, then they would go right ahead and do it the way they've been doing it since they started their business."

Gene laughed. "You're right. You're absolutely right."

They ate their breakfast in silence, reading the paper, then switching sections as they had done every morning for forty years.

"Are you going to the office today?" Sophie inquired, putting down the front page.

"I don't think so. I could tell when we got back that Fred's had a good winter. I knew this year would be the telling point, whether he was ready to take over or not. He can do it. He's there." Pride in his oldest son's accomplishments filled his voice.

"I think Bea and the kids might stop over tonight after school. Maybe I'll make some cookies later."

"How's their baseball coming? Shouldn't we be getting the schedule pretty soon? I'd like to go to some of their games." Their second-born was mother to several Baseball Hall-of-Fame hopefuls.

"Bea hasn't mentioned it, but it is mid-April. Seems like the games start any time now. I'll ask her to bring us a schedule."

Gene heard the noise of the old truck arriving.

"There they are. I'll give them a few minutes to get organized before I go out."

He stood and went back upstairs. Sophie had the oddest feeling pass over her again, as if something was not quite right with him.

Gene went into the bathroom. He had been having nausea and stomach pain after he ate for weeks now. Today it was particularly bad. Thinking it was too much coffee, he had tried to cut back without success. The burning felt like it was right in the pit of his stomach and he had to fight to keep his breakfast down.

*Okay, no more coffee today,* he promised himself.

"What do you think about the pouring this time?" James asked his brother upon their arrival, as they picked their way through what had become a huge stone field on one side of the lawn, the stones no longer in a pile but neatly arranged by Gene according to shape, size and color.

"How much help can Young James and John be this week? I don't think we can mix this much by hand without their help."

This surprised James. Never, ever, had Obie been willing to call for a cement truck to come to a site.

"I'll ask them tonight. We can decide tomorrow."

Obie went up to Michael's door and knocked. Michael appeared promptly, dressed and ready to work.

184

"Good morning, Obie," he said pleasantly, holding open the screen door.

"Good day, Michael. And how are you this fine day?" He entered and headed for the basement steps.

"I'm good today. I'm hoping to be of some real help to you this week."

"That would be wonderful. We need some strong hands. James and I were discussing whether to order a truckload of concrete this time. The planters are a big job, and I'm not sure how much time his sons can take from school."

James met Obie at the garage door with the extension cords in his hand, and by the time they were back out among the stones, Gene had joined them. Michael began to measure for lighting along the treads.

"What would you like me to do today?" Gene asked.

"We need to get the final framing done and the fill mix in. We might order a truck for Wednesday," James responded.

Gene was happily surprised, but tried not to appear so. "That might be a good idea with such a large project."

James shrugged. "I'm going to see how busy the boys are this week. I don't like them to miss their college classes to help us. Education is so important here."

"What do you think, Gene?" Michael called from where he was standing among the imaginary steps. "I want to go with recessed lighting in the stone, about a foot up on each side. Maybe two lamps on each wide step. Do you think that will do it?"

"That seems good. You'll have a porch light too, I assume? Then a pretty glow coming up along the planters. Good. Can I help you with the measuring?"

They worked until noon. Michael went into his house to eat and put his leg up for a while. Obie and James retreated to Madigan's tree to eat their lunch. Gene went inside his house, then reappeared with a cold drink. He came over and sat down beside Obie.

"Now, the woman who lives here, what does she do?" he asked.

"She works for the city. She's an accountant."

"You know, I've barely seen her all these years. But now that she walks that dog every day, I at least see her go past the house. How did you happen to do her driveway?"

"We did the driveway for the sister of her friend at work," James answered. "Madigan's feet were always wet because she had to stand in a puddle to put the garage door up and down—"

"The electric garage door opener wasn't working," interjected Obie. "And the water pooled at the door's bottom, so her feet were always being splashed."

"—so one day her friend suggested getting the drainage fixed so she would not have wet feet—"

"—and when we did the driveway, we fixed the door opener," Obie finished. "Only it was not really even broken in the first place. She never needed to get out of her car." He and James burst into laughter, though Gene missed the irony.

"But the drainage *was* a problem," Obie said more seriously.

James stood and excused himself. "I'm going to the hardware store to get the electrical parts for Michael. Do you need anything?"

"No," Obie said, leaning back against the tree, "unless the deli is on the way. Lilly's lunch was particularly healthy today. I need something a little creamy to get me going for the afternoon."

Gene moved around to get more comfortable, leaning his head against the trunk and closing his eyes.

"As I age," he addressed Obie, "I am beginning to appreciate more and more of your customs."

"Allowing the lunch a few moments to digest is a good one, is it not?"

"Yes, indeed. It's a good one."

"You're not feeling well today, I think," Obie said, his eyes also closed. Gene looked at him sharply, but Obie didn't move. "And I think that you haven't been feeling well for some time."

"It's nothing. I've never been sick a day in my life. My stomach's been upset for a few days, that's all."

"I think it's been longer than a few days. And I think you should ask your doctor about it." Now Obie opened his eyes and looked carefully at Gene.

"No, it's nothing. Too much coffee. I'm cutting back."

"Hmm." Obie made no other reply.

They sat in silence for a few moments, the wind moving the branches gently above them.

"Where would you live, Obie, if you could live anywhere on earth? Where is your favorite place?"

"I would go back home and live in my house with my wife and little children. Those were my happiest days, when my wife was alive and our children were young. What about you?"

"I don't know. I've been thinking about it lately. Our oldest son has pretty much taken over my business. I've cut back on my work hours, I could probably completely retire at any time. But what would I do? Where would Sophie and I want to live, that's the question now. Sophie goes south to appease me every winter. But she would rather stay here, closer to the kids and grandchildren."

"What do you like to do when you're not working?"

"I like to be outside. I like to be near the water. That's what I like about San Diego. The beaches are beautiful, the ocean is warm. It's a nice-sized city. But it's too far away from our children for Sophie." Gene stretched, then moved again, trying to get comfortable. He finally gave up, got to his feet awkwardly, and sat on Madigan's front steps.

"How many children do you have?" Obie asked.

"Four. Fred, the oldest, he's the one taking over the business. Bea is a teacher, she lives here in town with her husband and two kids. Then Emma, she's a legal assistant down in Portland. They've got three kids. And finally Jimmy, he works for Channel Two news here. What about you? What kids do you have?"

"A boy and a girl. They are both married and live in Hawaii where they work in the hotels. They have families and little room in their busy lives for our traditional ways."

"What is it about your home that you miss the most? Besides your wife, of course."

"The quiet. Even though the water is sometimes noisy when it crashes the beach on a windy day, there is still a peacefulness there that I have found nowhere else."

"I know what you mean. I love to sit on the shore and listen to the waves break. I love the sound of moving water. The children tease me because many years ago, before the remodels, we had an aluminum cover over our back porch. I loved listening to the rain beat on that old roof."

"Rain can sound both soothing and threatening, in my experience," Obie said thoughtfully. "There are some rain sounds that I would not like to hear again."

They sat for a minute. "Shall we get back to work?"

"Not quite yet. I'll wait for James to return." Obie set his thermos bottle down and closed his eyes again. "Now is the time I try to imagine myself on the beach, soaking up the sun's energy in my tired old bones."

Gene tried to sit quietly on the hard brick steps, but something about the way he was sitting made his stomach hurt more. He stood to go.

"You should see a doctor," Obie said, again without opening his eyes.

"If it's not better in a few days, I will."

"Go soon, Gene. I'm telling you this, go soon."

Gene felt unsettled, as if Obie's closed eyes were boring into him as he walked to his house. He went into the kitchen for a drink of milk, to see if that would help. Sophie had started to bake the cookies.

"Darling, what is it? You do not look well today," she said, interrupting her mixing to really observe him.

"Obie said the same thing."

"How long have you been feeling like this?" Her tone held growing concern.

"A few days."

"Are you sure? You haven't been eating as much lately. I noticed, but I didn't say anything. Have you lost weight?" She knew he weighed himself every morning before getting into the shower.

"Maybe a little."

"Gene! When did this start?"

"About two weeks ago. Before we started packing to come home."

"You should have been in to see a doctor before this! I'm calling right now to get an appointment." She wiped her hands on her apron and picked up the phone.

"It's nothing, Sophie. Too much coffee or something."

She waved her hand to shush him as she spoke into the phone and consulted their wall calendar. She covered the phone with her hand and turned back to him. "Wednesday morning is the first appointment they have, unless it's an emergency."

"That's fine. It'll probably be gone by then, anyway."

"We'll take it," Sophie returned to the receptionist. "Wednesday at ten. Thank you." She hung up the phone and studied her husband. "Get your prostate checked while you're in there. It's been three years at least since you've been in for a physical."

"Okay, I will." He felt her worried look on him. "It's nothing, Sophie. It's really nothing."

But he could not quite meet her eyes.

Chapter Twenty-Three
*Still Monday, April 16*

O BIE and James worked late. They needed to get the electrical laid out before Wednesday, if they were going to pour the stairs and planters at the same time.

"So, James, suppose that we do, this one time, get the truck for the concrete. Should we not go ahead and pour Madigan's sidewalk, and Frank and Liz's?"

"I don't think we can do that much in one day, on top of Michael's, do you? Even with Gene and Michael's help, that is a long day's work already."

"I know, but won't Madigan wonder why we cannot get her walk finished if we are having a truck?" Obie voiced his concern.

"Maybe we'll get the truck again to do her sidewalk and Liz's at the same time. That would be easy."

"All right. Perhaps she won't say anything." Though Obie strongly doubted it. Madigan had seemed busy of late, but even her patience most likely had its limits.

At that moment Madigan pulled into her driveway. She gave a wave as she ran into the house, then reappeared moments later with Roger. She walked over to say hello as Michael came out on his front stoop.

"Hey, guys, how's it going? Lots of progress today, I see. Hi, Michael. Did you hear from those people about the dog?"

"I did. They're bringing him to meet me tonight. And inspect the premises, I imagine."

Frank pulled into his driveway next door. He got out and nodded to the group, calling to Obie, "Did you see Kevin today?"

"Only for a moment. We were working quite hard to place the footings and could not stop to talk while he was walking Roger."

Frank approached them, pride evident in his voice. "He called me at work. He took first prize at the science fair at his school. He gets to enter his project in the district-wide competition this weekend."

"Congratulations! What was his final project?"

"How the eye works. His accident gave him a sudden interest in vision. You'll have to come see his model when he brings it home. It's quite ingenious, really. An actual working eye. Made of plastic, I mean." Frank had caught sight of Madigan's face paling when she misunderstood.

"While you are both here," James cleared his throat, "we have not forgotten your sidewalks. We want to get the steps finished for Michael."

"I know you'll finish as soon as you can," Madigan said amicably.

"Well," Obie said, slightly abashed at her graciousness, "it's possible that we will be having a truck bring the concrete for Michael's steps, because Young James and John cannot help this week, and we are ready to do it. But there will not be quite enough time to do your sidewalks at the same time."

"Oh," said Madigan, a bit less genial.

"It's not that we don't understand how long it's been," Obie was pacifying. "And I promise you, we'll do them the very next thing, right after the stairs are finished and the stone is set, right James? The very next thing."

"A little more time isn't going to bother us," Frank said. "Once the baseball games start we'll hardly be here."

"The games are at a time you can make this year?" Obie inquired, ignoring James' look.

"I plan to make most of them. My schedule has been rearranged by my wife and my lab assistant, and suddenly I seem to have some free evenings."

"That's good then. There's nothing like a comfortable game of baseball on a warm spring evening, the smell of the fresh-cut grass wafting up around you."

"You watched a lot of baseball, did you?" Madigan asked with mild sarcasm.

"I did. My children played. It has been years, of course, but—"

"—and they each only played a few summers," James finished for him. "Our sports were nothing like you have here. You picked up a bat and ball, called to your friends and went out to a field."

"I watched my children play," Obie said testily.

"I'm only teasing you, Obie," Madigan reached out and patted his arm good-naturedly. "Whenever you can finish the sidewalk will be fine. But soon, okay? Come on, Roger, let's go for a walk."

"And how is the garage coming?" Obie called to her back, getting in the last shot. "I see you still are not parking inside."

Madigan turned around. "It's coming along. One more section of boxes, really, that's all I have. I need to find a way to take a lot of it to the dump. I need a truck…." Her eyes came to rest hopefully on their truck.

"We'd be happy to help you, of course," James said.

"Although it may be awhile. We're busy right now," Obie added.

"Of course. In the meantime, I'll keep my eye out for another empty truck going down the street. Maybe I can snag it."

"You never know from where help may come," Obie granted.

A car came into view, moving slowly down the street, looking for a house number.

"I bet this is the couple with the dog," Michael said. He had been somewhat forgotten as he stood among his electrical lighting. He made his way carefully through the rocks with his crutches and came near the sidewalk. The car parked across the street, and Kristen got out first. She pulled the seat forward and the golden retriever hopped out.

"Hello, Kristen," Madigan called to her, joining Michael. Roger was tugging at his leash, trying to get close to the new dog.

"Hi," Kristen waited for Art before they crossed the street.

"Art, Kristen, I'd like to introduce you to my neighbor, Michael Stevens," Madigan indicated Michael, who held out his hand. "And," she bent down and rubbed the golden's big head, "this is Shiloh."

Frank said, "See you all later," and returned to his own house, while further introductions were made.

"This is a big project you've got going here," Art said to James and Obie.

After a short explanation about why his front yard resembled a rock quarry, Michael invited Kristen and Art into the house. James and Obie said they were about to leave, and Madigan continued on her walk with Roger. When she returned half an hour later, everyone had gone and only Michael was in his front yard, fooling around with the wiring.

"So what happened?" Madigan asked curiously.

"I guess I passed." Michael straightened up. "They're bringing him back a week from Wednesday. They seem like nice people. I wonder if Frank has ever run into them at the University."

"Yeah, I wonder. Well, Roger and I are going in for dinner. What are you cooking tonight?"

"I think it's hot dogs for me. What about you?"

"I've got leftovers from last night."

194

"Want to share?"

Madigan thought that what she really wanted to do was go in, take a bath, put on her pjs and relax. But Michael had asked so sweetly.

"Sure. My house or yours?"

"You come here. Bring Roger."

Madigan found herself smiling for no reason as she went into her house. There was no way Michael was the one with the anger problems. *Veronica had better watch her step, because this neighborhood will not put up with anyone messing around with Michael.* She laughed at the vision of a courtroom filled with Michael's friends and his faithful new canine companion lined up in his defense.

Chapter Twenty-Four
*Tuesday, April 17*

**O**BIE groaned as he got out of the truck.

"What's wrong? Are you hurting today?" James looked at him sharply.

"No, I'm just old. Too old for this, James. I'm not being a good help to you this week."

"You shouldn't try to do so much. Why are you in such a hurry, all of a sudden? It will get done when it gets done."

"I want to get it finished for Michael, to show his wife that it's a good project. And we need to keep Michael busy. Each day he has come out to help us now. That's good for him, no?"

"I'm not his doctor. I'm only trying to make a living pouring concrete."

"You are an artist, James. You never believe that about yourself!" Obie had to raise his voice at James' back as he walked up the wood steps to Michael's front door.

It was ten-thirty. Work a good hour, Obie told himself, then you can stop for lunch. He knew his muscles and bones were complaining about years of heavy work and carrying too much weight, and that pacing himself was the most important thing to avoid those odd moments of dizziness. But he didn't worry too much; their parents had lived long lives on the island.

He pulled the tools out of the back of the truck as James opened the garage door from the inside. In a few minutes he heard the front door of Gene's house open, and Gene joined them on the sidewalk.

"What's on today's schedule?" Gene asked.

Obie looked at him carefully. "How are you feeling today?"

"I'm fine. Sophie made me an appointment for tomorrow. I'm sure it's nothing. Now what can I do to help?"

"We're going to mix and pour the rest of the footings and set some rebar today, and check that the forms are in position. Then we'll be ready for the truck to come tomorrow."

The four men worked for an hour and a half. Sophie arrived with sandwiches and coffee. They retreated to Madigan's tree.

"This is a nice little spot you have for yourselves over here," Gene commented. He had carried over one of his plastic lawn chairs to sit on. Obie and James took their usual spots on overturned buckets under the tree, leaning against its trunk. Michael perched on Madigan's front steps.

"Are you sure you don't want me to get you a chair?" Gene asked him.

"No, I'm fine. But I'll take another half of one of those chicken sandwiches. They're great."

Gene held out the plate, then offered it to James and Obie, who shook their heads no, indicating their large lunches spread on their laps.

"So the truck comes tomorrow? I can't believe it," Michael said.

James swallowed his mouthful. "It will be a long day. I've ordered two loads to be delivered, one first thing, then one after lunch. If that is not enough, we can mix by hand to finish. I'm hoping my sons can stop by late. We'll see. If we get it all poured, then on Thursday we can begin to set the stone."

When they finished eating, Michael went to rest his leg, and James headed over to check on their morning's work. Obie looked at Gene carefully.

"It's good you're seeing the doctor," he said.

Gene sighed.

"You are having discomfort when you eat, right?" Obie looked at the sandwich Gene hadn't finished. "You're tired, and your stomach bothers you at night?"

"Yes."

"I've only met you. But have you lost weight?"

"Not really. Well, some, before we came back."

"Be sure to tell these things to the doctor. Don't say, 'Oh, it's not so bad.' Tell him everything you can think of."

Gene met Obie's eyes and looked into them for a long minute. "How do you know so much about it?" he asked quietly.

"We're not so lucky with doctors where I come from. There's not so much help. Be glad that you have it. Use it."

"Right. Well, I'm going in for a few minutes."

"We're thankful for your help. We wouldn't be so far along without it."

"That's okay, I like Michael. This was a good idea and I'm glad to be a part of it."

James sat down beside Obie as Gene returned home.

"What is it that you think is wrong with him?" he asked his brother.

"He looks the way Marie did, at the start. It will not surprise me if it's the same thing."

"Obie!" James was shocked. "You are so negative! He's only going to the doctor. It doesn't mean he has cancer."

"We'll know soon enough. There's something about him, the way he moves and eats, and his color, the color under his skin. We'll see. I hope I'm wrong."

"Let's talk of more pleasant things, and rest. There's much to be done yet today."

James feared his brother's predictions because Obie was so often correct. He observed things, or felt things, or somehow knew things about people he had just met in an almost frightening way. James had never been able to decide if this trait of his brother's was a gift or a curse; he was simply thankful that there was no bad news about himself or his family in Obie's expression each day.

They closed their eyes and rested peacefully for an hour, before getting up to work. Michael came back out, and Gene did also. By five o'clock, they had done all that they could do. They were ready to pour.

Madigan woke Wednesday morning to the familiar sound of the old truck parking in front of her house. She looked at the clock as she heard the doors being shut: only 7 a.m. She closed her eyes for a moment, but was awakened again shortly by the sound of a really large truck. This time she moved to the window. The cement truck, its giant tumbler rolling, was slowly moving into position as signaled by James.

*Well, I guess this is it.* She watched, fascinated, as the truck backed up Michael's driveway. Then the driver got out and extended a long boom and chute. Obie and James seemed to be in position, and then suddenly there was a different kind of noise, and the concrete was oozing slowly out of the channel. She watched as it filled the forms they had made for the top part of the stairs. She had to pull herself away to get ready for work, but she found it fascinating, this rush to keep ahead of the flow, to move it and spread it and smooth it just so. By the time she was out of the shower, dressed and ready to leave, the

199

truck seemed to have finished and the driver was hosing off the equipment.

"Do you think one more load will be enough?" James asked his brother.

"I hope so. I don't like working off the truck."

"There's only the bottom stairs, the planters and the pathway to pour. We'll mix the mortar for the stones by hand. Since Gene has laid them all out, it should go more quickly than I thought it would. But we could have waited until the boys could help," James said, giving a final brush to the upper stairs with a long broom.

"No, we can do it," Obie said, surprised at his own stamina and strength today. "Let's surprise them with how far two old men can get."

A few minutes later Michael appeared at the front door. "I didn't know we were starting so early! I'll be right out."

At nine-thirty they waved to Gene as he and Sophie backed out of their garage.

"It's looking good," Sophie called out her window. "We shouldn't be too long. Gene is anxious to get back to help you."

At ten-thirty, Obie and James rested under Madigan's tree and Michael went back into his own house. They ate some of their lunches. By eleven-thirty, Obie was beginning to worry at what was taking Gene so long at the doctor's.

"Maybe they stopped to do some errands," James suggested.

"Maybe, but I don't think so."

They rested until one o'clock, when the next load of concrete arrived. Then they worked hard for the next hour, getting the thick, gray mixture smoothed to their liking in the bottom half of the project.

"There," James said with satisfaction after the truck had gone and last portion was leveled just right.

"Yes, that is very nice," Obie replied distractedly. He was definitely worried now. It was past two o'clock.

Michael was ecstatic as he stood by the street and looked at the front of his house. "It's going to be beautiful," he told them. "Like your picture."

It was after five when Gene and Sophie finally pulled into their driveway. The garage door went up and the car pulled straight in without stopping. Obie, James, and Michael all paused in the rinsing of their tools, but it was several minutes before Sophie came out, a wad of tissue in her hand. All three men went to her.

"What is it?" Michael asked, reaching Sophie first and switching his crutches so he could put his arm around her gently.

"His stomach," Sophie said, the tears beginning to well. "They did a lot of tests. It's going to be a few days before we know for sure. But it could be stomach cancer. He didn't tell anyone about these symptoms he's been having." The tears were coming fully now. "He such a stubborn old fool!" She leaned her head into Michael's shoulder.

"I'm so sorry," Michael tried to comfort her. "When will you know?"

Sophie pulled herself erect, a long sigh escaping her, as she wiped her eyes and nose. "Maybe late tomorrow. Friday for sure. He took the news pretty well. If it's what they think, we're looking at surgery early next week. It's not an emergency, but the sooner the better. So we'll go get it taken care of."

Obie could see that she had been rehearsing this part, practicing the words she would use to tell their friends and children. Sophie looked into Obie's deep, kind eyes and saw the sadness there. "You knew about this, didn't you?" she said to him softly.

"Yes," he answered. "But you have good doctors here. Remember that—you have excellent care here. It will be all right."

Sophie nodded. "I do believe that. I really do." She wiped her eyes one more time. "I better go in." Her eyes fell upon the new stairs. "It's lovely, Michael. It's coming out nicely."

"Thanks," he gave her a quick hug. "Let me know if there's anything I can do."

Obie and James had gone when Madigan arrived home, but Michael was still out front. Madigan parked and then admired the new entrance.

"Gosh, Michael. It's going to be absolutely gorgeous. I had no idea it would be so stunning."

"I know. I can't believe it myself. I've been standing here looking at it for about an hour."

"What a change it makes for the house. And the stones aren't even in yet."

Michael gestured to the piles behind him. "Gene did a great job sorting the stones for us. Hopefully setting them will go quickly once the forms come out." His voice cracked oddly making Madigan look. "Gene might have stomach cancer."

"Oh, no. When did all this happen?"

"I guess he's been feeling a little off recently. He had the tests today. They don't know for certain, but Sophie seems pretty sure. I guess they'll do surgery next week."

"That's awful. But I think stomach cancer is something people can live with, you know, it's treatable and all that."

"I don't know anything about it. It was weird, though. Obie was reassuring Sophie about the good doctors we have here. Maybe he knew someone at home with it."

"His wife died several years ago. It could have even been her."

"Well, anyway, he was certainly worried about it most of the afternoon while we were working."

"You've been out here helping a lot, Michael. Seems to me you're getting around more easily, or is that my wishful thinking?"

"I think it's in your head. I'm still terribly slow." He tapped his crutches on the ground, then looked up at his new stairs again. He imagined the porch finished, the stones in place, the temporary wood steps gone, and the planters filled with attractive flowers. It was all going to look so good. Then his eyes fell on his driveway with its darkened concrete and large cracks. "This is all going to look great," he spoke his thoughts to Madigan, "except for this old driveway. It's going to ruin everything."

"Oh, no," Madigan sighed. "Here we go again. Did you come to this conclusion yourself, or did you have help from our friends with the noisy truck?"

"No, no, they didn't say anything about it. They're not looking for more work, Madigan. I'm sure they're trying to get finished up."

Madigan smiled and pushed her hair off her face. "I swear we'll be inviting them to New Year's Day dinner at this rate. You wait and see. Well, I need to get Roger out."

"See you later."

As Madigan walked back to her house, Liz pulled into her driveway, followed in a second car by Frank. Lauren and Kevin spilled out of Frank's car. "We won!" Lauren shouted, her baseball cap askew. "Madigan, we won for the first time!"

"They don't really keep score at her games," Kevin said confidentially, the experienced older brother.

"They do, too. And we won!" Lauren shouted.

Madigan exchanged hellos with Frank and Liz, and asked about Kevin's eye. It had been ten days since the accident, and it was no longer bandaged. Frank turned and waved to Michael. "Looks great!" he called over.

"But guess what?" Madigan said quietly to Liz. "Now he thinks his driveway looks bad. Does that sound familiar?"

Liz laughed. "It's sort of endless, isn't it? How's your garage coming, by the way?"

"I've only got one last section of boxes to go. What I need is someone with a truck to help me haul a bunch of stuff to the dump. Some of it I can get picked up by the charities, but there's a pretty good stack that needs to go out. James said he'd help. He and Obie are the ones who got me started on it in the first place."

"I don't have a truck, but if there's anything else I can do, let me know."

"Thanks. Well, Roger's waiting." She started to walk away, then turned back. "Liz, does Frank have any connections at the University in the medical school? Michael's neighbor Gene might have stomach cancer. I wondered, if it turns out to be bad, maybe Frank would know about some of those investigational studies people are always doing. Something that might help."

"I'm sorry to hear that; Frank reads a lot of the research, so I'll ask him. I hardly know that couple, but I've always been jealous of their landscaping."

"I know. Me, too." Madigan turned again to go toward her house. This time it was Kevin who called to her.

"Madigan! Did Mom tell you that I won the science fair at school? I get to go to District!"

"Your dad told me the other day. Congratulations! I'm glad it worked out."

"I still wanted to do a rocket, but there was no way Mom and Dad were going to let me." He bounded over to her, filled with excitement. "The eye turned out really cool, though. It shows how the image flips and everything. You'll have to come see it when I bring it home."

"I can't wait."

"The judging is this weekend. I hope I get First Place!" his voice carried over his shoulder as he ran into his house.

"The enthusiasm of youth," Liz said. "See you later."

"See you," Madigan headed for her front door one more time. *I've got to do something about this yard,* she thought, going up her front steps. *As soon as I'm done with the garage, I'm going to start digging out here.*

Chapter Twenty-Five
*Thursday, April 19*

O N Thursday morning, Michael sat at his kitchen table, waiting expectantly to hear the old truck on the street. When there were still no sounds by ten-thirty, he went out his front door and, averting his eyes, descended the wood steps, crossed to the middle of the yard, then turned to look at the previous day's work.

A smile spread across his face as he took in the new stairs. Double the width of the old ones, with only a six inch rise for each step, and alternating treads of ten and eighteen inches, he felt he could nearly run up them, even with his crutches. He pondered the planters for a few minutes. He would have to get help, someone who would know how to fill them so that they showed off perfectly against the house and the soon-to-be-installed river rock.

"Looking good, Michael."

Michael startled. "Gene, I didn't see you come out of the house."

"Sorry to make you jump. I went for a walk around the block."

Michael searched for the right words. "I'm so sorry, Gene. Sophie told us last night."

"Right. Well, sorry I was no help yesterday. I thought I'd never get out of the damn place, they poked and prodded and tested everything there is to test."

"You're expecting the results tomorrow?"

"Yeah. So it's just waiting around. The doctors are pretty sure it's cancer, though. I think they were trying to get us prepared. Sophie must have said, 'But he's never been sick a day in his life' to twenty different people. She took it pretty hard, but today she's pulling together. She's gone over to the library to see what she can find out. Our internet is down at the house, for some reason."

"Have you told the kids?"

"We're waiting till we have the results for sure. No sense having everyone upset and running over here before we know anything."

"Good idea."

"Well, where are the fellows today?"

"I don't know. They worked a long stretch last week and this. It's the most consecutive daily work I've seen them do since they started at Madigan's in February. But then I never know what other jobs they're balancing at the same time. Their schedule is...unpredictable, I guess."

Gene started toward his front door. "Well, it came out great. I like the look of the concrete so much it makes me want to do something over here."

"Your driveway is as bad as the rest of them. You could have it re-done using those decorative pavers."

"Now there's an idea. Wouldn't Sophie love me starting a big project like that right now? I think I either had a bathroom or the kitchen torn up every time she came home from the hospital with a new baby. There was always something."

"Before you go. I've decided I need help to make these planters look right. Do you think Phil and his son do any consulting? I'd need to do the work myself to keep the cost down, but I sure need advice on what to plant."

"I'm sure they do. It's Thursday, right? They should be by later today. You can ask them yourself."

"Great."

"And Sophie and I are sorry about Veronica. We've kind of figured out that she's split."

"Yeah. The accident changed too much for us."

Obie and James arrived then, and behind them the second truck with Young James and John.

"Good day, Michael! Gene! And how are you today?" Obie asked as he carefully extricated himself from the truck.

"How are *you?*" Gene replied. "You're moving slowly today. Your back?"

"I'm a little sore. The pace of the cement truck is different when you are not used to it. But today, today is the fun part. We will pull off the forms and lay the stone. James' sons have arranged to stay the day. By evening you will have your beautiful new planters!"

The boys, serious as always, were already beginning to remove the wood forms and carry them to their truck. James was unloading the mortar mix.

"What can I do to help?" Gene asked.

"You have done the hard work already, separating the rock. Now we will put it in place. Michael, why don't you decide the pieces you want here for the front, the first ones most people will see?"

And so the day went, with each piece of river rock carefully coated with mortar and pushed into place on the planters. After lunch Gene went in and did not return, but even with only the five of them working, it went quickly.

At the end of the day, Michael stood on the front sidewalk and admired the work. It was simply stunning. The stonework added depth and texture; the shades of the stone brought out the color of his paint and trim. Obie, James and the boys had left and Michael was heading in himself when Phil's truck pulled up.

"Hey, Phil, could you come look at this for a minute?" Michael called to him.

Later, Michael was watering down his new concrete when Madigan arrived.

"Hey," she called.

"Hi, Madigan."

"It's spectacular," she came up beside him. "The colors—they're exquisite. Aren't you pleased? Who would have thought it would look this nice?"

"Not Veronica, that's for sure."

Madigan was glad he could make a joke. "Now you have to plant something in there."

"I know. I was talking to Gene's gardener. His son Greg is going to come back tomorrow with some ideas. I want it to look right, you know? I've always admired Gene and Sophie's yard. It's gorgeous, but in a real natural way. Not fake like a magazine cover or anything. Phil's a terrific gardener."

"Phil's the owner, and Greg is his son?"

"Right. Greg's older than I am. I hadn't met him before the other day. Oh, look, here comes Sophie. She's been out all day. Have you ever been officially introduced?"

"No."

"Stay here. If she comes over, I'll introduce you."

Sophie pulled the Cadillac into the driveway, and got out carrying a cloth bag full of books. She walked over to Michael.

"Sophie, I'd like to introduce you to Madigan Gardner, my neighbor two doors down. Madigan, this is Sophie Phillips."

"Nice to meet you," Sophie extended her hand.

"And you," Madigan said. She glanced in the book bag and saw several titles with the word 'cancer' in them. "I'm sorry about your husband. I hope everything turns out okay."

"Thank you. After what I've read this morning, I'm not optimistic that it could be anything but cancer. It's strange, but somehow I think I knew something was wrong, but I was afraid to say anything. Head in the sand, I guess."

"Do you have family in the area?" Madigan inquired.

"Yes, three of our children are here in town, and our younger daughter Emma is in Portland."

"If I can be of help in any way, please let me know. I've got both an extra bedroom and a comfortable couch over there if you need to put some people up."

"Hey, me, too," Michael added. "I've got a guest room. You're welcome to use it."

"Thank you, thank you both very much. We've got plenty of room in the house. It would only be Emma who might come from out of town. I'm sure she wouldn't take her kids out of school even if she comes up for the surgery."

"If anything changes, I'd be glad to help." Madigan edged toward home. "I've got to go let the dog out. See you later."

"She's certainly a nice young woman, Michael," Sophie watched Madigan's retreat.

"Yes, she is." Michael became aware Sophie was waiting for more of a response. "We're friends, Sophie. I'm a good bit younger than she is, you know."

"I bet not even five years. These days no one cares about that anyway. Well, I'm going in to make dinner. Do you want to come over?"

"Thanks, but I'm going to stand here for a while and admire my stones."

Sophie laughed. "You should build a stone bench out of the leftovers so you can sit here all day and look at your house. Though I fear your social life might suffer."

"Sophie, haven't you noticed? I have no social life."

"That's what I mean, Michael. You've got to quit moping around the house all the time. Get out! Do something!"

Michael was a little hurt. "I helped a good bit with these stairs. That's the most I've worked since the accident."

"Good. Now what are you going to do next?"

"What do you mean?"

"What's the next project? You always have to have one you're working on, one you're thinking on, and one way in the back of your head you don't even know about yet."

"Is that the gospel according to Sophie?"

"Yes. Gene's trained me well. Don't let the grass grow under your feet! Keep moving along through life, no matter what. Which is what I'm going to do right now. Sure you don't want to come for some dinner? It's soup and sandwiches. Gene's appetite is still off; nothing tempts him."

"No, but thanks for the offer. Let me know tomorrow if you get any news."

"All right. I'm going to spend tonight going through these books I found. Even if it's cancer, there's a whole range that it could be, you know."

"I don't know anything about it, actually."

"Well," Sophie said as much to herself as to Michael, "there's just a whole range that it could be."

Chapter Twenty-Six

*Friday, April 20*

MICHAEL heard the truck roll up late morning and waited until both truck doors slammed, then opened his front door. Obie and James were standing in the yard, admiring their work.

"Good day, Michael! And how are you this fine day?" Obie called to him.

"I'm great." Michael came onto the porch. "So, how do *you* like it?"

"We have outdone ourselves this time, I think," James said. "And you are keeping it wet, I see. Now we need to finish the porch while the stairs are curing for a few days, then we can tear down the wood steps and you will be finished."

"Except for the flowers," Obie added.

"Right. I've asked Gene's gardener for some ideas. He's going to stop back tonight after his other jobs. Then I'll order some soil to fill the planters."

"We'll help with the filling," Obie said. "If Young James and John can be here, it will go quickly with four shovels. What are you thinking, perhaps five yards?"

"I have no idea. I was going to ask Greg when he comes by."

"Greg, the gardener's son, with the truck?" Obie said.

"Right."

"After work today? That would be good. Maybe we will stay a little later tonight, James, and meet this Greg again."

James ignored him and walked past to go through the house.

Obie smiled up at Michael. "That will be good, to meet Greg again. And what's the news with Gene?"

"Nothing so far. They might hear something later today."

"Come and look what I have here," Obie said, pulling a small, folded piece of paper from his back pocket as James came out of the garage.

"What is it?" Michael made his way down the wood steps.

Obie turned so they were both facing Gene's driveway as he unfolded his page.

"Goodness, Obie, what is it?"

"It's a fountain," Obie replied, slightly insulted.

"I know that, I mean, why, what is it...I mean...who is it for?"

"For Gene, of course. Don't you know that he loves the water? And he loves the look of the stone we have used at your house? And he will love the look of the stone when it's wet. And the sound of the water running, it will comfort him during his illness."

Michael didn't want to hurt Obie's feelings. But who in their right mind would begin such a project on the eve of receiving cancer news? Maybe this was one of those cultural things.

"Obie, it's really beautiful. But I'm not sure now is the right time to approach Gene about something like this. I mean—"

"Of course it's not a good time. It's a bad time. That's why he needs the sound of the water, to soothe him through his recovery. He needs to hear the sounds he loves from anywhere in his house. These are the things that will cure him. As well as your good doctors, of course."

"I...I don't know."

213

They heard a door close and looked up to see Gene coming across the lawn. Michael hoped that the piece of paper would magically slide back into Obie's hip pocket, but it didn't.

"Obie, what a job you and James have done here," Gene started before he had even closed the gap between them. "It came out so handsomely. I'm sorry I wasn't of more help to you."

"You had already done a lot of the work, choosing and organizing the stones. That's why it went so quickly. It went together well, don't you think?"

"Very nice. What's that you've got?" Gene was already peering at the page as Obie handed it to him.

"It's a fountain. A fountain for your front yard."

"For us?" Gene was surprised, but he couldn't pull his eyes away from the drawing. "It's impressive." He studied it and then talked to himself. "Simple lines, the size not too overwhelming, but the stonework gives it a solid feeling that would go well with the house. Where were you thinking it would go?"

Michael's jaw dropped.

"Right here." Obie walked over and indicated a circle on the lawn, a little offset from the front door and surrounded by flowers. "You could add a stone bench, if you wanted."

"But why not the back yard? Perhaps that would be the better place."

"Perhaps, but no one can see your backyard. And your living room looks out this way, doesn't it? And isn't that your bedroom up there, right above?"

"Yes, you're right. And except for the kitchen nook, most of our sitting areas do look out on the front yard." He glanced up and looked around his yard. "You've given me something to think about. May I show this to Sophie?"

"Of course. It's yours. Let us know what you would like to do."

Gene headed back to his house, raising his hand in a distracted wave to Michael as he studied the picture.

Obie turned to Michael and smiled his broad grin. "So, he liked it."

"I can't believe it. He was saying yesterday how much he loved the stone—"

"—this we could tell when he was helping us—"

"—and I knew he loved the water in San Diego—"

"—that he told us while we were working—"

"—and a fountain *would* look lovely nestled over there among his flowers—"

"—this we also realized—"

"—but I can't believe they'll start any kind of project now if he's going to be sick."

"Sometimes a project is a good thing to have when you're sick. It makes you anxious to get better to get it finished." Obie was looking at Michael pointedly.

"Are we going to do *any* work today before lunch?" James finally called over.

"Yes, I'm coming," Obie replied. "Gene liked your drawing, James. I think we will be making a fountain."


Hammering and pounding together through the afternoon, the new porch was finished.

Madigan arrived home after work. Sophie came out of her house at the same time.

"The doctor called. It's stomach cancer. The surgery will be Tuesday. Gene's inside calling the children, so I need to go back in. And Obie," she pulled the drawing of the fountain from her pocket, "I like it. We can start when Gene gets out of the hospital, if that's all right with you."

"Of course." Obie took the drawing back. Madigan put her hand out to take it. A sigh of wonder escaped her. "It's gorgeous," she whispered to no one in particular.

"We'll have good thoughts for you on Tuesday," Obie said to Sophie. "It will be all right, you'll see. I firmly believe this."

"Thank you." Tears started coming and she hurried back inside.

"That's too bad that it's cancer," Madigan said.

"But I think they've caught it early. At least I hope that's true." A landscaping truck rolled up. Madigan turned to see a man about her age hop out of the cab.

"Hey, Greg," Michael called. "Thanks for stopping."

"That's okay," Phil's ruggedly handsome son responded, digging into the front seat of his truck and pulling out a notebook. "I made some preliminary suggestions. I don't know if you're going to recognize these names or not. Maybe I need to find you a flower picture dictionary. My dad's is being used by a new client. Do you have one?"

"No."

"I bet we could find one at the library for you," Madigan spoke up.

Greg glanced at her for the first time and extended his hand. "Hi, I'm Greg."

"Madigan," Madigan put her hand into his calloused one. "I live two doors down."

"Oh, yes. You were the first one to do your driveway, right?"

"Right," Madigan laughed. "That seems like a long time ago."

"Madigan," Obie called from where he was gathering up his tools, "did you find someone with a truck to help you to the dump yet?"

Madigan glared at him. "No, I'm not quite finished cleaning out the garage, Obie, but thank you for asking. I know you said you'd help as soon as I finish." She gave him a forced smiled that dared him to say one more word.

"Oh, yes, as soon as you finish. If we're available, we'd be happy to help," Obie answered nonchalantly.

"Here are the rest of the ideas," Greg went on talking to Michael. "Do you want to look them over, then we could talk about them? It's fairly straightforward."

"Okay. Let me get the book of flowers, then I'll get back to you if I have questions. And we can decide about ordering the soil."

"All right, then, I'll be off. I've got one more stop tonight." He nodded to the group and returned to his truck. Obie felt disappointed. Greg pulled the door open and was about to swing up into his seat when he stepped back and looked right at Madigan.

"And say, you're welcome to borrow my truck anytime you need it. It's so old nothing can hurt it."

"Thank you, that's nice of you," Madigan mumbled, but by then Greg was up in his seat and the truck's engine had started. She was sure he hadn't heard her. She waited until he pulled off before marching to Obie.

"Now why did you do that? You put him on the spot. I don't even know him."

"But you will. I think that you'll know him. He's a nice man. He has a truck. You're a nice woman. You need a truck."

Madigan shook her head in frustration. "Obie, you know how much I care for you, but sometimes you are just weird." She looked to James for confirmation, but he only shrugged his shoulders.

"He sees a lot of stuff that we don't see. That's all I know," James said.

"I think the dog has worked out quite well," Obie called conscillitorially to Madigan's retreating back.

She refused to answer and stomped home to get Roger.

Chapter Twenty-Seven

*Saturday, April 21*

E arly the next morning, Madigan enjoyed the cool dampness as she took her long jog beneath an overcast sky. When she got home she brought Roger to the front yard to play, trying to imagine how she could turn the neglected space into something that might compare favorably to Michael's when he filled his planters.

Once the air's moisture turned into real rain, she brought Roger in, made a cup of coffee, and sat at the kitchen table with the paper spread out before her. A little voice nagged in the back of her brain as she tried to read...there was only one corner of boxes to go through in the garage. She was so close to being finished. Then she could finally make Obie help her get the pile to the dump, arrange for a charity to pick up what she wasn't keeping for herself or Lee, and then, at long last, park her car in the garage with enough room to walk without squeezing sideways.

Perhaps music would inspire her. She grabbed her boom box, found her favorite Beatles' CD, called to Roger, and headed for the garage.

There were only twelve boxes left, tidily stacked in a corner amid the piles of other boxes spread out everywhere. The first two turned out to be her father's accounting books, and the third box was filled with his framed diplomas. *These must all be from his office,* she realized, remembering exactly where the diplomas had hung on his wall. *How did they get here?* She looked through them carefully. She tried to remember the funeral, the hurried packing. But neither she nor Lee had cleaned out her father's office. Someone else must have brought these boxes to the house to be put on the moving van. Probably Herb, her father's best friend at work. *What shall I do with these?* she wondered, counting six certificates in the stack, all in identical black frames. She set the box aside and looked in the next one. The first was a tumble of paper clips, pencils, a calculator, note pads, a small planning calendar. There was a file with work-related IRS information. *Now I find it,* Madigan thought. It had taken her forever to gather the information to do her parents' taxes for the year they died, all the more frustrating because she knew this very file existed, she simply couldn't find it. *It was in his desk drawer, of course. Right where I keep mine.*

The fourth box held all her father's old day planners. He used the medium size, always a black canvas cover. She picked up the top one, feeling as if she were holding his life in her hands. She flipped through the pages to her birthday. The day was marked, as she expected. And her mother's, and her brother's, and their anniversary. Her father was far from perfect, but he always made a big deal about family occasions. A smile crossed her lips as she recalled receiving cards and flowers on her birthday from him, even when she had moved away from home. She half-heartedly shuffled through the rest of the box. At the bottom, beneath all day planners, was a bulky manila envelope. She pulled it out, opened it, and found two stacks of letters, bound with rubber bands. They were addressed in neat handwriting to her father at work. Pausing only a second, Madigan pulled the rubber bands from them and looked through the postmarks. There were two or three a year for the fifteen years before her father died. The postmark was San Francisco. Her hand shook a little as she turned over the top envelope and slid the letter out.

*June 21, 1996*
*Dear Father,*
*I hope this finds you well. Thank you for the birthday check. The year has gone well. My work continues to be interesting. I received a promotion in May. I look forward to seeing you in September. Thieu and Meg send their love.*
*Love,*
*Anh*

Madigan felt the room begin to spin, and she kneeled on the hard concrete, letting her head drop for a moment, trying to take it all in. *What were these letters? What did this mean?* When the stomach-sickening motion stopped, she gathered up the letters and went into the kitchen, where she pushed the morning paper aside and spread them out on the table. She started with the bottom one from the other pile, the letter with the earliest postmark. It was dated June, 1983, a few lines in feminine handwriting, a thank you for money sent. The next two envelopes were similar, one from December and then one from the following June. In the fourth envelope was a picture of a beautiful young woman, probably in her late teens or early twenties, of Vietnamese descent, but with Madigan's father's eyes and dimple. Madigan felt her mind whirl as she struggled to figure out the dates. She knew her father had served in Vietnam as an advisor for one year, before all the ground troops were sent in. Wasn't that 1966? Because her brother was born just after he returned, in 1967. Her brother was thirty-six. Was this woman the same age now? How could that be? Her father was married to her mother when he was in Vietnam, wasn't he? *Wasn't he?* Lee had been conceived when her mother met her father on furlough in Hawaii. So who is this girl?

Madigan fingered the photograph as she searched for an answer in the girl's face.

She read through the rest of the letters. Each year there was a picture in the December thank you note. Madigan laid the pictures out on the table as she came to them. In one there was a young man with her. *Anh and Thieu* the note on the back said. Three pictures later there was a baby with the young couple. *Meg!* the photo declared on the back.

*There is a whole life here I know nothing about,* Madigan thought with despair. In the later letters, a September visit was mentioned, and yet her father had barely ever traveled. *The day planners!* She went back to the garage and found the most recent ones. She looked up September. And there it was, "SF conference" noted across a four-day weekend. She looked in the planners for the three years before that one…it was the same. But hadn't her mother gone on those trips? Madigan tried to remember…she was sure her mother would have gone, too. Did her mother know about this girl?

Madigan carried the top day planner back to the kitchen table and sat down. She reached for the phone and called her brother.

Her sister-in-law answered the phone.

"Is Lee there?" It was hard to hide the tremor in her voice.

"Yes, I'll get him. Is everything all right?"

"Well, I don't know. I found some stuff in Dad's papers that I don't understand."

"Here he comes…."

"Hey, Maddy, what's up?"

The familiar deep tones of her brother's voice brought tears to Madigan's eyes, and she struggled to keep control. "I was going through the boxes. I got to a stack of Dad's from work."

"Must be real excitement there. You know those CPA's—" it was a running joke between them, but she cut him off.

221

"Lee, I think Dad fathered a child while he was in Vietnam. She's your age. There are letters in this box from her to Dad for about the last fifteen years before he died. She lives in San Francisco with her husband and a little girl."

"Naw, that couldn't be. There's a mistake."

"I'm holding the letters in my hand, and she writes to him "Dear Father." But you were born in '67, and Dad was in Vietnam in 1966, right? I can't figure it out."

"Are you sure it's Dad's child? Not someone he's helping out? That would be so like him, to adopt someone."

"She has his eyes and dimple."

"Oh, man."

"Do you think Mom knew?"

"I don't think so."

"He saw her every year on that trip to San Francisco. But I'm sure Mom went on some of those."

"At first she did. I don't think she went as much later on."

"Tell me the truth, Lee, did you know?"

"Honest, Maddy, never."

"I've got to find out about her. Does she even know he's dead? She must, because the letters stop...and she's never tried to contact us. At least not me."

"Not me, either. Someone at the office must have returned the letters or notified her or something."

"Herb. That's what he would do. I'm calling him right now."

"Wait, Maddy," Lee tried to calm her, "think for a minute. Are you sure you want to find out? Like this? Can you wait till we come this summer?"

"No, I've got to know what happened. Lee, we have a sister. We have a niece. More importantly, there's a whole part of our father we know nothing about."

"Okay, call me back if you find out anything."

Madigan hung up. Her early shock was giving way to a rising anger. She found her address book and looked up the number of her parents' best friends.

"Aunt Marge, it's Madigan Gardner from Seattle."

"Maddy! How lovely to hear from you. How are you?"

"Is Uncle Herb there? I need to speak to him about something."

In a minute Madigan heard the distinctive voice of the man who had been as close to their family as any blood relative. He and his wife had single-handedly gotten Lee and her through the death of her parents. Taking on every detail and helping them through each decision. *And he was executor of the will* popped into her head.

"Uncle Herb."

"Maddy! So good to hear from you. What's going on up there?"

"Uncle Herb, I'm going through Mom and Dad's things. All those boxes that have been in my garage for five years? Dad's things from the office are here. I found the letters. Anh's letters. All of them."

There was silence on the other end of the phone.

"Did Dad have another daughter? With a woman in Vietnam? You must know."

Herb's voice was compassionate. "Madigan, I'm so sorry. He never would have wanted you to find out this way. I told him not to keep her letters. I should have known he would. I never had a chance to check his office before it was packed up; the assistants threw everything into boxes, we were in such a rush. I meant to go through them later, but they must have ended up at the house and on the moving van to you. I'm so sorry."

"Tell me what happened. *Exactly* what happened."

"Your parents had been dating the whole year before he left for Vietnam. They planned to be married when he got back."

"No, they were married before he left."

"No, actually, they weren't."

"But Mom met him in Hawaii half-way through his tour. She always told me how romantic it was, and that's where they conceived Lee."

"That's right, she went to Hawaii to meet him. It's all true, except they weren't married yet. They got married right away when he got back from Vietnam because she was already pregnant. Then they moved the marriage date back a year for you kids. It's so hard to explain. It wasn't such a big deal then, in the 60's, but as you kids grew up it was important to your mother that you think they were already married."

"Okay. They weren't married and she got pregnant. But what about this girl?"

There was a long pause on Herb's end of the conversation.

"Tell me. Please."

"As your father explained it to me, everything in Vietnam was so different than anything he had encountered before. It was culture shock, it was psychological shock, it was everything. He met a young woman who was helping in his office. She was young, he was young and lonely. It wasn't anything serious and it didn't last long. It just happened. Then she was transferred. He didn't know what happened to her. Your mother came to meet him on his furlough. Although they weren't officially engaged before he left for Vietnam, the visit solidified their relationship and he proposed. When they discovered Lee had been conceived, they got married as soon as he got back. They started their life together. Then in 1972, when the little girl was five, the mother wrote to your father. She found him through his work, somehow. That's the first he knew he had another daughter. It was a terrible shock. But things were hard for Anh at that time, being biracial. The mother had relatives in San Francisco. She needed money to send the girl there. That's all she asked of your father."

"Did Dad see her then?"

"No. He sent money to help support her. The mother stayed in Vietnam, married, and had other children. He didn't hear any more from her. He sent money twice a year to the relatives in San Francisco. But when Anh turned 17, she wanted to meet him. So he went."

"And Mother, did she know?"

"No. She never knew. He was afraid she might not forgive him, and, knowing your mother, she might not have."

"But Mom never suspected? The money?"

"He handled most of the finances. He kept a separate account for Anh."

"But what happened when they died?"

"His secretary gave me all his mail to deal with; when her last letter came, I returned it with a note telling about the accident. I said if she had any questions to call me."

"But what about the will? Did he include her?"

"He tried to do the right thing."

"But how could he have kept this from Mother?"

"By the time he found out there was a child, you were all established as a family. And he wasn't needed as a father, Anh came into a big extended family with an aunt and an uncle who raised her as their own. But he felt responsible to support her, and he did. That's all."

"But when she contacted him?"

"I think then he was ready to say, 'Who is this girl? What has she become?' And she wanted to know about her father."

"So he loved her like a daughter." Madigan said it without malice, but it tore her heart.

"Madigan, this is terrible to do over the phone. Come and visit us. We can talk about it."

"Aunt Marge knew?"

"She did. It was the only secret she ever kept from your mother."

225

Madigan's brain had been churning on something, and suddenly the answer popped forward in a burst of clarity.

"He left her a full share in the will, didn't he? Or, at least a full third of his half, I suppose, is that how it worked?"

"Madigan, I—"

"I could never quite put my finger on it, but the numbers you sent didn't seem to work out."

"Oh, Maddy—"

Madigan felt the tears starting to well in her eyes. "You know, this is terrible, but I thought maybe you took a big fee or something, as executor, but I didn't really know why you would do that. It didn't make sense but I didn't really want to know. I couldn't ask why the numbers didn't add up."

"I knew Lee would never notice, but you—I knew if you sat down and did the math you'd realize something was wrong."

"Were those even the real papers you sent?"

"They are, but I omitted a few. Listen to me: Your father never expected it to happen this way, of course. Early on he expressed his worry to me that if something happened to him, how could he leave something for Anh. We phrased it so his will clearly called for equal division among his children without naming them, and he knew I'd take care of it if he died first. I think he always wanted to tell you and Lee, he just didn't know how. And then, like that, they were gone. It was so shocking to lose them that way."

"Does she know about us?"

"Yes."

"Have you met her?"

"Only once. She was about twenty-four. I was at the conference with your father, and we had lunch."

Madigan found she couldn't speak.

226

"Are you okay, Maddy? You don't have to do anything about this. She doesn't want anything from you. That was the point of settling the will fairly, so she'd have no reason to contact you."

"I have a sister!" Maddy blurted through her tears. "Why would he assume that I didn't want to know about my sister?" Her sobs filled the space between them.

"I'm so sorry. Things were different then. It was not something to be proud of, the fact that you'd left a woman pregnant in Vietnam. It wasn't talked about. He did way more than most men. He took responsibility. He did everything he knew how to do. And it was enough for her. She had a family. She only wanted to know him a little."

It was after lunch before Madigan ventured outside again to walk Roger, having decided to skip the dog park. After talking to Herb she had stood in the shower for half an hour, the grief and tears that had been so tightly controlled at her parent's funeral pouring down the drain. Their sudden deaths in the car accident had forced her into a state of automation as she dealt with all the details and arrangements. She had walled off the part of herself that first received Lee's devastating phone call and hurt so badly. Even now, five years later, she couldn't think about that day.

Calling Lee back had not made her feel any better. He was much more sympathetic to her father's plight than she.

When she returned from walking Roger, Michael was out front spraying his new concrete and looking at his list from Greg.

"Hey," Madigan tried to put on a smile.

"Hi. Do you know anything about flowers?" He directed the hose spray away from her. "I'm trying to figure this out."

"Not much. Why don't you go to the library and get some books out?"

"Believe it or not, I don't have a card."

227

Madigan was incredulous. "You don't have a library card? I didn't think there was a kid left in America who didn't get a card by the time they could print their name."

"I didn't mean I've never had a card. I don't have a card for this library."

"Oh, well, that's different. I was beginning to think you were an alien or something. I have a card. I'll take you if you want to go."

"That would be great. I'd like to keep on this while there's enthusiasm. Obie said they'd help shovel the dirt into the planters. That's going to be a big job, so I want to get that done while they're still around."

"They still have to do my sidewalk and the Haffner's, you know."

"Oh, right. I keep forgetting about that. Your walks have been torn up for so long, they don't look weird anymore."

"That's certainly what worries me! Especially now that the fountain is in the queue."

"It will all get done, I'm sure. I'll actually be sorry when they're completely finished. They're awfully pleasant to be with all day."

"Spoken by someone whose job is almost finished," Madigan said dryly. "I'll go get my car keys. Wait, will you fit in my car?"

"Yeah, if you put the seat all the way back. I can bend this knee a little more lately."

Madigan drove to the library and helped Michael check out the flower books. He didn't ask why she had two books about Vietnam in the pile, and she didn't explain.

Chapter Twenty-Eight

*Sunday, April 22*

S OPHIE rolled over in bed to face Gene, still asleep on his side. He had been restless during the night, as she realized now he had been for the past few weeks.

It was supposed to be a nice day, with the sun breaking through the morning clouds by afternoon. Their last day of any kind of normalcy for who knew how long? The children would be over later for dinner, all except Emma, who wasn't coming up from Portland until after work tomorrow.

Sophie observed her husband's breathing, the gentle rise and fall of his chest. What would this be like, this path into the unknown? They had been lucky for so long; many of their friends had suffered serious illnesses; some had lost their spouses to heart attacks and cancer. At least Gene had never smoked. The doctors said his overall health was good, and that would help his recovery.

But how bad it would be they couldn't tell her until after the surgery.

She studied his skin in the growing light of the room. He had always been fair, but now there was a grayness to him.

She couldn't imagine life without him.

*Please, God, let it be curable. Let him survive the surgery. Then we'll take it day by day. Just let him make it through these next days.*

The thought of Gene down in bed for even a short time worried her. He was a goer, a doer, a well-paced worker who got the most out of every day. They had created a comfortable space for themselves, a comfortable life, a comfortable routine. Now what? *Let him be able to do the things he loves. Perhaps that above all.*

Gene stirred and opened his eyes. He smiled at her, rolled over on his back and slid his arm beneath her head. She put her head on his chest as she had nearly every morning for forty-five years.

"Hi," he said softly.

"Hi."

"Why are you awake so early?"

"I don't know. The light coming in, I guess. It's supposed to be nice today."

"That's good. I want to work in the back garden a little. Who knows when I'll be able to get out there again."

They were quiet with each other. Sophie felt tears begin to well in her eyes, and one fell onto Gene's cotton pajama top before she could catch it. He hugged her hard at the feel of it.

"It's going to be all right, Soph. It's gonna be all right."

"I know. I know."

"I don't want you to be scared for me. I'm not afraid. It's gonna be what it's gonna be, that's all, and they'll get it out, and I'll do whatever I have to do to get better."

The tears were welling faster now; Sophie squeezed her eyes shut tightly to hold them back. "I know," she whispered.

They lay together for another few minutes, the rise and fall of his chest and his heartbeat in her ear a comfort to her. *Remember this moment,* she told herself. She held perfectly still and tried to imprint every sensation of it in her brain. Then she felt a kind of peace go through her body, and she soaked it up and imagined it gently

230

covering Gene, as if some protective blessing had been sent. *It will be all right,* she could hear Obie's voice in her head. *You have good doctors here. It will be all right.*

Obie went out to the back yard of his brother's house and sat down in his favorite chair. The rhododendron and azaleas were all in bloom. The colors of the late season tulips were vivid in the afternoon sun, which had finally broken through. He closed his eyes and rested. A week of ups and downs, he reflected. Michael's new stairs and planters had come out so well, and Michael himself had been outside most of every day they had been there. Several times Michael had stood without his crutches and put a little weight on the bad leg, something Obie had never seen him do before. And Madigan had met the gardener's son Greg. Yes, that was going to work, he was sure of it. Madigan would forgive his boldness. You cannot be too angry at a man who still needs to finish work for you.

That left Gene. Obie had known it was cancer the day that Gene could not eat his sandwich, the way he was uncomfortable when he sat a certain way. How odd was this, to run into the same cancer again? Perhaps not so odd here in America, where there was so much more of everything. Perhaps not strange at all. But at home, it had been unusual, this cancer in the stomach. It had taken too long to figure it out. Marie had thought it was so many other things, womanly things. *Ah, well, that is over,* he sighed to himself. *It will be all right for this man Gene, with his wife and children, and his big hands that like to work with stones. We will build him a fountain, and the music of its water will bring rhythm to his healing.*

Lilly stood at the back door and observed Obie in his favorite spot. James came up behind her.

231

"You have worked him too hard this week, James. He is worn out," Lilly scolded her husband.

"Me? He is the one who set the pace. He would not wait for the boys. He would not mix by hand, he ordered the truck, so that we had to work at its speed. He insisted we finish quickly. I do not know what this urgency is in him all of a sudden. And then the fountain! Who would have thought of such a thing?"

"It's a beautiful drawing that you made," her voice softened now. "I'd like to have one like that myself one day."

"Well, there is much to finish on that street before we start the fountain. We're lucky that Madigan had so many neighbors with old concrete. They all like the look of the new. I'm betting that Michael will want his driveway done once we get the temporary steps taken down and the front yard all cleaned up. He will want everything to match the newness of the entrance."

"Hmm," Lilly smiled at her husband's good fortune. Steady work was not always so easy to find. Quite often they did two driveways on a block, but a whole street like this? Never before.

"When is the man's surgery?"

"On Tuesday, they said. But I think he checks into the hospital tomorrow."

"We'll put him in the prayers tonight at church. Him and his family."

James put his arms around Lilly and kissed the back of her head. "We must hope that it turns out better than Marie."


Nearly four o'clock and Madigan placed the phone back in its cradle, disappointed she had not reached Marilyn to talk. After twenty-four hours of struggling to come to terms with her knowledge of a sister, she was ready to see what counsel her good friend might have.

232

Frustrated and antsy, she decided to take Roger for a walk. They went the long route around the neighborhood, and came back past Gene and Sophie's. Michael was next door in front of his house, the flower books spread out before him.

"Hey," Madigan said. "How's it going?"

"Good. These books are a great help."

"Let me see," Madigan peered at the drawing Greg had made, then compared it to the pictures of flowers in the open books. "Oh, I like this one." She pointed to a purple English wallflower. "I'd like some of these."

"You can order when I order mine. Greg's going to buy them for me, he can get a good price."

"Let me think about it." She pulled Roger back from where he has started to dig in the grass. "I want to fix up my front yard, it looks so shaggy and overgrown. It will look even worse by comparison when your planters are finished."

Roger attacked Michael's shoelace. He shook his foot free, then bent to scratch the growing pup's ears.

"So what have you two been up to today?"

"Not much."

"Me, neither. I went to the store. Got a load of groceries. Even got them all inside by myself. Took four trips. I think going up and down the steps has made me stronger. This week is the best I've felt since the accident."

"That's great. There's nothing like a strong dose of 'Obie' to cure what ails you."

"Right. Oh, here come Greg and his dad. I wonder what they're doing here today?"

Phil parked in front of Gene's house, waving to Michael as he headed up to Gene's front door. Greg came over to Michael and Madigan. Roger made a lunge but Madigan made him sit.

"Hello, again," Greg said to Madigan as he glanced at the open flower books. "Hi, Michael. So what do you think?"

"I like your ideas, the way each level has its own special colors and height. But it's going to cost a fortune for all these plants, isn't it?"

"Not really. And you don't have to get them all at once. You can start with a few, then fill in as you go through the seasons of the first year. With a mix of annuals to add the color and perennials to tide you over between seasons, I think it should look good."

"I love this purple wallflower," Madigan pointed to the book. "I'd like to put some in my yard."

Greg glanced down the street to Madigan's front yard, strewn with remnants of Obie and James' work, patches of bad grass, and the holes Roger had started to dig.

Madigan followed his gaze. "I mean, I'd have to make some flower beds first, of course."

"Have you been thinking about working on your yard?"

Madigan could feel a blush start up her cheeks. "Seeing everyone else's has made me want to spruce mine up a little."

"It's a good yard," Greg said, still looking at it with a critical eye. "Wonderful tree. That's really the focal point of the whole place. Let's see." Before Madigan could say anything else, Greg wandered toward the front of her house. She shrugged at Michael and then followed, with Roger tugging on the leash. Michael returned to matching the names on Greg's drawing with the pictures in the books.

"What you want to decide first," Greg said to Madigan from behind the torn up sidewalk, "is what you want people to look at after they look at the tree. You could put a lot of color up by your steps, and that would draw their eyes up there and seem welcoming. Or you could do an interesting border down here along the sidewalk. That would both make the yard seem bigger, and sort of set a boundary between your lawn and the street."

"I'm not sure how long a row of flowers along the sidewalk would last with Roger around. I let him loose in the yard quite a bit. The kids next door play ball with him, and he runs everywhere. Never met a plant yet he won't either piddle on or try to eat."

"Well, then I think your best bet would be some beds up by the house and stairs. That would be easy to do. Looks like it gets a little sun, but mostly shade from the tree. You'd have to have the right mix, some low shrubs, some grasses and then flowers, but it could look really attractive."

"Thanks for the advice. I'll think about it."

"Sure." Greg suddenly realized he had gone off and left Michael. "Well, I need to talk to Michael a little. I'll see you later."

"See you. Come on, Roger. Let's go get you some dinner." As she went in the door, Madigan glanced back at Greg, now hunched over the books with Michael. *Maybe I could ask to borrow his truck if I need it. But only if Obie is too busy to help.*

Gene opened his front door to Phil's knock.

"I wanted to drop by and say good luck on Tuesday," Phil said.

"Thanks. Can you come in and say hello to Sophie? The kids are coming over and bringing dinner."

Phil glanced back at the street. Greg had strolled toward the neighbor woman's house. "Sure, I'll come in for a minute."

Phil was the first of a swelling group of well-wishers who stopped in that evening. By the time Gene and Sophie's youngest child Jim arrived, there was not a place to park anywhere on the street. Michael was coming out of the noisy house as Jim arrived after parking at the end of the block around the corner.

Michael knew this must be the youngest son, as he had seen him occasionally. Jim had never been at his parents' house as much as the other two siblings who lived in town. Michael nodded but didn't stop to introduce himself as he navigated on his crutches. Jim held the screen door open automatically, but then gave Michael a second look.

"Do I know you? I'm Jim, their youngest."

Michael turned back. "I'm Michael Stevens. I live next door."

"Oh, of course. I guess that's where I've seen you. How long have you lived there?"

"Two years, with my soon-to-be ex-wife, Veronica."

Jim was thoughtful. "No, I don't think that's it. Michael Stevens. That name is so familiar." His eyes fell on the crutches and the leg brace. "Accident?"

"Construction. I fell off a building in November."

"Of course, that's it! The building at 5th and Sitka. I covered that story. I work for Channel 2 News. Man, that was quite a fall. We didn't think you were going to make it, you know. I had no idea you were Mom and Dad's neighbor, or I would have let them know. They would have sent flowers and a card or something."

Michael laughed. "That's okay. I probably couldn't have appreciated them. It was about two weeks before I even knew who I was."

"Ever thought you'd owe your life to a convertible? You were lucky that car was there."

"I know."

"Well, hey, you're looking good. Really. There was a ton of human interest in that story. Calls kept coming in about it. I think you surprised everyone by pulling through."

"I guess so. Some firefighters who were here a few weeks ago said the same thing. I didn't realize the accident was so well-known among the first responders. If only there were some fortune to go along with the fame."

"Did they ever figure out what happened?"

"A couple of things, but basically a bad tie-off and a missing toe board. I should have caught within three feet when I slid under the scaffolding bar, but I kept on going."

"Huh. We got there really quick because the news station is around the corner. I literally grabbed the camera and came running. I got there before the medics, but they were right behind me." Jim seemed to be thinking, then nodded towards the house. "I gotta get in there. I'm already late."

"I'm real sorry about your dad. Everyone will be thinking about him on Tuesday."

"Thanks. It's tough. He's never been sick. There's a whole range that it could be, Mom says. So we'll wait and see what they find."

"Jim!" Sophie called to her son as he entered the living room. She came up beside him and he bent his cheek for a kiss. "Finally."

"Sorry, Mom, got stuck at work."

"Come into the kitchen. I want to ask you something."

"Sure." Jim followed his mother through the dining room and into the comfortably remodeled kitchen at the back of the house. Friends of his parents called his name as he worked his way through the throng, but he could tell his mother was on a mission and he didn't stop to talk.

"What's up?" he asked as the swinging door closed behind him, allowing them relative quiet.

"I want to ask you a favor. I want you to move back home for a few weeks, until your father is up and around again."

"Well..." Jim was surprised. "I guess. Sure. But why?"

"First, I want to know where I can find you. I don't know what's going to happen this week, and I don't know what kind of help I'm going to need here at the house. Unfortunately for you, your schedule is the most flexible, so I'm going to have to depend on you. Bea can take some days off, but I know it's hard on her class when she has a sub. Emma can only stay up for a few days at a time, and Fred—"

237

"Fred has to run the business. I know, I get it. Sure, I'll be glad to move back for a few weeks. My roommate has a new girlfriend and she's driving me crazy. It'll be nice to get away for a little while."

"Good," Sophie smiled at her youngest. "That's settled. Now what are you doing tomorrow? You're working?"

"Well, yeah, why wouldn't I? The surgery's not till Tuesday, right?"

"Right. But you've asked for Tuesday off, haven't you? I want you at the hospital. Early. So bring your things on over here, and you can drive me over Tuesday morning."

"How early?"

"I want to be there by six."

"Six?"

"Jim—"

"No, that's fine. Six. Okay, I'll get it squared away at work tomorrow. Don't worry. And I'll bring my stuff over tomorrow night.

"No, I want you at the hospital with us tomorrow night. The minister is stopping by at eight, and I want you all to be there."

"Mom, it's going to be okay—" but Jim looked at his mother and stopped. He had never seen quite this look of determination on her face before. He thought of his parents' friends who had been through this, and he thought of how often while growing up he had watched his mother head to the hospital to sit with a friend, or take a dinner to someone recovering at home. There was a rhythm to this process, he realized suddenly, a well-orchestrated pattern that began each time someone sat in a doctor's office and heard the word *cancer*. There was the medical response of tests and surgery and chemo. And there was the human response of sitting, and waiting, and hoping, and holding. He looked at his mother with new appreciation of what lay ahead. No, he was not going to be the one to disrupt the predetermined role that his mother had set in her mind for each of them to play.

238

"I'll tell you what. I'll go say hi to everyone, then I'll go home and get enough stuff to last a few days. Then I'll come back here and sleep tonight. Is that what you want me to do?"

Sophie smiled at her last one, her easiest to raise. He had a quick way of figuring out what was going on, and usually went with the flow.

"Yes, that's what I wanted. Now go say hi to your father."

Jim went back out the swinging door. Sophie reached up and took a clean glass from the cupboard, then filled it with ice and water. She held the glass to her cheek for a moment, the shock of the cold pulling her attention from the tears that were beginning to well up.

"Mom?" Bea, the oldest daughter, stuck her head in the kitchen. "Are you okay?" She came in when she saw her mother standing at the sink.

"I'm fine." Sophie wiped her eyes with the back of her hand.

Bea touched her mother gently on the shoulder. "It's going to be all right," Bea tried to sound reassuring. "It really is."

"I know." Sophie set her glass down on the counter and fished in her pocket for a tissue. "I've been through this so many times with other people. It shouldn't seem so astonishing that it's finally our turn. But your father...I always thought I'd be the one to get sick. You know, breast cancer or something. We've been lucky. We've been lucky for a long time. So," she wiped her eyes again with the tissue and turned to give Bea a bit of a smile, "we're just going to have to be lucky this time, too."

Bea's heart tugged as her mother spoke. She couldn't quite put her finger on what was wrong. Her mother was usually strong, up-beat, and in control. She had taken the cancer news well and had gone into preparedness mode almost immediately. But there was something beneath the surface. *She's really frightened*, Bea realized. *I've never known her to be less than completely confident about an outcome. But she isn't sure this time.*

239

The door opened and Bea's daughter came in looking for a drink.

"Here, darling, I'll get you something." Sophie found a plastic glass for the six-year old.

"Uncle Jim's here," the child announced to her mother.

"I know, I saw him for a minute out there."

"I've asked him to move back in for a few weeks," Sophie said.

"But why?" Bea was caught off guard.

"I might need help with your father at first. I don't know what to expect. And I want to be able to find Jim if I need him. He's been a stranger around here lately."

"Oh, Mom, he's a normal—"

"He's not a teenager anymore. He's thirty-four years old. He should be settled down and not living with a roommate in some flea-bitten apartment like he was still twenty-one."

Bea had no reply. It stunned her each time she realized that her baby brother was, in fact, aging at the same pace she was. She didn't know why he hadn't settled down. Two long-term romances had faded when he refused to commit, despite the heart-felt phone calls to her from his ex-girlfriends, begging for intervention. He was addicted to the news, and lived his life on the end of his camera.

Bea glanced at the kitchen wall clock. "We'd better be getting the kids home, Mom. School tomorrow for everyone."

"All right, dear."

"You're okay getting to the hospital and all that?"

"It won't be a problem, we don't have to check in till ten o'clock. He's got a few procedures during the day. Now you know I want you all there tomorrow night. The minister is coming at 8."

"I know, I know. And Emma will be up by then, won't she?"

"Yes, she should be here by four. She was going to get the children all squared away, work the morning and then leave after lunch."

"All right, then, we'll see you tomorrow night." Bea kissed her mother and hugged her. "Try not to worry."

240

Sophie followed her daughter and granddaughter out of the kitchen. Bea's exit seemed to be the signal, and their other friends began saying goodbye. Gene stood tall by the door, shaking hands with everyone as they left. Sophie looked at him, unable to believe that tomorrow at this time he'd be in a hospital bed. *Please, God, let it be all right. Whatever it is, let us get through it all right.*

Their oldest son Fred, his wife, and three daughters were the last to go. Fred came over and kissed his mother goodbye. "We'll see you tomorrow night, Mom. Eight, did you say?"

"Yes."

"Okay," he shook his dad's hand. "Well, we're off then."

Gene stood inside the screen door and watched them get into their car. Sophie came up beside him and he slid his arm around her. Petite by comparison, she had always fit neatly against him.

"That was nice, Sophie. Nicest funeral I hope to never be at."

"Gene! Don't say things like that! Honestly—"

"You know what I mean. We have a lot of nice friends. We're lucky. That's all."

But she had pulled away from him and was gathering up the coffee cups, fighting back tears again.

Chapter 29

*Monday, April 29*

"THIS will give us something to do until we can start the fountain," Obie said cheerfully late on Monday morning as he and James broke up the old concrete of Michael's driveway. "How lucky that Michael wanted his driveway done. I thought he would."

"I'll enjoy working at our own pace again. I didn't like working off the truck so much."

After lunching and resting, they labored another hour. About three o'clock, Young James and John arrived with the other truck, picking up the concrete pieces to take to the dump.

While James helped, Obie went over and sat under Madigan's tree to rest. The heavy work in the heat had made him feel dizzy, but he had refused to stop until his nephews arrived. Within a few minutes, Madigan pulled up. Saying only a quick hello, she hurried into the house, visibly upset. Obie waited patiently, and in another twenty minutes she came out with Roger on the leash.

"Good day, Madigan." His voice was soft and kind.

"Hey, Obie." Her usual smile was missing.

"What is wrong, Madigan? You are unhappy; I can see."

With tears close to the surface all day, Madigan had been determined not to begin a conversation. She had spent Sunday poring over the books about Vietnam and still she could make no sense of the situation.

"I have to walk Roger," she said, hiding her eyes from Obie.

"Sit, Madigan," he patted the seat beside himself. "Sit and talk. Whatever it is, let it out a little. You'll feel better."

The gentleness in his voice made the tears slide down her cheeks. Giving up, she sank down beside Obie, digging in her pocket for a nonexistent tissue. Obie offered a clean handkerchief.

"Thanks," she wiped her eyes and nose. "I'm sorry. I'm a mess today. I had to come home early from work. I couldn't concentrate on anything, and I was biting everyone's head off."

"Interesting expression, that one. So what has happened since last week to make you so unhappy?"

Madigan could not believe she was going to launch into this with Obie, but he waited so understandingly, she couldn't stop herself.

"I was cleaning out the final boxes in the garage. I found the things from my father's office. In one box…." It took a moment to compose herself so she could go on. "In one box there were some letters. It turns out he fathered a child in Vietnam. He and my mother weren't married yet. He didn't know the child existed until she was five, and her mother wanted to send her to relatives in America, so she searched out my father for help. By then he was married, and my brother and I were both born. At first, he sent money to the relatives who were keeping the girl, but then, when she was seventeen, they met, and then they met once a year until he died. She's married and has a child. Her name is Anh. She lives in San Francisco." She fought more welling tears.

"Hmm," Obie said. "That is quite a secret to discover in a box in the garage."

"I couldn't believe it." Madigan pulled a strand of hair away from her face. "I called my brother, and he knew nothing about it. My father's best friend is the only one who knew. Not even my mother…." She began to sob.

"Oh, Madigan, I am so sorry." Obie lifted his arm around her shoulders, and she leaned against him, his soft bulk a warm comfort. After a minute, she pulled away and straightened up, trying to find a dry spot on the soft cotton hankie.

"I can't believe I've had a sister all these years that I knew nothing about. I am so *angry* at him!"

"Which part makes you so angry?"

"All of it! He cheated on my mother. He had this great deception for so long."

"But, they weren't married when he left, correct? Perhaps not even promised to each other? Do you know for sure what their arrangement was?"

"No, because they told us they were married before he left. And that wasn't true, either."

"So perhaps it seems worse to you, because you think there was a commitment that was not really there yet."

"I don't know. But how did it happen?"

"He was lonely, perhaps." Obie shrugged. "And it is easy to have an accident. Things happen. Can you not forgive him an accident that he did not intend?"

"I don't know."

"What do you think is the part that you cannot forgive, that he kept it a secret from you or from your mother?"

"My mother," Madigan's tears started again, "she was such a wonderful person. I cannot believe that he never told her in all those years. That he held such a secret from her."

"Good. Now how do you know that he never told your mother?"

"Well," Madigan sighed and tried to think, "his best friend said that he and his wife were the only ones who knew."

"Ahh. So you feel your mother was left out of the secret. But how would this friend know what your parents spoke of to each other? What if your father did not want him to know, because he did not want it talked about among the four of them?"

"But Mom never gave any hint that she knew."

"And why would she, if she did not want you to know?"

Madigan shook her head. "I'm not sure."

Obie took her hand in his calloused one. "Was your mother the kind of person who could know about and forgive him this thing, but never say anything about it?"

"I don't know." Madigan felt as if her heart were ripping.

"Who would have an answer for you, do you think? Who would know this?"

Madigan thought for several minutes. "I guess Anh might. Whether they ever met. If my mother knew, she would have wanted to meet her, at least once."

"We cannot always understand why other people do the things they do, Madigan." Obie patted her hand. "But if you know the kind of people your parents were, and if you loved and trusted them, then you must believe that they did the best they could."

"I guess." Madigan gave a heavy sigh, not quite convinced.

"Do you want to meet this Anh, this sister that you have?"

"I don't know. I'm afraid what other secrets there might be."

"I wonder if she is just as afraid of you."

"I suppose." She leaned back against the tree again and closed her eyes. Could she meet this woman? Should she? What must it have been like for her, to suddenly lose a father she never really knew except for letters and a once a year visit?

"She is a part of your father, and deep inside you know that. And you will want to see her one day," Obie spoke quietly. "It doesn't have to be tomorrow. You will know when the time is right. Let it be for a little while."

"But how do you do that, Obie? How do you let things be when they're eating up your insides?"

"I think of sitting on a beach." Obie closed his eyes. "The sun is warm, the waves are hitting, and then rolling up the sand. I watch the water, I feel it on my feet, but I cannot change it. The water is life, Madigan. Sometimes it is still, almost like glass. Some days it crashes so hard you cannot even be on the beach. And you have choices: You can watch, you can swim, you can stay in your house and look at it from afar. But you cannot change it. The waves will come."

"I can't think of it that way. It seems sort of hopeless."

"Oh, no, the opposite! Full of promise, never-ending, always changing, refreshing, renewing. Do you have faith of some sort, Madigan?"

"We were Presbyterian. I haven't been to church since my parents died."

"Well, that is your answer to how you let those hard things be. The things you cannot change, you give to God. And you wait. There will be an answer. Not always the one you want, but there will be an answer. And a new path will open, sometimes a path so small you can barely find it, but the way is there to go on."

Madigan sighed again. Obie could make things sound so easy. It wasn't that easy. It just wasn't.

She stood and called Roger. Her hand fell on Obie's shoulder, the strap of his overalls warm from sun.

"I'll try," she said simply.

"I don't think this new sister is a secret that can hurt you, Madigan. Don't be afraid of her. Something good might come. Wait and see."

"All right. I guess I'll walk Roger. How long will you be here?"

"Not much longer. The boys are nearly finished. We'll be back tomorrow to frame the driveway, and then we'll pour on Wednesday."

"Okay, I'll see you tomorrow if you're here late. Thanks for your wisdom."

"Not wisdom, Madigan. Only a long life learning what are truly the worrying things."

"I'm not sure that's a lesson I'll ever learn."


Obie got up slowly, his knees letting him know it had been a long day. He packed up the tools with James. Sophie had arrived home a few minutes earlier and reassured them that Gene was resting comfortably after completing his pre-surgery tests. A small car pulled up in front of the house and parked, and Sophie greeted her daughter Emma.

"Mom." Emma was out of the car and in her mother's embrace, a little shocked at the dark circles under Sophie's eyes. "How is he? Can we go right to the hospital?"

"He's fine—resting comfortably. He's worried, of course. We all are."

Emma started to pull her suitcase out from the trunk when her mother stopped her.

"Actually, dear, you're not going to be staying here. Madigan, a nice young woman three doors down, has offered her extra bedroom to us, and I'm going to take her up on it. She left a key with me."

"But why can't I stay here?"

"Patty and Virginia are on their way from San Diego. We called them Saturday with the news, and they called back last night and said they'll be in late tonight. I'd already asked Jim to move back in for a few weeks in case I need him, and the other bedroom is so full of stuff I could never get it cleaned out in time for you. You understand, don't you, dear? All you have to do is sleep at Madigan's. And she has room for Max and the kids, too, if they have to come."

"What do you mean, if they have to come?" Emma had a sudden sick feeling in her stomach like she used to get in school when there was a surprise math quiz and she was caught unprepared. "How bad is it, Mom?"

Sophie looked at the top button of her daughter's shirt instead of into her eyes. "It could be pretty bad, Emma. They won't know until they've done the surgery and they can see how far the cancer has spread. It's possible it hasn't spread, but it's not likely. We're a little too far down the path for that."

"Why didn't you tell me? I would have come up right away on Saturday."

"There wasn't really anything to tell, Emma. We don't know for sure. That's the way cancer is. You don't know. You prepare for the worst, you hope for the best, and you pray like crazy every waking hour. And that's all you can do."

Emma stared at her mother. What else had she missed in the conversations she'd had with family since Friday? Was there some secret code being used here that she had misunderstood? She took a deep breath and tried to fight the nausea of fear that was coming in waves now.

"Are you all right?" her mother asked with concern.

"It's okay. It's fine to stay at, what was her name again?

"Madigan."

"Okay, well, let's go to the hospital, I'll take my things over later tonight."

Emma finally noticed the activity at Michael's house. "What going on next door?"

"Michael's having some work done. See the new stairs and planters? Did you know he was injured last November? Come on, I want you to meet someone," and she led Emma through the construction maze to where Obie and James were closing the tail gate of the truck.

"Obie, James, this is my daughter Emma, from Portland. Emma, Obie and his brother James, the finest concrete artisans you'd ever want to meet."

"How do you do," Obie said politely, extending his hand. "We were so sorry to hear about your father's illness and we will be thinking about him tomorrow."

After a short exchange about the drive from Portland, Sophie and Emma were in the Cadillac backing down the driveway, giving Obie a final wave.

"If it hadn't been for that man," Sophie said quietly to her daughter, "your father would never have gone to the doctor. But Obie's wife died of stomach cancer several years ago, and he somehow knew by looking at your dad that something was wrong. Your father never said anything until we were at the doctor's. He never said anything to me about it...." Sophie's voice trembled a bit and trailed off.

Emma's heart ached for her mother. "But Mom, that's so like Dad. He never complains. He's never been sick. He probably thought it was the flu or something."

Sophie's eyes didn't leave the road but her hands tightened on the steering wheel.

"He'd been throwing up blood for a month," she said quietly, the anger barely controlled under the surface. "And he never said a word about it to me."

"Oh." Emma couldn't think of anything else to say.

Emma quietly approached the front door at Madigan's, putting down her suitcase and purse and digging out the house key her mother had given her. The lights were still on inside, so she gave a little knock then inserted the key. Before she could turn the handle, she was greeted with exuberant barking and a woman's voice.

249

"Hello!" Madigan held open the screen door for her. "You must be Emma. I'm Madigan. Please come in, can I take your case? Down, Roger! I hope you don't mind dogs. I forgot to ask your mother about that. How is everyone doing?"

Emma was immediately taken with this friendly and gracious woman a few years younger than herself.

"Thank you. No, the dog is fine. Mom and Dad are holding up pretty well. I told Mom she didn't need to come over to introduce us. She's going to bed. It's going to be a long day tomorrow."

"Well, you're probably tired, too. Would you like some tea or something? Did you get dinner at the hospital? I could make you a sandwich."

"No, I'm fine, thank you. I'll probably head to bed myself. Mom and Jim are going over at 6 tomorrow morning, I guess I'll go then, too." Madigan was leading the way upstairs to the extra bedroom as Roger sat plaintively at the bottom step. "Thank you so much for letting me stay with you. I think Mom was quite surprised that these friends are coming from California."

"I know. I offered her the room last week, but she said, no, she had plenty of space. Then last night she called and said their old friends were coming. That's quite caring, don't you think?" Madigan pushed the bedroom door open and placed Emma's suitcase on a small stand.

"I guess. I keep wondering if there's something they aren't telling me. I didn't have a chance to learn much about stomach cancer before I came."

"From what your mother has said to Michael, our neighbor, they won't know anything for sure until after the surgery."

"But, I mean, people live through the surgery. I know people whose parents have other cancers and live a long time."

"Of course. Not knowing and the waiting are making it hard right now. By tomorrow night things should be much more clear, I would think."

"Right."

"The bathroom's here. Those green towels are for you. And you have the key, obviously. Make yourself at home. I keep the dog in the kitchen during the day and he's not allowed upstairs at all. The kids from next door come in each day after school and take him out for a few minutes, so don't let that startle you if you happen to be here. Come and go as you please. Don't worry about waking me or anything. Help yourself to whatever's in the kitchen."

"You're so kind."

"Okay. I'll be thinking about your family tomorrow. We'll all be anxious to hear the news."

"Thank you. I guess there's nothing else to do but go to sleep." She sank onto the edge of the bed and pulled off her shoes. "The traffic was bad driving up here this afternoon. I'm beat."

Madigan put Roger out for the last time and turned off the lights, musing that the experience of watching your parents become ill was one that she would never have. She tried to imagine what her parents would be doing right now if they were still alive, and a wave of grief enveloped her. What had Obie said to do? Think of the beach, of the waves, of the water rushing over her and then retreating back along the wet shore. This rhythm of life. It wasn't that easy.

Chapter Thirty

*Tuesday, April 24*

MICHAEL, who had been impatiently waiting at the window, came out to greet Obie and James as soon as he saw their truck come down the street at eleven o'clock the next morning.

"Any news yet?" Obie asked as he lowered himself stiffly from the truck.

"No. The family's all at the hospital, and their friends from San Diego are at the house. They promised to let me know as soon as they heard anything."

"Hmm," Obie said. "The time will go faster if we work. We'll get the framing of the driveway done today so that we can pour tomorrow."

"What can I do?" Michael asked.

James and Obie shared a look before James headed inside to open the garage door.

"It seems to me we are done with your temporary wood stairs. Why don't you start to take it apart? Save as much wood as you can. It can be reused."

"Sure, I can do that. Do you have a crowbar in the truck?"

Within minutes Michael was busy, starting at the bottom and prying away the wood sections. Obie observed Michael seemed infinitely more happy with a tool in his hands, rather than the flower books of the days before. As the sun approached noon and then beyond, Obie wondered why there had been no word about Gene.

"Do you think you should go over and ask?" Obie said to Michael at four o'clock as they finished their late rest.

"I could. But they promised they'd come out and tell us any news —oh, look. That's Sophie's friend Patty now."

The men all stood as the older woman approached.

"Hello," she said. "Sophie called." Obie could tell there was not good news. "The surgery was extensive, more than they thought it would be. He's gone to recovery. But he's hanging in there. Sophie thought she would hear again from the doctor pretty soon. The kids are all with her. They're just waiting."

"Thank you," Michael said. "We wondered what was happening. Let us know when she calls again, would you please? And send her our best."

"Of course. All Virginia and I are doing, really, is fielding phone calls. It's what Sophie did for me when my husband had open heart surgery. She was a godsend. I'd never let her go through this alone."

Obie had gone back to work, the bad feeling still in his stomach. Michael continued to pull apart the ramp and stack the boards, pulling out as many nails as he could.

James came past Obie and said quietly, "Why is he bothering to go back and pull out the nails?"

"It's good for him. Let him work at it. I told him to try to save all the wood."

The last square frame was in place when the souped-up Honda raced past and pulled to the curb two houses up, on the other side of Gene's home. As soon as the car stopped, the passenger door opened and the teen girl got out, her hair swaying in the wind. They could hear the raised voice of the boy who was driving.

"Sierra, will you wait a minute? Wait a second, will ya?"

"Go away! Take your stupid car and go!" She slammed the passenger side door as he hopped out his side.

"Sierra. Come on. Let's talk about it for a minute."

She ignored him and went up to the front door hurriedly, digging in her pants pocket and coming up with the key.

The boy reached into the back seat and pulled out her backpack. "You left your backpack!" He tried to catch her but she was in the house and slammed the door before he could reach her. He sighed, then placed the pack by the front door.

"Here's your pack," he called through the door. He stood there for a few minutes, then returned to his car, still staring at the house. Finally, he drove off slowly, but in a minute came around the block again as if hoping to catch her with the door open. But the house was closed up tight.

"Stormy weather over there all of a sudden," James noted.

"I think so, too," Obie replied. He stood up straight and tried to rest his back a bit. They were finished, but he did not really want to leave without further word about Gene. As they were putting the last of the tools in the truck, Patty came out again. He did not like the look on her face.

"He's still in recovery," she relayed as Michael came closer to listen. "He hasn't woken up yet, and Sophie won't leave until he does. That's all, but at least he's apparently stable. So that's good."

"Yes, that's good," James agreed. Obie was silent. He didn't like this. He didn't like this at all. But there was nothing to do but go home and say some prayers for the family. Surely by tomorrow there would be good news.

Chapter Thirty-One
*Wednesday, April 25*

A NXIOUS to hear news about Gene, as well as to get Michael's driveway poured, Obie and James got an early start on Wednesday morning. Young James and John had been by before their classes, leaving a tidy stack of pre-mix concrete waiting by the cement mixer. They would be back later to help.

Obie admired the new stairs and planters as he made his way up to Michael's front door, but his pleasure was short-lived when he saw the expression on Michael's face.

"Good morning, Michael. What's happened?"

"He still hasn't woken up after the surgery. Kind of a coma, I guess. They're not sure what's wrong. Madigan called this morning. The daughter never came home last night, and only came in this morning for a minute to change clothes. I don't think Sophie has been home at all."

Obie brushed his hand across his forehead. "But it has not yet been twenty-four hours since the surgery was finished, correct? Perhaps by this evening he will awaken?"

"They hope so. I'm glad you're here, I need something to do. How can I help today?"

"We're ready to pour. If you can mix concrete, it would be most helpful to have another pair of hands at the mixer. We will work slowly today and get it right. And think good thoughts for Gene as we go."

Obie and James began their familiar routine, teaching Michael how to add just enough water into the mixer for them. They worked on the driveway section by section, breaking for lunch. Patty came out at noon to give them the hospital report: no change. Obie was disheartened, but the arrival of Young James and John perked him up as the new energy spurred the rest of the afternoon's work. By four-thirty they were finished, the new driveway smooth and perfect. While Young James and John cleaned up, the others sat under Madigan's tree, but Michael was fidgety.

"I can't just sit here. I think I'll run those plant books back to the library. Do you need anything at the store?"

"No. We'll wait a little bit longer before we go home, in case there is some news," Obie said.

"That dog I'm taking is coming tonight. I don't know if I'm doing the right thing getting involved with a dog right now." Michael wished he'd never let Madigan talk him into this crazy scheme. How was he ever going to care for a dog when he could barely care for himself?

"Helping a dog can't be a wrong decision," Obie asserted.

"Like that time on the highway up north?" James asked dryly.

"That was an honest mistake," Obie replied firmly.

"What happened?" Michael encouraged them, ready for any good story to relieve his anxiety about the dog.

"When Obie first arrived I drove him around a bit. We were traveling up north when there was what looked like a big, dead dog in the middle of the highway, in the grassy part. Obie insisted we stop to see if it was still alive. It was, so we took it to the next town and found a vet. It turned out to be a wolf that had been hit. It was far

256

from home, no one knew how it could have gotten there. They said they would send it to a wildlife center to recover. But we ended up making a hundred dollar donation to help with the expenses."

"Wolf, dog, it doesn't matter. If you can help, you help," Obie put in obstinately.

"I like it better when it doesn't cost so much to help," James replied. "We were not working so steadily, right then."

Michael gazed fondly at these brothers, so similar but so different. What had he done before they came into his life? And all because of cracked driveways and sidewalks.

"All right, I'm off to the library."

Obie called him back. "Did you ever look up the news articles about yourself?"

"No. I didn't want to spend the time the day I went with Madigan. Maybe I'll look today."

"Good. Then you will understand why you are a famous person. A miracle on two feet and two crutches."

Michael doubted that very much, but he would look.


It didn't take long for the reference librarian to show Michael how to use the microfilm and find the articles from the November paper. He thanked her, then eased himself into the swivel chair, pulling up to the desk to look at the computer screen.

Michael was surprised to find his hand shaking a bit as he scrolled down the dates. He found the day after the accident, and a small picture in the bottom corner of the front page, with a reference to the first page of the local section. He looked with disbelief at the picture of his own body, seemingly lifeless, crumpled onto the convertible, the torn fabric roof around him, the struts bent beneath him. The shot must have been taken from overhead somehow. Maybe even from one of the news crews' helicopters with a telephoto lens. He tried to see his safety harness. He enlarged the picture, but he couldn't tell. ***Did** I have it fastened right? What did I do that day?* These were the questions he had asked himself a thousand times, until he had decided the answers made no difference in the outcome. But still, he was hoping to find some piece of information that would show he hadn't made a mistake, that he had in fact tied off correctly just as he had every morning for the past eight years. Why would he have done anything differently that day?

He read through the articles in the paper for that week, following his progress. No wonder people were amazed: broken legs, crushed knee, broken ribs, punctured lung, ruptured spleen, concussion. A short quote from Veronica with an update. The early prognosis had seemed quite grim. Yet here he was, "up and about" as the firefighter had said.

Michael closed out of the file, got his crutches in place and left the library. He *was* a miracle, he understood that now. So what would he do with his life?


He was sitting at the kitchen table after dinner contemplating that very question, when the doorbell rang. It was Art and Kristen with the dog. Kristen looked as if she had been crying. Art had a dog bed in his arms.

"Come in," Michael opened the screen door. "Hi, Shiloh. Welcome to your temporary home."

Shiloh came in tentatively and sniffed him, then went through the first floor of the house, smelling everything.

"Checking it out again," said Art. "Is it okay if I put the dog bed in the kitchen?"

"Yeah, sure. Come on back." Michael led the way down the hall.

Kristen wiped a tear off her cheek as she followed. "I'm sorry. It's so stressful trying to get ready to go. I didn't realize it would be like this. And it's harder to leave Shiloh than I thought it would be."

258

"That's okay. I imagine I'll get pretty attached to him myself, once we get used to each other."

Art set the bed down near the floor's heating vent and then went back out to the car.

"I know it probably seems ridiculous to have so much stuff for a dog," Kristen apologized. "They really do become like your children."

"So I've heard," Michael said.

Kristen pulled a neatly stapled stack of papers from her purse. "Here's all the information you'll need. This page has how we can be reached. This is the secretary at the university who will always know where we are. Here's the vet's number, and the emergency after-hours hospital vet. This is our good friend's number. She has dogs. If you have a question, you could call her to ask. Now, page two has the feeding and snack schedule. See those little treats?" She pointed to one of six boxes Art was setting down on the kitchen counter. "You stuff those into his red bone, into the ends. He loves that. I give him one after dinner. Or if you're going to be gone for a while and he might be bored."

Kristen flipped the sheet of paper to bring up page 3. "Now here are his medical records. He's all caught up on his shots. And it tells you when to give him his heart worm and flea medicine. Those are the little boxes in the bag Art has now." Art was placing another bag that looked like grooming tools on the counter. "We did this month a little early, so you won't have to worry about those meds until the end of May. Once a month is all you have to do it."

"Here's his water dish." She took the larger aluminum bowl from Art who was struggling in with a twenty pound bag of dog food. "And that's the food bowl. And here's the measuring cup. So about two scoops in the morning, and then again in the evening. If he eats too much at one time, he can get a bad stomach ache. We would have bought you one more bag of food, but it goes stale." Art was making another trip in with a half-bag of food and a cloth bag of toys.

"Will you have trouble buying the dog food?" Kristen looked at his crutches as if seeing them for the first time. "I didn't even think about that."

"I think I can get Madigan to help. She's the one who got all this going. I'm sure she'll be glad to take me to buy food, and I think she'll take us over to that dog park she likes so much where you all go. So Shiloh will get to see his friends."

"That would be wonderful. However much you can keep to his routine would be great. I mean, I realize you have your own life. And dogs are pretty adaptable." She leaned down and petted the golden's large head gently, gazing into his dark eyes. "He'll probably have forgotten us in six months...." Her tears started again.

"Oh, I doubt that," Michael tried to sound cheery, despite his small panic at the enormity of the stuff that had arrived in the house. "Why don't you write down your address? Then I can take him past your house every once in a while, as a reminder."

"Oh, would you? I'll put it on the emergency page." She dug in her purse for a pen. Art came in with one last load, the dog towels and blankets.

"Did you tell him about the ear wash?" Art asked, finding a place on the floor for his armload.

"Ear wash?" Michael asked with a forced smile.

"If you think you can. If his ears start to smell stinky and there's black yuck on the inside—" Kristin glanced up from her writing. Michael's face indicated a line had just been crossed. "Never mind. If his ears smell, call my friend. She'll come do it for you."

"I know it looks a little overwhelming," Art said, trying to relax the tension that black, stinky ear yuck seemed to have brought to the room. "It's really not that complicated. Just feed him and let him out. You'll be fine. C'mere, Shiloh. Let's say good-bye and get this over with. It's not forever."

260

The dog came at his call, tail wagging as he was stroked lovingly by Art and then Kristen, who was fully crying now. Michael felt completely helpless. He had not been prepared for this show of emotion over a dog. *What if something happens to him while he's with me? They'll never forgive me.*

"Thank you again." Art made his way down the hallway to the front door, pulling his wife with him. "I'm not sure how the communication will be. But we'll try to drop you a line when we can, and maybe you could let us know how he's doing."

Kristen gave Shiloh one last, loving stroke along his sleek head. Then she faced Michael.

"I know that you'll take good care of him, but dogs sometimes get sick. So if anything happens, we've talked about that, and we trust you to do the best you can. That's why I left all those numbers. Dogs are basically pretty healthy. But if he starts acting weird, throwing up a lot, diarrhea, acting lethargic, anything unusual like that, please take him to the vet. We'll take care of all the bills, I promise. Oh, here, I almost forgot." She dug into her purse again. "Here's a check for $500 to cover your expenses for food and the vet or anything else. Keep a list and we'll reimburse you for anything over this."

Shiloh had followed his owners to the door. "Now stay," Art said to him.

"Be a good boy," Kristen added, giving Shiloh one last pat. Then they were out the door and gone.

Shiloh watched them and whined at the door. Once the car had driven out of sight, Michael called his house guest to come along to the kitchen. He pointed to the dog bed and sat down at the kitchen table and wondered what to do next. Shiloh sniffed around the kitchen, went to the front door and back, then finally curled up in his bed, still watching Michael.

"Welcome to your new home," Michael said.

He was still sitting at the kitchen table twenty minutes later when Madigan phoned.

"Hi," she said. "Your driveway looks nice. What's happened today with Gene?"

"Still no change as of dinner time."

"That's terrible. That poor family."

"I know. I don't think Sophie has even left the hospital."

"I wish I knew something to do for them."

"The waiting is the hardest part, at least for me. Oh, by the way, the dog is here."

"Good! How are you two doing?"

"I'm sitting here going through the twenty single-spaced pages of instructions Kristen left for me."

"I know you're exaggerating. But he is a well-loved pet."

"You should see the stuff they brought. I need a bigger house to fit him."

"Now you are absolutely stretching the truth. I'm going to eat and then take Roger for a walk. Are you up for visitors? We'll bring Shiloh a welcome bone."

"Yes, please. Anything to keep this dog from staring at me like he's lost his best friends. Whatever made you think that this was going to work?"

"You'll get used to each other, don't worry. In three days you won't be able to imagine life without him. See you in half an hour."

Chapter Thirty-Two

*Thursday, April 26*

OBIE and James arrived early. They knocked on Michael's door and were greeted by loud barking.

"Your new friend arrived, I see," Obie regarded the shiny-haired golden retriever wagging its tail.

"Yes, this is Shiloh." Michael patted the large head and made room for Obie to enter.

"And what news from next door?"

"I haven't heard anything since before dinner last night. I think Sophie might have come home late with Jim, because I heard a car, but then they were gone already this morning when I got up."

"They do not know what is wrong?"

"I don't think so. Patty said there's plenty of brain activity, but he isn't coming back to consciousness."

Obie had so hoped for good news today. Feeling his disappointment, James said to him softly, "We don't have much to do today. We will take out the forms from the driveway and wet it down. Maybe there will be better news later."

They worked for an hour, then went over to their familiar spot under Madigan's tree. Michael came out and joined them after lunch. About two o'clock, a car pulled up at Sophie's, and the four adult children disembarked. Fred, Bea, and Jim headed into their parents' house, while Emma came to Madigan's.

"What's the news this afternoon?" Michael asked.

"No change," Emma said. "Mother sent us all home to eat and rest awhile. I'm going to try to get her to let me spend the night at the hospital so that she can come home to sleep."

"We're sorry about your father," Obie said. "But it can still turn out all right, correct?"

"I guess. It's hard not to be discouraged, but the doctors are being positive. Well, I'm going to go in and get a shower and maybe a quick nap."

Michael headed home while Obie and James stayed under the tree. A while later Emma came out with half a peanut butter and jelly sandwich in her hand and sat on the steps near them.

"That was a short nap," Obie remarked.

"I couldn't sleep." She took another bite. "Time passes so slowly at the hospital. I don't know how Mother can stand it."

"It's a hard time," Obie said compassionately.

"We were all starting to get on each other's nerves. I think that's why she sent us home. She said she wanted to be alone for a while."

"It must be stressful for all of you."

Emma ate the last bite, looking at Obie. "Mother said it was because of you that Dad even went to the doctor. So thank you for that."

"I didn't do anything. Everything I said your father already knew. It's fear, I think, that keeps people away."

Emma looked at her house.

"Here comes Jim. He's the youngest. Works at Channel 2 here in town."

"Hmm."

"Hey," Jim nodded to the men, but asked his sister, "What are you doing?"

"Just sitting here. Jim, this is Obie and his brother James. They're the ones who are going to build the fountain for Dad."

"Hi," said Jim. "You're getting quite a stretch along this street."

"It works that way, sometimes," James replied modestly.

Jim looked at Emma. "Bea wants to know if you're coming over to eat. Patty and Virginia have a whole spread laid out. You'd think they're feeding an army."

"I made myself a sandwich. I could use a little space, to tell you the truth."

"I know. I forget how bossy Bea is."

"And Fred's no better. I thought if I heard him say 'I'm going to insist on another opinion' one more time today, I'd deck him."

"He's upset."

"We're *all* upset." Emma looked over at the house. "Oh, shit— excuse my language. Here comes Bea."

Bea made her way along the non-existent sidewalks to the small group.

"What are you doing?"

"Sitting here," Jim answered his older sister.

"Bea, this is Obie and James," Emma introduced them. "They're the ones who are going to build the fountain for Dad."

"How do you do?" Bea said politely. "It sounds like a lovely idea. I'm not quite sure about the timing right now. But mother was quite taken with it." She turned expectantly to Emma and Jim. "Are you coming to eat?"

"I'm going to sit here for a while," Emma answered.

"Me, too," Jim replied.

"You have to come. Patty and Virginia have everything ready."

"I don't feel like being with anyone right this minute, Bea. I can't be in a crowd." Emma crumpled the napkin that had held her sandwich.

"It's no crowd. It's us and Virginia and Patty. What's the matter?"

"Well, our father is in a coma."

"You know what I mean. Is something else wrong?" Bea demanded.

"No—oh, now, here comes Fred." Emma caught sight of Fred coming out of the house and looking for everyone. He walked over to Madigan's tree.

"What are you guys doing? We're ready to eat."

"They don't want to come," Bea complained to him. "I think it's rather rude—"

"Give us a break, Bea," Jim interrupted. "Patty and Virginia don't care. If Emma wants to sit, let her sit."

Obie and James seemed to have been forgotten in the middle of the siblings' discussion.

"Is something wrong?" Fred asked.

"*Nothing* is wrong," Emma said forcefully, near tears, "except that our father is in a coma. Don't you guys get it? COMA!! What if, you know, he never comes out of it? Or he's not the same, or he slowly gets worse and worse—"

"Don't say things like that, especially around Mother," Bea reprimanded her.

"Emma's right, though," Fred argued. "We should really be talking about what if we have to make some hard decisions."

"*We* won't be making any hard decisions," Jim said. "Mother's the one to do that."

"But she'd listen to us. She might need help working it out," Fred spoke again.

"I don't want to talk about this," Bea said.

"You never want to talk about difficult things," Fred replied harshly.

Bea faced him, hands on hips. "That's not true. How can you say that?"

"You've never been around for the difficult discussions."

"Excuse me?! When was *I* ever invited? You and Dad always have your heads together about the business. It's not like the rest of us have a say in anything."

"Do you know how hard it is trying to take over the business from Dad? It's impossible to please everyone the way he did. His standards are so high, I feel like he's second-guessing everything I do, even when he's out of town. By the end of our Tuesday/Thursday phone calls I've got a knot in my stomach."

"Tough. You're the one who wanted to work with him. Some of us never got a chance."

"Oh, here we go again. If you wanted to work in the business, Bea, all you had to do was say so. It's not fair, now that I've put in all this time, to all of a sudden want in."

"*I'm* not being fair? When was it considered that any of the rest of us would want to share the business? It was always assumed it would go to you...or you and Jim if he'd ever shown any interest. Emma and I never had a choice."

"Leave me out of this," Emma said.

"Me, too," Jim added.

"Oh, stand up for yourself for once, Emma," Bea was angry now. "You always take the easy way out."

"Now wait a minute—" Jim protested.

"And you, too, Jim. She's all the way in Portland, and you can't be found even though you live in town. Where did *you* disappear to today, I'd like to know?"

"I had to check in at work. I wasn't expecting to be out this long."

"You could have lived anywhere you wanted to, Bea. Nobody made you stay in Seattle," Emma said.

"It so happens I like it here. I like being close to them. And you two could be a little more involved with the family." Bea was close to tears now.

"Harruum." As Obie cleared his throat, the four siblings remembered that he and James were there. "It's the nature of families to push and pull against each other," Obie said. "And times like these make little things seem very big. You each care for your parents. I think that's all that is important to them right now."

There was an awkward pause.

"I'm sorry," Bea apologized. "I know I try to run the show. It's one disadvantage of being a teacher. I want him to be better." Her tears fell freely now. Emma offered a tissue from her pocket, and Fred put a consoling arm around her.

"It'll be all right," he said. "They'll figure out something." He turned to Jim and Emma. "We're going back to eat, then I'm going to sleep for a while. What about you two?"

"I'm going back to the hospital now. Maybe I can get Mom to come home for a bit," Emma said.

"Will you come over and have something to eat?" Bea invited Obie and James. "We might as well wait together over there."

"We'll put our tools away and then stop by," Obie accepted graciously.

When Madigan arrived home, she observed Obie and James, Michael, the San Diego friends, and several other people she didn't recognize, seated on lawn chairs in Gene's front yard. Concerned, she walked over before going into her house.

"Hey," she said to Michael, who was sitting on the edge of the group. "What's going on?"

"I guess we're having an impromptu vigil. People keep dropping by and staying. I think Emma went back to the hospital, but the other kids are here."

"So still no change in Gene?"

"No."

"That's too bad. Do you want me to walk Shiloh for you?"

"That would be great. I'll go get him hooked up and meet you out front."

Having eaten and then slept for two hours, Jim and Fred went back to the hospital and managed to talk their mother into coming home with Emma. As they approached the house, Emma was overcome by the crowd sitting in the dwindling daylight talking quietly.

"Who are all these people?" she asked her mother.

"Our friends, dear," Sophie said rather matter-of-factly, getting out of the car slowly. Virginia and Patty came to her immediately and she was swallowed up by a circle of women. Emma got out of her side of the car and walked to where James and Obie were sitting.

"Where did all these people come from?" she asked them, looking around.

"After you left, people started coming. I think the word must have spread that your parents were in difficulty."

Emma looked at her mother in the midst of a sisterhood of older women who were escorting her inside. She had a sudden memory of being young, her grandmother gravely ill, and people sitting in a parlor, talking in hushed voices. The same sisterhood had existed then, this web of human kindness that materialized overnight whenever there was a need. Emma pondered whether this was lost to her generation, her busy, day planner-addicted, always-in-the-car driving someplace generation. An impromptu vigil like this was unlikely unless previously scheduled.

"It's a different kind of family, that's all," Obie said to her, watching her observe the group and feeling her uncertainty of where her place would be.

"Yeah, I guess so." Emma yawned in exhaustion. "I'm going to sleep for a while. Aren't you two going home tonight?"

"We'll wait a little longer. It's a common thing on our island for families to sit and wait in times of need. Maybe all the prayers of these people together will help your father."

"That's a nice thought. Well, good night for now."

Emma walked wearily to Madigan's, then turned and looked across the yards at the quiet assembly. She realized with both sadness and an odd relief that it would not be she or her siblings, but rather these people, gathered on the lawn on a warm spring evening, who would care for her mother if her father died.

Chapter Thirty-Three
*Friday, April 27*

A RRIVING early the next morning, Obie and James could tell by the number of parked cars that there were already a few people at Gene and Sophie's. They joined Michael, who was sitting on the lawn with Shiloh.

"It's not good for this to go on so long," Obie said, carefully lowering himself onto a wooden picnic bench that had been brought from the back yard. "I never thought it would go this way. I somehow felt he would have a better result."

"Sophie thinks because the surgery was so extensive, that his body has shut down from the shock. Because he's never been sick or anything before."

"I would think being so healthy would work more in his favor," James eased into a white deck chair.

Obie shook his head. "You have good doctors here. It does not make sense to me. It should go better than this."

They kept vigil all day until four o'clock, with Obie becoming increasing agitated throughout the afternoon. The crowd swelled and then diminished, Patty and Virginia came to each group with food offerings, but nothing could calm Obie's unease.

"This is not good," he said again to James and Michael.

"There's nothing we can do," James said. "You know that. We've been through this waiting before. What's wrong with you today?"

"I need the keys to the truck," Obie stood suddenly.

"Why, where are you going?"

"Give me the keys. I'll be back soon."

James looked at Michael and shrugged as he handed over the keys.

When Obie returned in the truck, Madigan had arrived home and was sitting with Michael and James for a moment before going into her own house.

"What do you have there, Obie?" she asked as he walked up to them with something in his hand. He held it out for them to see: a perfectly shaped, cream-colored oval stone, the size of a slightly flattened large pear.

"A rock?" Madigan reached for it. The weight of the larger end fit neatly into her palm.

"Not a rock. A stone. A perfect stone. Feel the texture of it."

She rubbed across the stone's surface, then passed it back and forth from one hand to the other. There was something about it: smooth with the slightest texture, cool but not cold.

"What is it?" she asked, running her fingertips around its edge.

"A rubbing stone. Are any of Gene's children here?"

"I don't think so," Michael said. "They've all gone back."

"Well, then, Madigan, I must ask you a big favor."

Madigan tore her eyes from the creamy stone and looked at him expectantly.

"Me?"

"I want you to take this stone to Sophie at the hospital. Tell her to rub it in Gene's hand, to talk to him about stones and the fountain and water."

Madigan returned the stone to him. "Obie, I can't do that. I don't know them well enough."

"You are the only one to send."

"But they'll think I'm crazy."

"Say you are coming for me."

"Why don't you go yourself? You and James?"

"We are in our work clothes. It would be disrespectful to go to the hospital like this."

"That's not a good excuse."

"Really," Obie indicated the dirt and dust on his pants from digging through the rocks at the nursery and his big work boots, "it would be bad luck to do that."

"I'll ride along with you," Michael offered to Madigan. "It can't hurt. We've got to try something."

Madigan looked at Obie, knowing she couldn't refuse him. "Fine. Let me go put Roger out for a minute, then we'll go. Michael, you be in charge of the rock."

"The stone," Obie gently reminded her. "Remember, tell them to talk to him of stones and buildings and water."

"They are going to think I am nuts," Madigan muttered, still unconvinced.

"You'll be surprised about that. They will be thankful for any little thing to do."

Madigan couldn't find a place to park near the hospital entrance.

"Listen," she said to Michael. "I'll drop you at the door, and you take it up to them. I'll wait over there. It shouldn't take more than ten minutes."

"I'm not sure I can carry it with my crutches and I don't have a big enough pocket."

"Here," Madigan twisted around and felt along the floor of the back seat until she found a small plastic bread bag. "I always have bags for Roger's walks. Put it in here."

Michael got out of the car, held the bag top under his hand on his right crutch and made his way into the hospital, the stone swinging against the aluminum support with each step. He asked at the reception desk where to find Gene's family and was directed to the fourth floor.

The smell of the hospital overwhelmed him. Although not the same hospital where he had been taken after his accident, the odors were the same. His chest tightened as he crowded on the elevator with the other visitors, and he had to remind himself to take some deep breaths as the doors closed.

The people in front of him stepped aside so he could get out on the fourth floor, and he cautiously made his way to the nurse's station. Before he could inquire, he saw Emma and Jim sitting in a small lounge area nearby.

Emma noticed him first.

"Michael! What are you doing here?"

"Obie sent something he wanted your father to have." Michael balanced himself with one crutch under his arm and shook the stone from the plastic bag into his other hand. "Here," he handed it to Emma.

"What is it?" she inquired, captivated by its weight, simplicity, and pale color.

"Obie said it's a rubbing stone. He said to put it in your father's hand, to rub his fingers on it, and to talk to him of buildings, of water, and of stones, things that he loves."

Mesmerized yet skeptic, Emma felt the texture with her fingers, and admired the smooth, round edges.

"What made him think of this?"

"You don't know Obie very well, yet. Things come to his mind. And no matter how crazy I think some of his ideas are, he's usually right. Like with the fountain, I thought it was the wrong time to even suggest it to your parents, and yet both took to the idea immediately. He thinks out of the box in a big way, I guess."

Jim reached over and took the stone from his sister, turning it over to look at the underside, then weighing it in his hand.

"Thank you for bringing it, we'll take it right in. Do you want to stay awhile?"

"No, Madigan drove me over, she's waiting out front."

"Thank you." Emma hugged Michael. "It certainly can't hurt."

Michael watched them go down the hall and then returned to the elevator. He was relieved when he cleared the front doors and saw Madigan double parked nearby.

"How did it go?" she asked as he opened the door and backed into his seat, then lifted his leg and the crutches inside.

"Emma and Jim were in the hallway so I gave it to them. They said they'd take it right in. It was strange, Emma was just like you, sort of rubbing the stone and turning it over between her hands. Maybe there *is* something magical about it."

"I think it's river rock, but I've never seen such a perfect shape. I wonder where he found it."

"He was gone over two hours. He must have gone through the whole pile at the nursery until he found the one he wanted."

Madigan looked at her watch as they sat at the stop light.

"I need to take Roger around the block when we get home. Do you want me to take Shiloh for you?"

"Are you sure you don't mind?"

"No, I'm the one who got you into this. How's it going?"

Michael started to reach for the scar on his face, but instead let his hand come to rest on his knee.

"All he does is sleep and eat and go out in the yard. We play fetch every day in the back with the tennis ball. He brings the ball all the way up the steps to the door. He's easy to have around. Hasn't chewed up anything yet. Comes over and lies by my feet in the kitchen, and I moved his bed into my room for overnight. He seems to like that better." The vision of the sandy-colored, large ball of fur curled up in his bedroom brought a smile to his face.

"Oh, I can see you are hooked already." Madigan pulled up in front of Michael's. "We better start lining up another dog for when he has to leave."


Madigan was getting into bed when she heard Emma come in. She greeted her as Emma came up the stairs with heavy footsteps.

"Hey, how are you holding up?" Madigan asked kindly. "How did the stone go over?"

"We put it in his hand and rubbed his fingers on it, like Obie said to do, then left it there with his hand resting on it." Emma reached the top step and leaned tiredly against the wall. "Poor Mom. You could tell she's ready to try anything. She had really prepared herself for almost any kind of news after the surgery, good or bad, but I don't think she ever expected this no man's land of not knowing what is happening. And I think we're all afraid that when he comes to, he won't be himself."

"It's really tough. What have you decided about having your husband and kids come up tomorrow?"

"I don't know what to do." Emma went into the bedroom with Madigan following. She put her purse on the night stand and sat on the edge of the bed, rubbing her forehead. "I know Max would like to come, but there's nothing to do at the hospital but sit and wait. I can't leave the kids unsupervised over at Mom's house, they'd drive Patty and Virginia crazy. I suppose they could go to Bea's house and stay with her kids, but Bea's mostly at the hospital so Max would have to stay with them. The cousins are all close in age and they get along pretty well, but, I don't know." She glanced at the clock. "It's too late to call tonight anyway. I'll decide in the morning."

"Could I go make you a cup of herbal tea or something? You look beat."

"That sounds wonderful. I'll change and then be down. You're sure it's no trouble? You were probably going to bed."

"No trouble at all. And how about a sandwich or something? When was the last time you ate?"

"I had a sandwich from the cafeteria at four. You've been so kind, Madigan. Everyone has. I don't know how we can ever thank all of you."

"I'll make some eggs. How about a fried egg sandwich, does that sound good? Pure comfort food—with ketchup on white bread?"

"That sounds perfect."

Madigan and Emma sat in the kitchen and talked until nearly two. Madigan slowly gave out the details of her own parents' deaths, and Emma tried to imagine the shock of losing both parents at once. Emma talked about her brothers and sister, how they had fought with each other growing up but had finally settled into some typical birth-order roles that seemed to keep them all functional, even if Bea and Fred were the parental figures to herself and Jim. Their discussion made Madigan wonder if she could ever have any relationship with her half-sister, functional or not. Obie's words sounded in the back of her mind: *something good might come*. Well, she hoped so.

# Chapter Thirty-Four
## *Saturday, April 28*

T HE telephone rang by Madigan's ear. Deep in her last dream of the night, it took her a moment to realize what it was. She finally woke up enough to grab it from the bed stand and her eyes fell on the clock. Six a.m. *Who would call so early? Oh, no, it must be for Emma.*

"Hello?" she answered warily.

"Madigan? It's Jim. Sorry to wake you. I couldn't get Emma on her phone. I need to talk to her right away."

"I'll get her. Maybe her battery's down." She talked as she carried the handset to the guest room. She had to shake Emma awake. "It's Jim," she said, handing her the phone. She saw fear in Emma's eyes as she put the phone to her ear.

"Jim? What is it?"

Madigan watched as Emma's face broke into a broad smile and she relayed, "He's awake! And he's fine!" Then Emma's tears started to flow so fast and in such sobs that she had to hand the phone to Madigan.

"Jim? It's Madigan again. Emma's sort of overcome here. That's wonderful news. When did it happen?"

278

"About an hour ago. Now he's sleeping again. I need Emma to come over so we can send Mom home for a while. She's beat."

"I'll go start the coffee and get your sister going. Such wonderful news."

"And you know what he said when he woke up? That he was dreaming about the fountain, that it was all made and he was standing there with Obie looking at the water spraying on the stones. And then he woke up with the stone in his hand."

"That's sending a chill down my spine."

"What?" Emma had regained her composure. "It was the stone, right? It worked, right?"

"Bye," Madigan hung up and repeated what Jim had told her.

Emma dressed. "I wonder if they called the house yet? I suppose Mother would like to be the one to break the news. Oh, I wish I could be here to see Obie's face when he finds out. He'll be so pleased." She pulled on her socks and shoes. "I'm going to call Max and tell him to come up with the kids tonight. Would that be okay with you, you wouldn't mind a few more guests?"

"I'd be delighted. It will be the celebration you've been waiting for all week."

Arriving later in the morning, Obie immediately suspected that something was going on. The changed demeanor around Gene and Sophie's house was evident before he even got out of the truck.

Jim saw the brothers from the window and met them as they disembarked at the curb.

"My father woke up this morning! And he's fine! He woke up after dreaming about you and the fountain...the water on the stones, just like you said. Mother's sleeping now, but she can't wait to see you," Jim stuck his hand out as he spoke. "Thank you so much," he said quietly. "We can't ever thank you enough."

"I didn't do anything, but you are welcome," Obie spoke simply, overcome with emotion himself. "We are happy for your family."

"And finally back to work, then," said James cheerfully. "So much sitting around is not good for old men like us."

"Will you start the fountain?"

"Not quite yet. I think we must finish the sidewalk down the street first. Madigan has been patient with us. We should finish her job before we start your father's."

Jim nodded and shook James' hand, too, before driving off. Michael, who had heard James' truck arrive, came out of his house, Shiloh at his heels.

"The dog stays right with you, now?" Obie asked when he saw them making their way down the new steps.

"Yes, he's really good. I was worried he might try to find his way back home, but he's been quite content. It's surprised me."

"Perhaps he understands they are coming back. Or perhaps life with you is good!"

"I doubt that," Michael laughed, but his hand found its way down to the top of Shiloh's head, right beside his crutch. "You heard about Gene?"

"The son was telling us," James said.

"Well, now that you're getting ready to go back to work again, I want to do my sidewalk, too. Then there will be this whole stretch of new driveways and sidewalk looking sharp."

"We were thinking about pouring Madigan's and her neighbor's. They have waited a long time."

"I don't think they'll care. Pull mine up and do it all together. It wouldn't be that hard, would it?"

"No, we can do it," answered James. "There's plenty lumber left from your framing. Perhaps I can get my sons to come by later and help remove the old concrete."

Madigan was stepping out of the shower at noon when she heard the familiar sound of the sledgehammer breaking up concrete. She couldn't imagine what part of the fountain required concrete removal, and so was not particularly surprised when she looked out her window and saw Michael's sidewalk being torn up. But then, very little on her street could surprise her anymore.

After lunch, she picked up Michael and Shiloh so they could accompany her to the dog park. Roger eagerly shared the back seat with the adult lab. Madigan was somewhat unnerved by the large head that kept appearing in her rear view mirror or, worse yet, was thrust over her shoulder in slobbery glee as she drove.

"Sit, Shiloh," she said sternly, trying to push his head back. Shiloh promptly sat. "Good dog."

The day was overcast but not raining, and the park was filled with people. Madigan let the dogs off leash and then walked slowly along one of the paths with Michael, pointing out the dogs she knew as they went along. About halfway down one path she saw the yellow lab that Roger had first tried to steal the bone from, lying in the middle of the grassy stretch. "Hello, Sunny," she stopped to pet her. "Haven't seen you for a while."

"Hey, Madigan." Pete, the owner, approached from the other side, walking with a woman a little younger than himself.

"Hi, Pete, I've missed seeing you this spring."

"My wife and I have been traveling a bit." Madigan's eyes went to the face of the woman with him. She stuck out her hand.

"Hi, I'm Madigan Gardner. Nice to meet you."

"Oh, no," Pete interrupted with a smile. "This is my sister, Carol. She has those two big Great Danes over there by the tree."

Madigan glanced at the large dogs sniffing their way around the evergreen's base. Then she remembered Michael beside her. "This is my friend and neighbor, Michael Stevens. And that's Roger, my dog," she pointed to where Roger was circling Sunny, attempting to grab her bone. "And Michael's dog is—" she looked over her shoulder the other way but Shiloh had run over to the Great Danes, tail wagging.

"I know who you are!" Carol said to Michael.

Michael prepared himself to repeat the accident story again and his hand self-consciously came up to his scar.

"Right, I fell off the building at 5th and Sitka last November. That was me."

Confusion crossed Carol's face. "Oh? No, I don't remember that. I meant you're the one who took Shiloh, Art and Kristen's dog."

At the sound of Carol's voice, Shiloh came running to the group and bounded into her legs. Carol leaned over and rubbed him fondly on his chest.

"Oh, right. Yes, Shiloh is staying with me."

"How are you, old boy? You doing okay? You look good." After holding Shiloh's head still and looking carefully at his eyes, and giving a quick flip up of his ears and looking for wax, she finally addressed Michael again. "I'm Kristen's friend. I think she gave you my number, in case you had any questions? I can't tell you how relieved I was that you could take the dog. They had a terrible time trying to leave, everything kept going wrong. And I'm indebted to you, too. If they hadn't found someone to take him, he probably would have ended up at my house. But I've already got those two big lugs, so my house is pretty full. Kristen never mentioned you'd been injured."

Michael traced his facial scar again in his habitual pattern and considered the two times Art and Kristen had been at his house with the outside stairs in progress and his slow movements with his crutches.

"So how's it going?" Michael realized with a start that Carol was still talking to him. "You haven't had to call me yet."

"It's fine," he offered truthfully, somewhat surprising himself. "It's great. I'm enjoying it." He looked around for Madigan, but she had gone off after Roger.

"Do you want to meet my dogs?" Before he could answer, Carol had called them over and Michael found himself trying to maintain his balance among dogs that were nearly the size of small horses. He had to brace himself not to be knocked over by their excited jostling.

"Whatever made you decide on such large dogs?" he asked, finally confident enough to hold his crutches in one hand and attempt to pet the dogs with his other.

"I had a Great Dane growing up. So as soon as I could, I got one as a puppy. The second one I got from purebred rescue. Do you know what that is?"

Michael found himself totally involved in conversation with this young woman, and didn't even realize forty-five minutes had gone by until Madigan came back. Pete and Sunny had already left, but Carol accompanied them as they made their way to the parking lot.

"I told Kristen I would come by and check on Shiloh every once in a while. She gave me your address and phone. Would you mind? That whole earwax stuff can be pretty gross for a newbie."

"I wouldn't mind at all," Michael said.

"Maybe we could walk them together or something."

"Uh, I haven't really been able to walk Shiloh yet. Madigan's been doing it for me."

"Oh, really?" Carol seemed surprised. "I wouldn't have guessed. You've done great over here. Shiloh's pretty easy. It's not like he pulls your arm off the way he did as a puppy."

Michael realized that, in fact, Shiloh had simply trotted along beside him for most of the walk back to the car. Maybe he *could* get him out for a bit of a walk each day.

"It was nice meeting you," he said to Carol, once they had navigated the double gates at the fence line. "Please, come by any time."

"Okay, I'll call you!" She walked toward the smallest car in the front row of the lot. "Come on, guys," she called to her companions.

Madigan and Michael stood dumbfounded as the huge dogs crowded into the non-existent back seat of the minute automobile.

"Now those are dogs," Madigan said in awe as she opened her car door and let Roger and Shiloh hop in. "I can't imagine what it costs to feed them."

Michael wasn't really listening. He was thinking about Carol, and that he would very much enjoy it if she happened to stop over sometime.

"Is she married, do you think?" he asked, easing himself into the passenger seat.

Madigan looked at him. "Aren't you?"

"Not for long," he said, pulling the door shut with a smile.

Chapter Thirty-Five

*Sunday, April 29*

A FTER the mid-day meal, Obie rested in his garden chair as usual. The sky was unusually clear, with clouds barely peeking around the horizon. He adjusted his great bulk to a more comfortable position; his back muscles were still complaining from the effort of pulling up Michael's sidewalk.

Closing his eyes, he thought happily of the look on Sophie's face when they had spoken the day before. Yes, things were good. Things were very, very good. He and James would pour the sidewalks, they would build the fountain, then they would be done.

The spring sun warmed his face and chest, and he drifted off into contented sleep.

A knock roused Michael from his kitchen table. Jim stood at the front door, videotape in hand.

"Come on in," Michael stepped back to make room. "What's up?"

"I was talking to Obie the other day about your accident. He mentioned that until recently you hadn't looked up the news reports about it."

"Right." Michael leaned against the wall. "I did finally check out the news clippings. They were a little hard to look at, you know?"

"Well, like I told you, I was one of the first on the scene, camera in hand. OSHA asked for my tape, so I made them a copy. Then I got to thinking, maybe now you'd like to see it, so I made another copy for you."

"Thanks," Michael took the offered cassette. "My memory of that whole week after the accident is fuzzy. I remember thinking 'Oh, shit' when I started to slide and realized there wasn't a toe board, then desperately trying to grab anything on my way down, but I was out too far. And that's it."

"Well, maybe the tape will help."

"Thanks, Jim. I appreciate it. How's your dad today?"

"Improving rapidly. Quite amazing. Even considering how extensive the surgery was, they think they got all the cancer and everything hooked back up the way it should be. It turned out about as well as it could have, Mom says."

"That's great."

Jim left and Michael placed the tape on the VCR, then walked into the kitchen. Out the window he could see Frank, Lauren and Kevin playing basketball on their driveway. Farther down, Madigan was digging her new flower beds, a shovel in hand and a basket of gardening tools at her feet.

Shiloh interrupted by nuzzling Michael's leg. He rubbed the big head and then reached for a dog biscuit on the counter top, a calm resolution enveloping him. He could look at the tape. It was time.

The camera angle was different from those in the newspaper. Jim must have been less than ten feet from him, standing on the street and shooting straight at the convertible, with its ripped canvas, bent struts, and Michael's body dropped like a rag doll into the back seat. Then, as the sound of sirens increased on the audio, the view switched to a higher station, but Jim still had a good shot. The firefighters were first, the medics right behind them, the construction crew and bosses also in the mix. The camera zoomed in, and there he lay…his entire harness still attached, the tether in a heap beside him. Then the camera panned straight up. There were guys hanging over the scaffold on each floor, looking down. There was the third floor, where he had gone airborne. Now the camera was back on him as the medics started cutting off his harness. Then that was it. Michael watched it one more time, paying special attention to his harness. But the harness was right there, and it was in one piece. Nothing had failed, nothing had broken. The tether and connectors were all in place. So it was as they had told him, the board where he tied off had a knot on the back right at that point. He slipped on the wet board, there was no toe board to stop him, and he slid under the rail. If he had tied off someplace different, if there had been horizontal safety lines with anchors, he would have stopped within six feet. But all the guys tied off on anything they could find up there. It was his bad luck to have picked an imperfect spot. And worse luck to have slipped where there was no toe board.

*I picked the wrong place to tie off.* Under ordinary circumstances, not such a horrendous mistake. Anyone could have done the same thing.

He had secretly hoped OSHA would find a bad tether, or a bad line stop, or anything that would make it not his fault. But no, it was right there on the film: The harness came down in one piece with him, sliding right off the broken board.

Shiloh came and nuzzled him again. Michael petted him and looked into the dark eyes of this new companion.

"Come on, boy, let's go for a walk."

Madigan was perched on her front steps. Greg had stopped by and they were talking plants. She liked his easy manner. She glanced up as Michael came out of his house with Shiloh. He gave her a wave, but went the other direction, moving well on his crutches, Shiloh at his side sniffing along the grass.

Madigan marveled how much better Michael was walking than only a month ago, and she wondered if he realized how much stronger he had become.

.

Chapter Thirty-Six

*Monday, April 30*

O BIE was sitting under Madigan's tree when she pulled up to her house after work. By the time she had changed her clothes and leashed up Roger, Michael and Shiloh were under the tree, too.

"That's good news for you, then," Obie was saying.

"What's that?" Madigan asked, sitting down on the steps to tie her shoes. Roger bounded over to Shiloh for a greeting sniff.

"I met with the claim manager and a financial advisor, and I think I've got a handle on the future. The immediate future, anyway."

"That's probably more than the rest of us have," Madigan joked. "What's the good news?"

"With the disability award and the pension for the severely injured from my company's insurance, I've got enough to live on and go to school for the next two years. I can find a new career. And I can stay in the house. Veronica's father is going to lend me a little for the mortgage until I'm working again."

"Wow, that's generous. I thought you two didn't get along."

"We didn't. But at least I was always fully employed and I did take care of his daughter, unlike her current guy who does nothing but play...on her money."

"He didn't appreciate you until he found out it could be worse, huh?" Madigan stood and stretched while pulling Roger off Obie's lap.

"Something like that."

"And what have you decided to study?" Obie inquired.

"I'm thinking about architecture, or maybe teaching math. I had started a few teaching courses before I got into construction. I'm not sure how much more it will take to finish. I might need a fifth year."

"I'm about to walk Roger, want to come? And I'm glad you can stay in the house, especially after all that work on the new entrance."

"Sure, we'll go part way with you." Michael headed for the street with Shiloh to get past the torn-up sidewalks.

"Soon you'll have a beautiful stretch of sidewalk to walk on," Obie called after him. "We're going to pour tomorrow."

"I can hardly believe it," Madigan looked at his gentle, worn face, "I don't know what we'll do without you around here."

Obie laughed. "Oh, it will be awhile. We have the fountain to do yet."

"I know, but you'll probably sit down there in the middle of Gene's gorgeous yard instead of under my tree."

"Soon you will have magnificent flowers in your own yard. The gardener's son is going to be a help to you, yes?"

"Yes," Madigan smiled, "Greg's helping me, *and*— we're going to take a load from the garage to the dump next week, too."

"Ha!" Obie looked at the arriving James in triumph. "I knew we would find a nice person with a truck for her. Was I not right?"

James nodded his head in surrender.

Madigan let her hand fall softly on Obie's shoulder. "You were right about a lot of things, Obie. You are incredibly wise."

Unaccustomedly embarrassed by her praise, Obie shrugged his shoulders and indicated she should catch up with Michael, who was now two houses down the street.

"I see things sometimes, that's all," he said simply.

Madigan impulsively kissed his cheek before calling for Roger to come. She would miss these two, that was for sure. Tomorrow was the first of May. It had been three full months since she looked out her window to see their truck pulled up in front of her house, wondering what she had gotten into. How much had changed since then! As if to accentuate the point, Roger stopped, sniffed, and pooped along the grass line. When Michael looked back, Madigan held up a plastic bag to show him she'd be there in a moment. He smiled and continued slowly so that she could catch up.

Chapter Thirty-Seven

*Tuesday, May 1*

O BIE, James, and James' sons had started early to pour the stretch of sidewalks. They started with Madigan's, then completed Liz and Frank's before lunch when the boys had to leave. Having eaten and rested, now it was time for Michael's.

The girl Sierra came home alone again. Obie and James had not seen the boy for a week, since the day of the argument. The mother came home later as usual, and in a few minutes the girl came out and stood by them.

"My mother sent me out to ask. She wants to know about our driveway. How much would it cost to do?"

"We could do a very nice job," Obie straightened and looked her in the eye, but she quickly broke contact. "Your driveway has many cracks. We could make it much better."

"How much would it cost?" Sierra asked again.

"Oh, not too much." James took over now, as usual. "Tell your mother she will be happy with the result."

"But the cost?"

"It's hard to say. We can come look at it tomorrow and talk to her. We can't stop right now while we're pouring."

"Okay, well, thanks." She began to walk away.

"So the father," Obie spoke to her back as he returned to leveling the concrete with the spreader, "he is not going to be around, then?"

Sierra whirled and looked at him sharply, this elderly man with the gray curly hair, stooped over his work. *How could he possibly know?*

"He seems a nice boy. Maybe you could give him a chance to become a good man."

She studied Obie while he continued smoothing the concrete over and over. Finally he looked up at her and smiled. "I think it's a boy. Two parents to love him, that could only be good, no?"

*Just like that, he had an opinion! As if he knew anything about it at all. Anything!*

"I don't know," she answered so softly he could barely hear.

*Maybe.*


The End

# Acknowledgments

This book has been a long time coming and received much help along the way. My family has been invaluable: husband Richard; adult children Katie, Roxanne, and Brian; sons-in-law Matt and Matt; and two joyful grandsons. All have encouraged me in various ways from reading the manuscript, to helping with technical difficulties, to simply delighting me with smiles and hugs.

I would like to thank Phil Spadaro and Fritz Anderson for advice about construction accidents; to firefighter Marvin for responder vocabulary; to Jennifer James' book *The Slug Manual* for perfect imagery about critical personalities; to Lynn Krog for assistance with medical details and proofing; to Kathy Brandstetter and Julie Pierce for first draft reading and proofing; to Betsy Best, artist, who led by example; to Jim Musar, Aspects Inc, Architecture, for the house drawings on the dedication page; to Lynn Newcombe, whose driveway experience gave me the idea; to Riley Roberts, for help with the design, layout and finishing process.

To my writing group: Donna, Petra, Gerrit, and Jim.

To all those who promote reading at Faith Lutheran Church, Seattle; to the FLC Book Group, which has discussed what makes a good read for over twenty years.

To my friends and large extended family, all of whom continue to put one foot in front of the other despite the uncertainties of daily life.

To my editor Ariele Huff, whose ear for language is unequaled.

However, all errors, grammatical failings, and modern rule avoidance are my own.